HARLE

AMERICAN

D0052100

Leandra Logan

THE LAST BRIDESMAID

1♥800
HUSBAND

Pages
& Privileges ™

See inside!

You're About to Become a

Privileged Woman.

INTRODUCING

PAGES & PRIVILEGES™.

It's our way of thanking you for
buying our books at your
favorite retail store.

**Pages
& Privileges** ™

Enrollment Form

☐ *Yes!* I WANT TO BE A *PRIVILEGED WOMAN.*
Enclosed is one *PAGES & PRIVILEGES*™ Proof of
Purchase from any Harlequin or Silhouette book currently for
sale in stores (Proofs of Purchase are found on the back pages
of books) and the store cash register receipt. Please enroll me
in *PAGES & PRIVILEGES*™. Send my Welcome Kit and FREE
Gifts -- and activate my FREE benefits -- immediately.

More great gifts and benefits to come.

NAME (please print)

ADDRESS   APT. NO

CITY   STATE   ZIP/POSTAL CODE

**NO CLUB!
NO COMMITMENT!**
*Just one purchase brings
you great Free Gifts and
Benefits!*

Please allow 6-8 weeks for delivery. Quantities are limited. We reserve the right to
substitute items. Enroll before October 31, 1995 and receive one full year of benefits.

Name of store where this book was purchased_____

Date of purchase_____

Type of store:

☐ Bookstore   ☐ Supermarket   ☐ Drugstore
☐ Dept. or discount store (e.g. K-Mart or Walmart)
☐ Other (specify)_____

Which Harlequin or Silhouette series do you usually read?

Complete and mail with one Proof of Purchase and store receipt to:
U.S.: *PAGES & PRIVILEGES*™, P.O. Box 1960, Danbury, CT 06813-1960
Canada: *PAGES & PRIVILEGES*™, 49-6A The Donway West, P.O. 813,
North York, ON M3C 2E8

HAR-PP6B

▼ DETACH HERE AND MAIL TODAY! ▼

Jill put her hands on her hips and continued. "We've already agreed."

"You can't mean it!" Matt thundered in correction.

"I know my own mind," she threw back, embarrassment heating her cheeks. Was it her mind...or her libido? After his kiss last night, she wasn't so sure anymore.

"Look, Mr. Travis, the wedding is just weeks away and I've already paid—"

Matt couldn't resist a trace of mockery. "Ah, yes, the down payment on my devotion. Well, I guess the important details are already settled." He leaned down close to her and flashed a row of gleaming white teeth beneath his mustache. "Well, lady, congratulations—you've just bought yourself the big bad wolf."

She flinched, and struggled to keep her voice steady. "Wonderful. Then it shouldn't take me more than a few hours to mold you into the man of my dreams."

Dear Reader,

Whether you want him for business or for pleasure...one month or one night, we have the husband you've been looking for. Call 1-800-HUSBAND.

We're so glad you decided to call the matchmaking Harrington Agency, along with five desperate singles in the 1-800-HUSBAND miniseries. This month we join author Leandra Logan on a trip down memory lane. In fact, she's got more than her share of bridesmaid dresses!

Leandra Logan is the bestselling author of a previous American Romance and numerous Harlequin Temptations. You can contact her at: Leandra Logan, c/o MFW, P.O. Box 47888, Minneapolis, MN 55447.

Don't miss any of the remaining 1-800-HUSBAND titles. We know you'll love this extra-special miniseries!

Regards,

Debra Matteucci
Senior Editor & Editorial Coordinator
Harlequin Books
300 E. 42nd St.
New York, NY 10017

Leandra Logan
THE LAST BRIDESMAID

Harlequin Books

TORONTO • NEW YORK • LONDON
AMSTERDAM • PARIS • SYDNEY • HAMBURG
STOCKHOLM • ATHENS • TOKYO • MILAN
MADRID • WARSAW • BUDAPEST • AUCKLAND

For Mary Drewing Garlough,
a dear old friend who manages
to keep the good times going
for all of us!

ISBN 0-373-16601-X

THE LAST BRIDESMAID

Chapter One

"Tangerine dream taffeta."

Jill Ames's fingers curled tightly around the telephone receiver as she absorbed her old friend Penny's simple, loaded message. She remained frozen in her chair even as the dial tone buzzed in her ear. Voices rose above her head as the uniformed police officers milling around her cramped glass office realized that she'd been disconnected.

"Detective Ames, did you wish to make a point?" Bob Williams prodded plaintively. The big balding detective had been her partner for a couple of years and had stepped up to her desk and was staring into her blank face.

"Oh, yes." Jill hastily hung up the phone and lifted her eyes to her restless subordinates. "Sorry."

"They're all off duty as of five minutes ago," Williams pointed out with a meaningful look. In other words, they weren't married to their jobs as Jill was and were anxious to go home.

"I won't keep any of you longer than necessary." Splaying her slender hands on her tidy desk top, Jill rose to her feet. She knew from experience that standing toe-to-toe with the members of her team of burglary investigators gave her a more commanding presence. Not that she needed much of a boost. She was commonly known as the cool blonde of San Francisco's Bayside Station, the princess of precision, the wonder detective with eyes of laser blue.

At the age of thirty, Jill had already risen through the ranks and out of the standard-issue uniform. She still had a personal dress code of her own, however, consisting of earth tone gabardine suits, white blouses and midheel leather pumps. Her fair hair was maintained at shoulder level and a dash of coral blush and lipstick provided her lovely features some definition.

"I am concerned about the quality of your written reports," she began, hanging tough against the onslaught of moans. She strolled over to her bookcase piled high with weighty blue books. She lifted one in the air. "Remember this text from the academy?" The groans deepened in affirmation. Her voice rose with firmness as she flipped through the pages. "Effective writing saves time, clarifies cloudy issues." She scanned them over her wire-rimmed glasses. "Folks, it means upward mobility. Improving your image as effective law enforcement personnel. I want all of you to review it cover to cover. Especially the chapter on expository style. Let's put a stop to inconclusive narrative—"

The telephone bleeped again. Jill moved through the crowd with strained aplomb, smoothing her gray skirt as she edged her hip onto her desk. She absently noted that her furniture and suit were the same drab shade. Far from tangerine dream taffeta, the private crisis brewing down the coast in her home town of Santa Barbara. She snagged the receiver with a pounding heart. "Detective Ames."

"Organza half-sleeves."

Jill was quick on the click this time, dropping the receiver in place like a red-hot branding iron.

Before she could catch her breath, it rang again. "Ames!"

"May twenty-ninth."

"Dammit!" The expletive slipped out as she hung up again.

The officers were eyeing her with open curiosity now, suddenly more eager to linger and learn. Jill tucked her flaxen hair behind her ear, fighting off a flush. They'd never seen her really flustered, not in her eight-year tenure at the station.

Bob Williams leaned over the desk, using his body and saggy brown suit jacket to shield her from the troops. "You okay, Jill?"

"Of course," she assured him evenly. But the news that her best friend Penny Richman was getting married in two weeks had left her shell-shocked.

Jill had nothing against matrimony, in general. But this ceremony was a particularly painful milestone, for it would leave her the last single bridesmaid in their girlhood clique. How uncomfortable to take the news in public this way, in a room full of men who were, for the most part, her subordinates. But Penny assumed she'd be alone by now, Jill realized. Her pal sometimes called at this time, just to scold her for being too dedicated to her job. As close as they were, however, Penny didn't understand that being the last single was her Achilles' heel.

The phone bleated again. Jill didn't even bother to say hello.

"Organza bodice etched with roses."

Jill cleared her throat. "Anything else for now, ma'am?"

"Thought you'd be alone."

"Not today."

"Minilength skirt. Bye-bye."

Jill broke up the meeting several minutes later, insisting that all the officers take a copy of the textbook from the stack. After all, no personal circumstance could be allowed to interfere with her work. It hadn't happened yet. Not once. Mainly because she had no substantial personal life to disrupt! But that was beside the point. Expressing

one's real feelings only led to trouble, revealed a weak spot
for people to prey upon.

Anxious to do her crumbling in private, she dropped the
white blinds on her glass walls, then sank back into her
chair with a frustrated noise.

It was foolish, but she felt like the old maid in the children's card game!

It hadn't been so bad when she and Penny had been a
pair of bachelorette holdouts. Whenever one of their Santa
Barbara schoolgirl pals sent out the bridesmaid alert in the
past, Penny would send word to Jill in San Francisco
through the phone call game, doling out details one at a
time about the often gawdy dresses.

They'd shared their horrified delight over and over again.
Giggling like thirteen-year-olds over extravagant bows and
ruffles.

The dress didn't sound half bad this time and belonged
to Penny herself!

Jill didn't care much about most of those women taking
the plunge before her. But their tight group was a different
matter entirely. They'd always been friendly competi-
tors—as close as sisters. And in the long footrace to adult-
hood, Jill had always managed to come in last. Raised by
her terse aunt Wilma and a weak uncle Art after the death
of her parents in a sailboat accident, she was disadvan-
taged right down to her foundation. How she loved to hang
out at the others' homes, enjoying the love emanating from
their families.

Deep inside, Jill had always felt there was more of everything waiting for her someplace else. Anxious to test her
wings, she'd opted to earn her degree in criminology at
UCLA. She been at San Francisco's Bayside Station ever
since.

She'd made it her business to be first, or close to it, ever
since. It was an impossible habit to break at this late date.

If only husbands grew on trees! She'd pluck one for the weekend and take him home. A strong handsome man who could shock them senseless with his wit and strength, prove to them that she was lovable after all—no, downright irresistible.

Hell, who was she kidding? She didn't even have a tree of her own, being an apartment dweller. As far as dredging up a male stand-in, the last date she'd had was with Bob Williams's neighbor, a forty-year-old man who lived with his mother and shared her twenty-year-old station wagon.

JILL'S CHICKEN SANDWICH matched her mood as she stayed on to go over a stack of reports filed by her officers. It was uncharacteristic of her to dodge trouble, but right now she would've rather chased a burglar down one of the steep city streets in spike heels than return to take Penny's call. She loved her friend with all her heart, and it was imperative that she come off as a good sport when they did eventually talk.

So she chose to stew, allow the reality to sink in as she critiqued writing technique, noting flaws in margins. Unfortunately, two solid hours at this chore didn't make a sport of her, so she forged on to create a prototype report for her team, using a job pulled that morning in a Russian Hill neighborhood. She had everything she needed for her example, right down to the stolen items, promptly recovered thanks to the home's silent alarm.

Feeling far too edgy to sit any longer, she decided to pay a visit to the property room with her clipboard to double-check all the items, giving the report the clearest descriptions possible. Sergeant Mel Clooney, a staple on the afternoon shift, was on duty behind the counter fronting the secured department, humming along with some country-western tune blaring from the boom box beside him.

"Evenin', Ames." The small wiry desk clerk greeted her, looking up from the newspaper splayed beneath his spindly forearms. "No big plans on a Friday night?"

"Overloaded with cases." Jill reached across the counter and turned the radio's volume down a notch, forcing a smile to his sardonically set mouth. A staple of the day-shift crew, she rarely had contact with Clooney, and she was glad. He gave all the women in the precinct a rough time simply because of their gender—a barefoot-and-pregnant promoter to an irritating degree who deemed himself an expert on a woman's place. As it was, he had a hell of a lot of trouble keeping a woman at his place. At fifty-five, Clooney had already been to divorce court three times and was supposedly at odds with his fourth wife. A rather satisfying bit of irony to Bayside's female personnel.

Though she was generally capable of managing him, he was the last person she cared to deal with tonight. Due to Penny's news, she was already feeling extremely vulnerable and unappealing. He was watching her closely, his small dark eyes scoping for a weakness to disrupt his boring routine. She refused to be his diversion—in any sense of the word. She set her clipboard on the counter with a brisk slap to set the tone. "I'd like to see the recovered items on this morning's Russian Hill job."

He gazed down at the case number on the clipboard. "Want to dust it?" he quipped, turning to punch in the number on his computer.

"I hope that wasn't a derogatory remark about woman's work," she queried smoothly.

"Hell, no," he flippantly teased over his shoulder. "I meant dusting for prints. Like we sometimes do in our business."

"Sure, Mel."

"Well, the evidence for that job is in aisle seven," he said, intently peering at the screen. "Section F."

"Okay. Just let me in. I'll find my way."

Clooney deactivated the steel door from a keypad as she rounded the counter. "Wouldn't dream of it," he intoned. "You're the first person I've had to talk to since I got here!" With a firm grip on his boom box, he stepped aside to usher her inside.

Clooney trailed after her like a snappy puppy, his heels clicking on the concrete to the beat of his tinny music. The property was locked away in a padlocked cage, which Clooney had to open with a key on his huge ring. He thrust his radio into her arms to free his hands for the task.

"Damn it all anyhow!" he erupted suddenly.

Jill didn't understand his agitation. He'd no sooner opened the cage than he abruptly whirled around with a grabbing motion. She wasn't sure what he was reaching for. She swiftly jammed the black box into his hands because it was a large, solid barrier.

"Thanks, Ames," he said with all sincerity, scrambling onto a bench behind her. "Didn't realize it was nine o'clock already!"

Jill released a deep breath of relief. He actually wanted the damn radio! "What's so important?"

"The Dr. Love program on KZZZ, of course!" He dropped his eyes to the radio, fiddling with the tuning knob.

"Doctor who?"

"Love. You've heard of love, haven't ya?" He grinned, revealing crooked teeth. "Well, this chick is the utmost authority on the heart."

"Oh." Her flat, single-word statement oozed volumes of disinterest. Jill didn't think much of the show biz hype surrounding problem solving. There were too many talk shows these days, tackling bizarre topics. And every cop in the building knew that a lot of that stuff was rigged.

Despite Clooney's lavish praise for the good doctor, she set her clipboard on the bench and began to rummage through the stolen items. Two watches, diamond-studded, one pearl choker necklace . . . As she took silent inventory,

Jill couldn't help but note that mouthy Melvin had fallen completely silent as a rich feminine purr erupted from the radio's twin speakers.

"Welcome to the 'Ask Dr. Love Show,' coming to you on KZZZ FM from the City by the Bay, San Francisco. We're on the air from nine till midnight. I'm Dr. Love, on hand to help you with those glitches that befall all relationships from time to time. Lovers, spouses, families and friends. We all have troubles and we all need a boost. Let's talk, San Francisco. Let's help one another. The lines are open."

Tonight's main topic proved to be stepparenting. Jill listened to several callers with half an ear as she took copious notes on the inventory. It was a tough admission, but she had to concede that the show seemed on the level, that Dr. Love seemed quite sincere. And the callers were obviously legit. Nothing far out or overly dramatic. Just regular people struggling with everyday life.

A commercial break began, leading off with a pitch for Surfside after-shave. Mel wasted no time in lavishly reviewing the good doctor's performance. "You know, I've gathered up a few children through my marriages and I know just what the doc's talkin' about," he assured her, shifting on the wooden bench. "Personal problems can be hell."

Jill, leaning against the wall, rearranging her adverbs in a quest for stark accuracy, looked up from her clipboard. "I'm impressed with her, okay? But I have to concentrate on my work."

She lowered her blond head, scribbling on into the second commercial. Low classical music swelled up in startling counterpoint to the jazzy Surfside jingle. It faded into the background as a man's deep voice rose up out of nowhere.

"Need a man in your life?"

Jill's spine stiffened as the husky-edged question filled the quiet, hollow room. There was a brief, on-air pause to let the question linger. Melvin filled the void with snicker. Jill fought back a scowl as she pushed her glasses higher up her nose and jammed her pen into paper. Thankfully, the sergeant was seated behind her and couldn't see her expression.

"Are you a happily single businesswoman who occasionally needs a partner for appearances? An unattached female who is weary of scrambling for that last-minute escort for a personal engagement or business function? If so, the Harrington Agency would like to help. We understand the stress society can place upon the upwardly mobile female of the nineties. We offer a practical solution for those awkward situations in the form of a temporary partner. Let one of our husbands act as your other half, with the finesse and intelligence worthy of you. Confidential and uncomplicated. Dial 1-800-HUSBAND now. The lines are open twenty-four hours a day."

Jill remained stock-still as the music faded away and Dr. Love again took the airwaves. Melvin was the first to speak.

"Bunch of hooey, isn't it?" he said with his first inkling of criticism. "All my wives managed to find a man in me, didn't they?"

Jill turned to face him, welcoming the unintentional comic relief brought on by his words. All his ex-wives were as single as Jill herself was. "Not everyone out there is as lucky as all your women have been," she returned sweetly, tucking her clipboard under her arm. "Let me outta here, will you?"

"There's more show," he protested. "Till midnight."

She gazed down at the silver watch on her slender white wrist to find the hands resting on the nine-thirty mark. "I can't sit in here another two and a half hours, Mel. I have things to do."

He rose from the bench and replaced the padlock. "As much as I like the show, I don't get that commercial. There's plenty of us guys out there for you girls."

"I know, Mel, I know," she said with a wry twinkle in her eye.

He grabbed his radio by the handle, pausing to smirk at her. "Well, we both know you'd never consider a sappy place like that. You are married to your job."

Jill marched up the aisle in front of him, hugging the clipboard close to her chest. 1-800-HUSBAND was written in a bold scrawl along the side margin of the top page...and she'd have rather died than allow him to see it.

Jill made a dive for the radio the moment she was back in her glass sanctuary that would've put a linebacker three times her size to shame. She fiddled with the FM dial—perpetually set on the news channel for accurate world event updates—grinning with touchdown triumph when she stumbled across the confidently feminine voice of Dr. Love. The doctor was presently in a deep discussion over the trials of relocating to a foreign country.

Jill sank into her chair with a huff. Where was a commercial when you wanted one?

She tapped the tip of her pen on her slate desktop with anxious anticipation, staring down at the only framed photograph on her desk. It was a picture of her with her four high school cronies, Penny, Gayle, Rebecca and Alison. Along with their parents and siblings, they were as close to family as she'd probably ever come. They'd all understood about her coldhearted Aunt Wilma and her passive, now deceased Uncle Art. They'd included her at every turn, made sure she felt wanted.

She was grateful, but it bothered her that they all pitied her. It had enhanced that tag-along feeling all the more.

Jill picked up the gilt-framed photo for a good hard look, her coral-colored mouth thinned in a bittersweet smile. She'd always tried to be philosophical about her needy position. When a girl of humble beginnings hung out with the cream of the class, she had to expect to fade a bit into the background.

But the one scenario she'd always fervently wished to avoid was just on the horizon. Jill Ames, the last brides-maid. It would open the door to a fresh batch of discomforts. All her friends would be married from here on in, leaving her set apart like the old days. A new generation of families would be seeking to include her in special occasions. Her eyes widened in horror. The smell of sympathy would be in the air again. Strong enough to taste.

Jill simply could not face her friends at this impending wedding without a man of her own. He couldn't be just any man, either. She needed a husband with a passion to die for, who would wipe the pity off their faces with a lazy look or a possessive squeeze to her waist.

A fantasy man...

Again she turned her attention to the program. Dr. Love was counseling somebody on the pitfalls of hair replacement. No sign yet of the husband-for-hire commercial. She used the time to ponder, seek a more sensible solution.

Perhaps someone in the precinct could serve as her devoted better half. A friend who understood about such awkward situations, a subordinate who would gladly put her in an indebted position.

But someone like that might walk away from the weekend with a few of her secrets under his belt, Jill countered in final rejection. Her ice-maiden reputation served her well on the job. Reaching detective status was a long, hard climb, despite her education. Backsliding with a show of vulnerability was unthinkable.

But could she bring herself to go all the way with the charade by hiring a husband from a professional agency? Jill sighed hard, propping the frame in place beside her pencil jar. Dr. Love murmured on in the background, a constant reminder of the ultimate fantasy option.

The classical intro did eventually play again, after an advertisement for a local health spa. She listened to the escort pitch once more, weighing the words with care. Admittedly, the Harrington Agency sounded ideal. A no-strings husband—strictly for appearances. That was exactly what she wanted, wasn't it? A made-to-order man she could bring to Santa Barbara for show, then graciously drop off afterward, with no further involvement?

She closed her eyes, blissfully envisioning herself floating up the aisle in her tangerine dream taffeta without the piteous smiles from friends, waltzing into place near the altar before an agog Aunt Wilma, sure to be planted in a front pew in an outdated pillbox hat from Jackie Kennedy's heyday.

Jill swiveled sideways in her chair. It brought her closer to the console-style telephone, but even closer to her computer. Before she got her hopes up, she was going to check the records to see if the Harrington Agency had had any brushes with the law. Wouldn't that be dandy, hooking up with that place, only to end up in some sort of scam. Her station cronies would never let her live it down.

The agency proved to have no record. And Jill had no more excuses. Her finger shook as she punched in the number. Ironically, it was the same finger that had held steady on the trigger this morning at the Russian Hill burglary.

The contrast was staggering.

No wonder her career was far in advance of her personal relationships!

Naturally, at this hour there was a recording. Jill took a deep breath as an efficient female voice identifying herself as R. Harrington dictated instructions about leaving a message.

Jill surprised herself again as she launched into her crisis with a burst of emotion. "Yes, this is Detective Jill

Ames of San Francisco's Bayside Station. It is urgent that I speak with you, about hiring a companion—''

"Detective?"

Jill started as a truer version of the same voice broke into the line. "Ms. Harrington?"

"Yes, this is Rachel Harrington. I live here at the agency and sometimes monitor the calls."

"Oh, I see," she said breathlessly.

"Yours, of course, caught my attention immediately." The voice was openly loaded with concern and doubt. "If you're looking for a companion in some official capacity, we can't fit the bill."

"Oh, no," Jill promptly assured her. "It's personal. Just the sort of average call you receive every day of the week, I'm sure." She winced, sensing that she was babbling like an idiot.

"Please tell me about it," Rachel urged pleasantly. "Chances are, I can be of help."

Jill released a slow breath, immediately impressed with Rachel's pleasantly professional demeanor. Without further hesitation she launched into a brief sketch of the dilemma in a hushed, small voice.

"I imagine Penny will be calling you back tonight," Rachel predicted.

"Yes, it's only ten," Jill concurred with a glance to her watch. "She's so excited and I want to share in her joy...." Her voice trailed off doubtfully.

"But you want to save face with your peers at the same time," Rachel said, swift on the pickup.

"Exactly!"

"Well, it's not my policy to conduct business at this hour, but I'm willing to make an exception, if you'd like to stop by right now."

Jill gasped at her generosity. "How kind of you, Ms. Harrington! Just let me pinpoint your location."

Rachel laughed. "Pinpoint my location? Are you sure this isn't an official call?"

Jill laughed, but it drove home with a sting just how thoroughly her job consumed her life. She rephrased the request with good humor. "Directions to your place, if you please."

Chapter Two

It turned out that the Harrington Agency was only several blocks from the police station in an upscale section of the Bay Area. Jill knew the posh neighborhood well enough, occasionally shopping and lunching along the quaint cobblestone streets at the noon hour.

She slowed her white Lumina to a crawl, keeping her eyes peeled for 10 Harrington Court in the glow of the black wrought iron streetlamps. The grandiose turn-of-the-century splendor of the district was still miraculously intact, despite a century of progress. Many of the mansions tucked behind walls and fencing were the original structures, as were the huge trees lining the street. Naturally the space was more efficiently utilized these days to match San Francisco's population growth and the country's tighter economic situation. The homes that had once been single-family dwellings were now converted to businesses by shrewd entrepreneurs like Rachel Harrington. But considering the common name between the woman and the mansion, Jill suspected old money and bloodlines had kept this particular property in the hands of the same family through the generations.

A very affluent family, it seemed. Ten Harrington Court proved to be one of the most impressive properties on the street. The gray stone structure stood behind an eight-foot privacy wall, but the two upper stories were visible from Jill's vantage point in the car. A steeply pitched roof climbed into the starry sky and a series of high narrow windows gleamed in the muted light.

Jill parked at the curb and strolled up to the arched entrance. All the while she marveled at the enormity of the place. Judging from the position of the roof, the house was obviously set into an impressive plot of land. Her own modern apartment on the top floor of a boxy building several miles away was postage-stamp size in comparison.

Jill couldn't imagine such deep roots, such an expansive heritage. Presumably Rachel Harrington had plenty of wonderful things to remember. An enviable position to Jill.

The moment she appeared at the wrought iron gates, a front light flashed to life at the house across the courtyard. A feminine figure in gold lounging pajamas emerged through the front door and skimmed down the steps. Jill watched her graceful shadow move through the courtyard, a bright splash wending around towering trees before appearing in front of the statue midway between the house and the gate.

Jill automatically pressed the leather wallet holding her badge against the gate. "Jill Ames. Sorry to disturb you at this hour."

"Oh, Detective," Rachel admonished with a laugh. "Put that thing away."

"You can never be too careful at night, Ms. Harrington," Jill schooled, tucking the wallet inside her purse.

"You're right." Rachel relented, unlocking the gate. "But please, call me Rachel. I feel we already know each other too well for formalities."

Jill grinned wryly. "Yes, I guess you have a point."

Jill studied Rachel in the spare light as the other woman fastened the gate lock. Rachel was close to her own age of thirty, matching her in weight and height. Her eyes were a striking brown, and gleamed along with her smile, encouraging faith and sincerity.

Rachel led the way through the sheltered yard, cautioning Jill to watch her step. They climbed the steps and Rachel pulled open the heavy wooden doors to the house, graciously beckoning Jill inside.

Jill took in her lamplit surroundings with keen but discreet perception. The room had presumably been redesigned to serve as a reception area for the agency. It was far larger and airier than the average old-world sitting room, and had a fresh, redone look. The hardwood floor had been reworked with a high polish, with strategically placed Persian rugs of rose and blue hue. The furniture might well have been original with the house. A brocade sofa and chairs in harmonizing shades were clustered off to one side. Darkly stained side tables held delicate vases of roses. An impressive cherrywood desk sat off to the right, an obvious station for a receptionist during business hours.

The after-hours feel of the place prompted another apology from Jill.

Rachel offered swift comforting support. "My entire business is centered around helping ladies in need. And to be quite frank, I've become quite adept at sensing acute desperation...." She trailed off with a hesitant smile.

Jill shifted uneasily.

"It's natural to feel awkward. Most of my clients initially do. But that feeling goes away once they understand my service." Rachel's brown eyes hardened slightly. "Career women in our age bracket are struggling with a pair of obstacles. We want to be considered equals in the workplace and we want to be accepted as singles-of-choice. Unfortunately, all is not fair yet. We can land the decent job, but we're perceived as inferior if we don't have a partner behind the scenes."

"Exactly!" Jill agreed with a vigorous nod. "A male can attend any sort of function alone without fear of being criticized. Society's expectations for us are far more traditional. The little woman is nothing without the big, strong man to make her whole. Oh, I don't know, maybe I'm making too much out of this dilemma. It isn't job discrimination, or anything that serious.''

"But it is serious to you, Jill.'' Rachel replied. "Just because it is a strictly personal situation doesn't mean it is any less important. From what you told me over the phone, the idea of returning home single, the last bridesmaid of the bunch, is killing you inside. That's terrible. Here you are, a respected police detective, and presumably you feel you will be judged by your single status! It is another unjust trap set in our path. That's what the Harrington Agency is all about, Jill. A tailor-made service meant to even the odds a bit, no matter what the reason or the function. Strategy is my strong point. I love my work. And I'm good at it.''

"I believe you,'' Jill marveled, her defenses melting in the hands of this persuasive woman.

"Come along to one of the offices.'' Rachel veered down a wide hallway on the left, her hard-soled slippers clicking in harmony on the wood with Jill's sensible pumps. Despite her lounging outfit and compassionate words, Rachel moved as briskly as Jill, with shoulders erect and chin level. Jill could identify with that kind of on-the-job savvy. If Rachel's moves reflected her professional acumen, Jill was as good as married—to just the right temporary husband!

The same decor from the reception area flowed into the meeting room, but the ambiance was disrupted by some very modern equipment. A computer, a multiline telephone and a fax machine were incorporated into the area surrounding a Queen Anne desk. Rachel sat down in the work space and Jill paced around the room.

Rachel swiftly booted up the computer and typed her way into the proper program. "Do you know the date of the wedding?'' she called out, her eyes never leaving the glowing monitor.

''Monday, May twenty-ninth,'' Jill replied as she examined an antique spinning wheel positioned under one of the long narrow windows.

''Ooh, that's the holiday. And it's coming right up,'' Rachel murmured, busily scrolling through a list of names on the screen.

''Is it possible on such short notice?'' Jill blurted out in distress. ''I mean to find a man who could play the role well?''

''We can cover you easily,'' Rachel said with assurance. ''With somebody who is just absolutely crazy about being your man.''

Jill erupted in laughter. ''That'll be a first for me!''

Rachel turned on her swivel chair slowly, tossing her dark mane over her shoulder. ''You should smile more. It becomes you.''

''Thanks.''

Rachel consulted a notepad on the desk. ''I wrote down a few details during our call. This man will have to be available to travel, as well, correct?''

''Yes, down to Santa Barbara for, say, a long weekend. Four days, perhaps. I'll pay your flat fee and any travel expenses beyond that, of course.''

''Here is a fee scale,'' Rachel said, digging into the top drawer of the desk.

Jill slipped into the wing chair opposite her and picked up the textured sheet of paper. The price for saving face was high, but within her means.

Rachel watched her study the sheet. ''So, Jill, is this a workable option?''

''Yes,'' she promptly assured her. ''I would like to start the preliminary paperwork.''

''Wonderful. Let's just verify a few dates here.'' Rachel reached out to flip through the pages of her appointment calendar. "Today is the twelfth. That puts the wedding seventeen days away."

Jill swallowed hard. Hearing it from someone else made it all the more real in her mind.

"She certainly is in a rush," Rachel remarked, again focused on her monitor. "Not your average bride."

Jill nodded. "Not by a long shot. I imagine she's kept the deal hush-hush to fend off reporters."

"Oh?" Rachel's fingers froze on the keyboard and she turned to Jill with heightened interest.

"She is Penny Richman, host of a children's show on public television, 'Kid Konnection,'" Jill explained.

"Ah." Rachel's tone was one of respectful surprise. "I've heard of it."

"Penny and the show have won numerous awards from children's organizations," Jill confided with open pride. "The public has put Penny on a pedestal, and that, of course, means her privacy is invaded at every turn."

"So discretion is paramount."

"Exactly."

Rachel bit her lip in thought, then typed in a particular name. "I believe I have just the man for you. He's flexible, good-natured, but sharp enough to avoid any limelight himself, draw questions away from your situation."

"This will be a challenging assignment," Jill cautioned Rachel, "far more complicated and longer than a dance or corporate dinner. This husband will have to be an exceptional actor, quick on the uptake day or night. My friends will find it astonishing that I married secretly for one thing, and to tell you the truth," she went on awkwardly, flexing her fingers in her lap, "they will be shocked that I found somebody special. I've always been considered the lame duck of the bunch, you see."

"I find that difficult to believe," Rachel soothed. "But Matt Travis could handle such a situation. As a history teacher and track coach at Hill High School, he's become a master at public relations. It isn't every man who can get teenage girls to do push-ups and boys to dress up in Edwardian costumes! He's respected because he's involved. He never asks them to do anything that he's not willing to do himself."

Jill did have to admit that he sounded well-rounded. An educator introspective enough to care about history. An athletic figure who would complement her active life-style. "Some of the teens in my building attend that school," she said with growing interest. "The staff is supposed to be topnotch."

"And Matt's thirty-one, just a shade older than you are." With another keystroke, she brought up a computer image of him. She turned the monitor on its pedestal so Jill could have a look.

"He's promising," Jill admitted, her heart leaping at his image. Clipped brown hair, medium sized mustache, firm chin.

"The only hitch is his schedule," Rachel commented as she realigned the monitor. "Matt works for me exclusively over school holidays, and only then when school sports don't interfere. Summer is his most available time."

"School is still in session Memorial Day Weekend."

"But they have three or four days off then, just the same," Rachel assured her. "I'll check it out. At the worst, he can find someone else to cover for him over at Hill."

"But will he want to go to the trouble?"

Rachel was close to her husbands, considered them pals, so she was certain of her facts when she nodded. "He's the one for you, Jill. Trust me."

Jill shifted uneasily in her chair. She hadn't relied on one particular male to come through for her socially since high school, when things went sour with her boyfriend, Roger Bannon, senior year. And it went totally against her grain to leap into this without further proof of his appositeness.

"Time is of the essence here," Rachel coaxed in the silence. "Naturally, I am accustomed to booking jobs at the last minute, but they are usually one-night affairs, without the complication of travel. Matt will need time to make arrangements for a four-day absence."

Jill's knuckles whitened as she flexed her fingers in her lap. This situation was agonizing! She'd already exposed herself to this new acquaintance way beyond her normal limits. And to hire a stranger to play her man would be the most insane thing she'd ever done. But ultimately, her pride won out. She had to return home a winner in the romance game.

In a brisk motion she removed her checkbook from her shoulder bag. "I am going to give you a down payment now, if that's all right. Then I will pay the balance when we've settled the details."

Rachel handed her a pen. "That is perfectly fine. And we'll shoot for Matt as first choice. In any case, however, you won't be sorry. All my husbands are exceptional, each in his own way. I guarantee that we'll see you through."

Jill couldn't resist a wistful retort as she scrawled in the blank check. "If only it was that simple to find a genuine Mr. Right."

Rachel beamed. "Yes. But the trick is to hold out for the real magic. In my own little way, I make it easier for women to do just that. Sit tight now, and I'll print up a contract and a bio on Matt."

THE TELEPHONE was ringing in her studio apartment as Jill wrestled her way through the dead bolt lock on the door. Her machine was on a ten-ring delay, so she managed to scoop up the cordless in the living room before her recording kicked in.

"Hello," she huffed, moving around her cramped quarters, turning on lights.

"Hi. Where on earth have you been?"

Penny, of course. Jill sank down at the drop-leaf maple table in the kitchen. The clock over the white porcelain sink read midnight. "Working late. Sorry. But I was planning to call you tonight, honest."

Jill's teeth sank into her lower lip as that last word slipped out. This was where her sterling forthrightness was going to haze over to a cloudy shade of gray. She hated the idea of lying, but she felt so trapped.

"So, you must have figured it out," Penny went on merrily. "I am getting married!"

"Congratulations, honey," Jill replied sincerely. "I'm really happy for you."

"I've found the man of my dreams. Finally!"

Jill lightly drummed the surface of the table, her system humming with the jitters. "Who is he? Anyone I know?"

"Oh, no. His name is Bruce Kildare. It was just like in the movies, Jilly," she marveled, a note of disbelief in her voice. "We met at a children's hospital fund-raiser in San Diego. I was giving the keynote speech and he came up to speak to me afterward. I've been a blubbering idiot ever since!"

The sleek, elegant celebrity had never been blubbering or an idiot, but Jill wasn't about to spoil her story. "Sounds like a military man," she surmised, well accustomed to all the navy personnel combing the streets of California's coastal towns.

"You guessed it. He's a lieutenant, stationed at Point Loma."

"When did this happen?"

"Our meeting?"

"Yes, Penny," Jill prodded with a laugh.

"I've known him since January," she reluctantly admitted.

"So you've been dating him steadily for months, without a word," Jill scolded. "You sneak!"

"Yeah. But you know how it goes with the two of us," she rushed on apologetically. "I was afraid it wouldn't work out, and I figured the fewer people watching and judging, the better."

"Yes, that's exactly how it goes with the two of us," Jill conceded with a sigh. Or did until now. Penny was joining the other side now. The married, happily-ever-after side.

"My situation has always been worse than yours," Penny complained. "Sure, we both have the old crowd looking over our shoulders, but I've had the media to contend with, as well. My reputation is at stake every time I walk out the door with a new man. Keeping my image snowy white for the sake of my young viewers is tough, with reporters hovering for scandal, speculating on the future of each and every liaison. It'll be a relief to settle down, live in peace for a change, like everybody else."

Jill inhaled shakily as Penny pushed one of her more vulnerable buttons. "It hasn't been easier for me, Pen."

"Not exactly easy," she returned, openly anxious to please. "But, well, living alone seems to suit you so well. I've always been the mad scrambler, dating a host of guys in the hope of finding that special one. It's been murder to do with the limelight tracking my progress for seven years, since the inception of my show."

"I know, honey, I know," Jill soothed. "You're a wonderful role model to children around the world, and it's admirable that you work to keep a spotless image for them."

"You are happy for me, aren't you, Jill? Even if I do sound like a self-centered prima donna?"

"A bride has a right," Jill assured her.

"You can make it, can't you? I chose Memorial Day Monday because I figured most people would be free."

"I wouldn't miss it for the world. When do all the festivities officially start?"

"The preceding Saturday, with a bridal shower at Alison's apartment. She'll be calling you with details. Then Sunday night there's a groom's dinner barbecue at Rebecca's. Bruce is from New York originally, with no family to speak of, so Bec's offered to do the honors. She's also my maid of honor. Seemed only fair, since she had me," she babbled on. "And let's face it, she puts on a hell of a bash!"

Jill understood being passed over for the first-attendant slot. She'd always been too far away to serve as a competent backup for any of them. It was simply one of the prices she paid for living in another city. "Rebecca will do a lovely job of organizing everything," she promptly agreed.

Penny went on to fill her in on the buffet meal she'd chosen for the reception, and talked a bit more about the bridesmaid dresses. A local seamstress was making all the dresses under a veil of total secrecy. Penny explained that she was keeping the press at bay until the last minute. No one outside their close circle knew of Bruce or the impending nuptials.

Jill politely listened to all the details, her mind straying to her own position. If she was going to proceed with her plans to spring a "husband" on the gang, she had to say something in advance. She hardly knew herself right now— as the impulsive scheming stranger!

"You just can't imagine what it's like to find that perfect someone, Jilly," Penny said blissfully. "Someone who cares only for you."

"Well, Penny—" Jill murmured indecisively, the lie bubbling in her throat. "I happen to—"

"I know you're liable to feel a little awkward, being the only single, but I have a little surprise for—"

"As it happens, I have a surprise for you," Jill blurted brightly, her patience finally snapping from the strain. "I've gone and gotten married myself. Eloped just last week."

"No!"

"Yes," Jill insisted over her pal's squeal of disbelief. "A crazy coincidence, isn't it?"

"I'll say," Penny declared bluntly. "Hey, you're kidding, aren't you?" she said after a short pause. "Stringing me along as part of our phone game?"

Jill's heartbeat accelerated. Penny was already doubting her! "I would never do that, Pen. That's the kind of stunt you might try to pull!"

"Okay, okay." Penny instantly backed off with a laugh. "Can't blame me for wondering."

"You never doubted my word before," Jill said pouting.

"It's just out of character, you eloping," Penny insisted. "You're our old reliable!"

"I'm also notoriously honest," Jill blurted, her blond head bobbing in a nervous jag. It was a good thing she was on the side of the law. She'd make a crummy con artist!

"I can't wait to hear some details."

Details? Right now? Jill quickly reached across the table for her purse. She rummaged through it for the Harrington printout.

Penny's delighted laughter filled the line. "Like his name, for instance!"

"Didn't I say?" she airily bluffed. "It's Matt Travis." She studied the computer image of his face again, startled by the sensual tug in her belly. He was quite good-looking. The kind that turned heads on the street.

"And, and?" Penny prodded.

"Well, he's on the staff of a high school not far from here," she said, scanning the printout for accuracy. "History teacher and track coach."

"But what about the goodies? What's he look like?"

Jill's earnest blue eyes flew over his statistics. "He's thirty-one. Six foot three. Brown hair and eyes." She released a slow breath, hoping she sounded natural enough.

"Impressive," Penny raved. "I'll bet he's really nice, too. Just what you deserve."

Jill closed her eyes, wondering for a moment what it would be like to share this moment in a genuine way, as though they'd both truly found their dream lovers. Her eyes soon popped open again to face reality, though. It wasn't real. Matt Travis was a computer image on a piece of paper, and the excitement she was sharing with Penny was contrived.

"Why did you go and elope?" Penny asked. "Cheat us out of an extra gaudy dress?"

"Well, Matt and I both like the simple life," Jill hedged. "And Matt has to be at school. Has so many duties. It was a miracle we could coordinate our schedules to tie the knot!"

Penny released a relenting sigh. "What a chance to make a show, though, for the folks back home."

"You're the showman of our crowd," Jill countered dismissively.

"I suppose," Penny agreed. "So, do you think he'll be able to make my wedding?"

"As it happens, we've already adjusted our schedules for some holiday quality time," Jill improvised proudly.

"Is he there? Put him on the line."

"He's not home right now, Pen," she hastily denied. "There was a late meeting at school. Something about the track team."

"I suppose it's tough for two people immersed in separate careers to juggle it all."

"Yes, but it is possible," Jill agreed, her confidence growing. This wouldn't be so bad, if she kept on her toes.

"Where did you meet, how long have you known each other?"

"Hey, that kind of stuff can wait until we get there, Pen," she insisted evasively. "This is your moment, not

mine. I insist you tell me more about Bruce. All the goodies."

Jill managed to squeak through the rest of the conver-
sation without making a blunder. She remembered that
Penny had mentioned a surprise and asked her about it, but
Penny laughed it off, saying that Jill had misunderstood.
And maybe she had. She'd been in a tizzy, trying to play the
newlywed role with feeling.

Some great pretender! she lamented, rubbing her temples. This one conversation had left her pooped. And it was
only the beginning. Once back home in Santa Barbara,
there would be countless questions to answer about her
courtship, immeasurable moments to fill with blissful
marital exchange.

But the cop in her was speaking loud and clear above all
else. There was some pressing preliminary groundwork to
cover on this end, long before a bag was packed. Matt
Travis needed a thorough going-over, to make certain he
was everything he advertised to be!

Chapter Three

"You in trouble with the cops?"

Matt Travis was taken back fifteen years as he whirled on his Nikes to confront the young eager members of his varsity track team. Taken back to a time when such a question would've been justified. Several of Hill High's athletes had clustered around him on the grass beside the school's oval shaped track to point out the policewoman seated on a bench outside the school's chain link fencing. Their young voices rose in the warm springtime air, boys and girls anxious for the end of the school year, hungry for a diversion to cut short their daily program of warm-ups and practice runs.

Matt saw right through the ruse. But it was just the sort of distraction that could divert him from his iron-man routine. He raised the small binoculars hanging around his neck to his squinted eyes, first focusing on a few students jogging round the lanes, then ever so carelessly settling in on the lady in question, several hundred yards away on the tree-lined boulevard.

A stunning blonde in a navy suit. A pencil-thin body in a straight skirt. Matt liked blondes a lot. But this one was far too restrained for him. Her hair was pulled back in a confining knot. And her suit was too dark and too tailored. The jacket had thick shoulder pads and the white blouse underneath it was buttoned up to her throat.

She was sealed up tight. And it made him uptight. As though he was dressed in a straitjacket himself, rather than loose gray sweats, hacked short on the thigh and biceps with the school-issued scissors from his desk.

The kids couldn't wait to fill him in, he soon came to realize. Jill Ames was the detective's name. It seemed they knew her by sight, for she lived and worked in the area. Matt couldn't challenge their information, or the fact that the light blue unmarked vehicle parked at the curb was standard issue of the Bayside police department. One or two could often be found after hours at his father's bar and grill downtown.

But trouble with the cops was a yesterday deal. Shiny questioning eyes were watching him closely, looking for a response from their resident hero. They didn't know he had a rocky beginning, and he was determined that they never know. They might stop believing in him and that would destroy him.

He lowered the binoculars from his face, letting them dangle loose on a cord against his solid stomach. "What division is she from?" he inquired evenly.

"Burglary."

"Burglary!"

"Can't you make it with your coaching and teaching salary?" Krista Sundin teased, not a bit put off by his volcanic eruption.

Matt released a low, bearlike growl in the tall skinny blonde's face. "Maybe it's you she's after, Sundin."

"She can nail me anytime," Krista answered, wrinkling her nose. "Lives in my building. We're good friends."

"Well, I know I'm clean," he announced grandly with a show of white teeth beneath his dark mustache. "Maybe it's our assistant coach Mathers she's after?"

Doubt rumbled through the crowd. Chuck Mathers was too straight to cause trouble.

Matt rubbed his large callused hands together. "What say we get to work? Start tuning up."

As everyone started to assemble in their proper rows on the lawn, Matt's assistant coach sidled closer.

"Weird, huh, Matt?"

Matt glared at the smaller, stockier man dressed in a red and white Hill High T-shirt and shorts like the kids. "Burger King is right across the street, Chuck. Lots of people sit on those benches at noon hour."

Chuck shrugged. "A reasonable deduction."

"Thank you very much."

"But somebody was asking questions about you in the office yesterday," Chuck reported, toying with the bill of his baseball cap.

The news sent a jolt of electricity through Matt's body. Playing dumb seemed best. "Huh?" He dropped his jaw and his shoulder.

"I overheard Russell Dearborn discussing you on the telephone. With an obliging tone the principal of this zoo doesn't use too often. And I did hear the word detective as often as I heard your name. It was all good, of course," he hastened to assure Matt.

"Of course," Matt snapped, running a ragged hand through his short brown hair.

"Nothing to worry about."

"Hell, no." Hill High's principal did hold him in the highest regard, knew nothing about his juvenile record. There really was nothing to worry about, except the prospect of being misunderstood as he'd been the last time. What could the lady's motives be? With hands clamped to his lean hips, Matt looked into the brilliant bright sky, then at the ancient, four-level brick school to the right, then at his aligned troops on the green grass. This was his life, his kingdom, his dream come true. He tried not to stare at the invader beyond the fence. But he couldn't help it. Even without his binoculars, he could make her out more distinctly than he wanted to.

Just as he could make out the hulking, balding form of Detective Bob Williams, lumbering across busy Filmore Avenue with a large white fast food bag in his hands. He hadn't spoken to him in years. But you never could forget the cop who ran you in as a boy. Not even fifteen years had dulled the memory.

His fists tightened at his sides in unconscious resolve. They better not be misunderstanding anything about him all over again. Because he'd take a whole lot of pleasure in straightening them out this time around as a grown man.

JILL HAD some binoculars of her own. Compact, foldaway opera glasses, perfect for discreet spying. She turned from the street toward the school grounds and held them up to her face, just in time to see him fall in line before the six rows of students. They all began to exercise, stretching their limbs in impressive sync.

He was a beautiful male specimen. And so much the sort of man she truly hoped to marry one day. Steady, reliable, strong in physique and character, according to Mr. Dearborn. And good with people large and small, according to Rachel Harrington. Why, he currently had sixty hormone-charged youths hanging on his every word, on a day just made for daydreaming about the summer ahead. She couldn't hear what he was saying, of course. But she could see his lips moving through her lenses. Hard looking lips on a chiseled face. Her hand stole to her own soft lips, fleetingly wondering how it would feel to kiss a scantily clad jock on such a warm sunny day. Feel his strong tanned arms around her.

Matt Travis seemed perfect for the husband position. He'd dazzle the hometown folk all right. Make them sorry they ever doubted her worth.

"Gotcha!"

Jill squeaked in surprise as Bob Williams crept up on the bench. She quickly stashed her opera glasses in her roomy purse. "How'd you get across the street without my seeing?"

"I'm light on my feet," he said with a wink.

Jill frowned at her large partner, snatching the sack from his hands. "You jaywalked!"

"Prove it, Detective."

"Let's eat."

Bob sat down beside her on the bench, accepting the drink and sandwich she doled out. "Thought we could share the fries. My treat."

She waved a slender hand. "None for me. I'm watching it."

"You're always on a diet, Ames."

She tossed her head back, taking a bite of her burger. "No, I'm not," she distinctly denied as she swallowed, "It just so happens that a friend of mine is getting married in two weeks, and the bridesmaid dress is already in the works. I just have to make sure I keep a steady weight."

"You're too punctilious to vary more than eight ounces at time," he mumbled under his breath, snatching the bag back to snag some fries.

"What did you say?" she asked with suspicion.

"I said you're so perfectly gorgeous you could very much land on a dime."

Her tawny brows narrowed. "Liar."

His high forehead creased as he answered. "Look who's talkin'! You suggest we eat outside on some bench today, then have the nerve to pretend this is a random choice. I don't know why you're snooping over here at the school, but—"

"I am not snooping."

"You are. I don't see no opera around here to justify those glasses of yours," he taunted, scanning their surroundings with mocking perplexity.

"It has nothing to do with you," she declared flatly, giving up on the denial. Bob knew her well enough to know when she had ulterior motives. She busily adjusted her paper cup on her lap, taking a long draw of soda through her straw.

He chomped on his burger. "C'mon, give."

"It's personal, Bob."

He wiggled his brows against his broad forehead. "Sounds promising already."

"Please don't ask."

"I won't quit until you explain. And you know what a relentless interrogator I am," he added on a threatening note.

Jill huffed in resignation. "I'm checking out a teacher over there."

His gaze shifted to the school property. "Who?"

"Oh, he's the track coach. Shoddy outfit," she clarified with a wave at the field.

"Are you dating this guy? Is that why you're running a check on him?"

"I don't run checks on my dates," she retorted.

"Maybe you should. What's his name?"

"Matt Travis."

Bob chomped thoughtfully on his sandwich. "I know the family. The father, Chet, owns a busy grill downtown."

"Oh, really?" Jill brightened. "Hard workers, I imagine."

"Yeah, it's a tough business. I worked that precinct for more years than I care to count. Chet's always been a worker. It's a tough life down on those streets. Makes kids tough, too," he added ruefully.

"So you know of Matt Travis, then," Jill prodded with growing interest.

"Yep. The son. Haven't thought about him in a good long while." He winced, as though not caring to do it now. "Haven't thought of him since I ran him in."

Jill gasped in mortification. "You must have the wrong man! He's clean."

"It was ages ago," he clarified. "He was a teenager then—"

"And those records are sealed," she said, finishing his thought for him.

Bob nodded, snagging some fries. "In his case, I assure you it's the fair thing. Matt Travis deserved a second chance. Obviously he went on and cleaned up his act."

He had an act to clean up.

Disappointment deflated her. She'd made a down payment on an ex-thug! So much for the perfection dream. He could very well still be causing trouble. He might just be a whole lot better at it!

Williams shifted on the bench, running his arm along the back, poising his features in parental concern. "If he isn't a date to you, Jill, just what is your connection?"

Jill tucked her silken hair behind the shell of her ear, turning away.

Bob's large face hardened. "If it's police business—I'm making it my business, too."

Jill sighed hard. So much for a little undercover work. All she'd wanted was a look at the man. Now everything was amok.

"I'm waiting, Jill."

Her lower lip extended poutily. "You'll laugh if I tell you."

"I doubt it." She still hesitated, and he didn't bother to hide his annoyance. "If that kid is off the rails, I need to know. Now, Ames."

Kid? Of course, to the fiftyish detective, Matt seemed like a youngster, just as she did. "All right!" she huffed in livid resignation. "I am hiring him on as my fake husband, okay? For my friend's wedding back home in Santa Barbara. Satisfied?''

Bob Williams's laughter rose over the traffic. "He's into a sideline like that? I can't decide which of you surprises me more.''

"I'm not looking for commentary from anybody at the station,'' she answered with icy blue fire in her eyes. "Promise me you'll keep quiet about this.''

"I will,'' he promised between gulps of laughter. "Partner's honor.''

"And who knows,'' she declared with a stiffened spine. "I might not go through with it, after all.''

"Odds are you won't,'' he agreed.

She gasped at his cocky assurance. "And why not?''

"Because you don't have a wild bone in your body, Ames. And to tell you the truth,'' he confided with a pat on her hand, "I hope and pray both my daughters grow up to be as sensible and predictable as you are. I won't have a moment's worry between the two of them.''

Jill balled up their lunch sack in her hands, despite his protest that there were still delicious French fries in the bottom. Denying him those last slices of potato was the only retaliation she could think of. She'd have preferred to shoot back some kind of retort, but his clever backhanded compliment left her completely stymied, just as the news of Matt's record had left her frazzled. She knew better than to ask Bob more about it. Unless Matt was in real trouble again, she knew Bob wouldn't reveal a thing. She'd have to dig into the matter herself.

They rose from the bench and headed for the car.

"What's the name of that family bar of his?'' she asked in the silence.

Bob paused at the driver's door. "The Green Door. Why?''

Jill tossed the bag in a refuse container near the curb with a frustrated sound. "Because my investigation obviously isn't over yet. I can't rest until I find out just how imperfect this perfect husband of mine really is.''

They eased into the front seat, another lingering pause between them.

"Why not play it straight, Jill?" Bob suggested.

"With Travis?"

"With your friends and family! Wouldn't it be easier to just forget this charade, return home as the proud, unmarried detective you are?"

Jill twisted her purse strap in her lap, erupting in a small but stubborn little no. The plan was still sound in her mind. Her only mistake was giving her best friend a vivid description of him.

"Take a little fatherly advice," he said on a gentler note. "Don't delve too deeply into Matt's business, like a sightseer or something."

Jill frowned at his pudgy profile. "That's funny, coming from the man who busted him."

"I just believe everybody deserves a second chance. It's my understanding that he still doesn't like cops one little bit."

Because of Bob, no doubt. And Bob obviously didn't want to make it worse. Another silent moan seared her insides. "Thanks for the parental interest," she returned in rueful dismissal. "It would've been nice twenty years ago."

"Smooth brush-off," he remarked lightly. "Never too late, though. Think about it. We know you always think before you strike. Always."

Until now, partner. This little social situation was already way out of control.

"PRETTY GIRL over in booth seven, son." Chet Travis paused from his bartending duties at the Green Door that night to make the observation.

Matt grunted as he drew two ales from a spigot a few feet down the bar. "I know, Dad." He plunked the foamy mugs on a tray for a hovering waitress, then glanced at the small, wiry man with the closely clipped crew cut. Chet was smirking as he proceeded to make change for a regular at the register.

So much for disguising his motives in the dimly lit din. Even his father noticed his interest in Jill Ames—while catering to fifty of his favorite customers, currently clamoring around the dark-paneled place. Matt figured she might show up. She'd been to his neighborhood, his school. The family grill was the last stop on the tour. If you were interested in everything there was to know about Matt Travis. If you suspected him of a crime...

She angered him with her invasion, her persistence. Sorely disappointed him with the need for further verification of his integrity.

But there was an undeniable energy humming beneath the anger and disappointment. An energy even his spry old dad obviously picked right up on.

On the outside, Jill Ames was just his type. Long, leggy and blond. Young enough to do the town, old enough to do other things. Under other circumstances he might have been over at that booth by now, offering dinner and a decent bottle of wine.

Chet was closing in on him now, a crafty look on his narrow, lined face. "I couldn't help but notice you noticing her," his father teased.

"In that little white skirt and yellow tank top, I'd have to be blind not to notice," Matt returned smoothly, clearing empty glasses and several soaked napkins from the bar.

"You've been staring at her for an hour," Chet stated confidently. "Is she the reason I'm getting an extra hand on a Wednesday night?"

"Yeah." Matt added a grim grin to the blunt admission. "But don't kick a gift horse in the mouth."

"I won't," he vowed with humor. "Hell, I'd just as soon have her park it here Fridays when it's really busy. I mean, if this is going to be a regular mating dance between the two of you."

Matt's jaw tightened and his eyes darkened a shade. "We are not a pair. And it's going to be a one-time deal. Whatever she's after."

"Sure, sure. But she's pretty cute."

"She's a cop."

"Huh?"

"C-O-P," Matt said, spelling the word.

"What a shame, sonny. What a rotten shame."

"Quit mocking me," Matt cautioned on a menacing note.

"I don't mean to," Chet quickly assured him. "Just wish you'd shake that attitude." He inhaled sharply all of a sudden. "You aren't in trouble?"

"No!" Matt threw his hands in the air. "You're hopeless! I get into one jam at the age of sixteen and I'm labeled for life!"

Chet shook his gray head. "Your grudge against authority is your own doing. Half my business is the police on their off hours."

"Yeah, yeah. Spend a couple of months in juvenile hall and see how you like it."

"Now, Matty." The fact that Chet was fifty pounds lighter and six inches shorter than his son didn't stop him from grabbing the lad's denim shirt between his old fingers. "You took a wrong turn, you paid your debt. Shake it off."

Matt had shaken it off. But being watched, investigated, brought the whole ugly incident flooding back, recharging long forgotten emotions. "She's Bob Williams's partner, Dad."

Chet's expression clouded. "Maybe there is a problem," he slowly conceded, "a misunderstanding, I mean."

Matt's eyes slitted with resolve. "If there is, I'll take care of it."

HE WAS WATCHING her, all right. Jill shifted on the smooth wooden seat, taking a nervous sip on her glass of soda. She hadn't expected Matt Travis to be here. Her intention was to ask a few discreet questions, as she did in his neighborhood and over at the high school. But she couldn't very well do it with him bearing witness, could she?

Her honed instincts were sending her disturbing signals, flashing the warning that he was ready to pounce. His movements had grown stiffer over the passing hour. His glances her way increased by the minute.

But that was impossible. They were strangers. She had the advantage of anonymity. He couldn't possibly know who she was. And she couldn't possibly dig into his business if he was around. Three diet Cokes in an hour's time and she'd come to suspect he was settled in for the night. What a waste of time. She had stacks of laundry and unpaid bills to tend to at home, and a host of other Wednesday night tasks. And she wasn't a step closer to clearing his name to her satisfaction.

Why had she allowed Rachel to focus so totally on just one prospective husband? Jill knew better than to trust someone else's judgment so implicitly. But Rachel had been so effusive in her praise of Travis. She most likely didn't even know about Matt's sealed record.

In theory, Jill was all for giving youth offenders a break, a clean slate. But not the man who was to play her man! He had to be trustworthy, sterling, beyond reproach. Didn't he?

She soon decided to chalk up the night as a total loss. She drained the last of her Coke, then reached for her bag and the lightweight sweater draped beside her on the bench.

As she twisted to rise, she found herself confronted with Matt Travis himself. He was literally in her face, with his forearms flush with the table, his knee wedged on the edge of her seat. Jill made a small sound of surprise, her heart stopping in her chest.

"We don't like your kind in here," he murmured in a low, steely tone.

Her eyes widened as she stared into his. They were steaming coffee brown, full of rage and resolve. She was sure it wasn't deliberate, but his hair-dusted forearm had glided cleanly across her collarbone on its way down, leaving a burning brand on her skin. And his knee was currently nudging her thigh in a very cozy way. Despite the circumstances, she could feel her body responding with pulsing signals. This man was dynamite up close. She secretly wondered what it would feel like to be touched by him, what it would be like to touch him back. But she was a master of cool and wouldn't as much as wince.

"My kind?" she repeated in perplexity.

"I know what you are," he purred patronizingly. "Why you're hanging out."

Jill blinked and pondered. Why, the damn fool had to think she was a hooker! What else, with her watchful lingering? A hooker who had failed to find a client, too. Yes, she had definitely overstayed her welcome.

"Well, then, you'll be happy to excuse me," she said flatly, attempting to inch off the bench. But escape was impossible. Travis continued to use his body as a barricade.

"I can't leave until you move," she stated evenly, biting her lip as his arm again grazed her tender skin, this time at the throat.

"You can't leave until we talk. C'mon, outside."

It was an order, harsh and impatient. Jill swiftly weighed her choices. She could refuse to budge. Flash her badge. Or give him a good swift kick in the shins. But each one was bound to cause a scene. The easiest thing to do would be to hear him out.

"Yes, let's talk," she ultimately agreed, insinuating that she was in control of their encounter.

With a firm grasp on her arm, Matt steered her toward the back exit and the parking lot beyond. The area was fairly well lit, illuminating two rows of vehicles parked on a slant. Jill could see her Lumina in the center row near the front. She longed to make a dash for it, escape this awkward scene.

Matt Travis looked like a genuine con in the shadows. A far cry from the loose, clean-cut teacher on the track field that afternoon. There was a bristly stubble on his face, a murderous set to his jawline and a sharp arch to his brown eyebrows. The corded muscles in his neck were pulled so taut, he threatened to vibrate.

"I am not who you think I am!" she snapped.

His brow arched. "You're not Jill Ames, a detective with Bayside's burglary division?"

Amazement sheeted her lovely features. "You know I'm not a hooker then!"

He chuckled richly, beaming with triumph. "Is that the look you're shooting for?"

"No, of course not! I thought you made a mistake."

"I've made a few, as we both no doubt know—"

"Let's just forget I ever came here, okay?" She tried to wrench free, but he kept a tight squeeze on her bare arm. The tingle of the night air and his roughened fingers on her skin sent a jolt of lightning through her system, as well as a reminder that she'd left her sweater behind.

"So you've cleared me then, Detective?" he asked in mocking surprise. "You've poked your nose into my affairs, questioned my neighbors and my principal, cased out the grill. Sure you don't want to interrogate my dad before you go? I know, let's go over to my place and check it for hot merchandise."

Jill released a shaky breath. The hottest thing in this guy's place just had to be his sheets. There was a burning sensuality simmering beneath his temper, and a solid body hidden beneath his jeans and tan shirt to fulfill the promise. The combination was intoxicating.

So he did know exactly what she was up to. Rachel probably had already contacted him. "How did you find me out?" she couldn't resist asking.

"Some of the girls on the track team know you. Does it matter?"

She shrugged fluidly beneath her skimpy top. "Just curious."

"Too curious."

Her gaze sharpened. "You got something to hide, Travis?"

His mouth curled mockingly. "You find any dirt, Detective?"

"The answer is no."

"Well, my answer to your question is no, too." He raked a hand through his hair, staring off into the dark sky. "So, you going to tell me what this probe is all about?"

She rolled her eyes, more uncomfortable as they shifted to her delicate mission. "You know."

His glare held blankness. "No, I don't."

"Happens to you all the time, I'm sure."

His brows leaped. "Harassment?"

"I haven't been harassing you, Travis!"

"Only my friends call me Travis."

"What do your temporary employers call you? Honey?"

"Honey?" He paused, then slapped his forehead. "Oh, no."

"Oh, no, what?"

"You're not connected with the Harrington Agency?"

"Of course, I am! Why else would I be checking you out?" She paused, wondering, "You're not so paranoid as to believe a youthful slipup has me on your tail? That I suspect you of a crime?"

"No! Of course not!" He could feel a telltale flush climbing his face and could do nothing to quell it. "But don't you think you went a little overboard in your inquiries? Do you believe Rachel would allow just anyone to represent her agency?''

She managed a genuine smile. "No, I'm impressed with Harrington. And I would've been satisfied with your principal's praise, if I hadn't heard about your old record today—''

"Bob Williams, the T.J. Hooker of Bayside Station," he cut in. "Minus Hooker's toupee.''

"Bob's a good guy. And he's proud of the way you turned out.''

"Jeepers, I'm touched.''

"It's true, Travis," she persisted for Bob's sake. He cared and deserved the credit.

"Let's just skip the soft sell, okay? My hardhead phase is history!''

She rocked on her heels with a doubting look. "You're not acting like it's in the past.''

"It's really none of your damn business, Detective.''

She raised a finger triumphantly. "Ah, but I made a down payment.''

"Down payment?'' he repeated in hoarse disbelief, his heart slamming against his rib cage. This had to be the Santa Barbara job Rachel pitched to him! He'd half accepted during their brief conference call, scheduling an appointment with her to iron out the details. He hadn't used any caution, so accustomed to trusting Rachel's judgment in these matters. He shouldn't have this time, not for a four-day assignment.

"A down payment," she continued, "on four whole days of your undivided devotion.''

"Get a refund," he snapped.

Her jaw sagged open in disgust. "Maybe I don't want one.''

He studied her keenly. She wanted a refund, all right, but she was too stubborn to give in. The whole story was right there in the depths of her vivid blue eyes. Deep inside she was quivering over his unexpected outburst. Like all the others, she'd probably signed on believing him to be a clean-cut, all-American saint. His file read that way. A teacher with a nose for history. A coach who breathes lots of cleansing air.

Suddenly, she suspected him to be a sinner.

In truth, he was someplace in between, lurking in the gray unknown. To an orderly cop like her, that had to be the worst of the three options. He'd had a long talk with Krista Sundin, the senior who lived in Jill's apartment building. Krista liked her a lot, but it was clear that Jill lived in a black-and-white, law-and-order world that would make Joe Friday of "Dragnet" beam with pleasure. Quite simply, they couldn't be more mismatched.

Still, a little voice inside him played with the idea that she was intriguing. Damn pretty, and desperate, too, if he was any judge. His experience with women, with relationships at school, did give him some insight. He was willing to bet that the bravado hid a fragile, frightened woman. But wasn't that the way it often went with the strong career types? They worked like fiends to attain powerful jobs and recognition for steeliness, only to feel society's slap in the face when they came up empty socially. It was a composite of his average employer.

But Jill Ames was unique somehow. Yes, she had a savvy, collected shell like the others he'd escorted. But a current of electricity hummed around her, too, so subtle that only the most discerning male was bound to notice, so strong that it could stop the heart on contact. Matt liked high-voltage trouble, finding it a challenge to avoid electrocution. But not on the job! He'd always trusted his own self-control. Until tonight...

It would be wise to give her the brush now, before their initial tango here evolved into a full-blown mating dance. It was a cardinal agency rule, not to become emotionally involved, sexually connected with any client. Already, he was breaking that rule, with a captive eye on her luscious curves, luminous eyes and lush, pouty mouth.

But it would be far better with Rachel if Jill made the break. The quickest way to squeeze some reality into the situation just might be to give her a real squeeze.

Jill cried out as he seized her by the bare arms, pulling her up against his solid length. She gulped for night air, but was overwhelmed by a blend of smoke, liquor and masculine scent instead.

"I'm all wrong for you," he rasped. "Understand?"

"Maybe—"

His dark eyes glinted in lustful mischief as he stroked the gentle curve of her jaw. "Maybe I am still dangerous. Really, really dangerous. Maybe I rob stores at night or something."

Her mouth curled wryly as she saw through his bluff. "There's a difference between burglary and robbery—"

"And there's a difference between husbands. Even fake ones."

Jill's mouth puckered for protest, only to be covered by his. Lightning coursed her system as he kissed her thoroughly, his hard lips branding hers, his whiskers digging into her soft complexion. She tried to escape, but her head was firmly cradled between his hands. The searing burn, the hot wet pressure went on and on until she thought she would explode.

And then it was over.

He released her as abruptly as he'd taken her. She stumbled a step before righting herself.

"Some things can't be faked," he scolded on a hoarse, heaving breath.

"No, guess not." She stared at him in heart-hammering wonder, the back of her hand instinctively massaging her chapped skin.

"I mean, you want to convince people that we're a pair, right?"

"Right," she gasped.

"But who'd buy it? I'm not the man you had on order. You thought you were getting a mild-mannered teacher who can spout poetry and use the right fork, didn't you? Well, didn't you?" he pressed in irritation.

"Yes!" she confessed. "Dammit, yes!" She was counting on it so heavily that she'd spilled the details to Penny. One impulsive act and she was in the social jam of her life. Probably fate's hand steering her back to the conservative policies that suited her just right. But just this once, she wanted to be something more than last. If only she could somehow swing it.

"It's a clear case of deceptive advertising." He shoved his hands in his pockets, stared down at his ancient moccasins.

She frowned in uncertainty. "If you know there's more than one fork, you've got potential."

He shook his head with a thin smile.

"Look, I already told my best friend all about you," she explained. "Your name, your vital statistics."

"Vital what?" he asked in amazement. "You must be a real treat at a party." But that probably was why she needed him in the first place, he reasoned. Because she was too wrapped up in her job to play social games. He might have been amiable under other circumstances, but he didn't like the way she used her job to investigate him. In truth, he could handle two forks when pressured—even a third with dessert. But he wouldn't perform. Not for any hard-nosed cop.

"There are lots of other guys at the agency," he said.

Her gaze narrowed. "But I have your name on a contract."

"Burn it," he advised flatly. "Let Rachel start all over with you, steer you to the proper guy."

"But it would keep things so much simpler if you just played yourself," she reasoned. "The respected teacher, the admired coach."

"Coying flattery is beneath you, Detective," he scoffed.

"I happen to know those things are true about you."

"We can't make it work. I can't make it work," he specified, drawing a finger to his chest.

"You don't even know me yet," she sputtered in frustration. Her face was flushed now, too. She was so unappealing that she couldn't even hire a man to play her husband!

He made a vain attempt to control his temper by sinking his teeth into his lip. But his feelings flared just the same. "Look, I know cops. I know snoops. And you're both!"

"I'm cautious," she protested. "Just cautious."

"I hate cautious," he confided with vehemence.

"I hate jerks." She tossed her head with a nod hard enough to send her silky blond hair flying.

He offered her a slit of a smile. "Never mind, Ames. I'll burn the contract myself."

She folded her arms across her chest. "You can't. It's my decision."

Was it? He'd have to check with Rachel on the finer points. "Well, I suggest you sleep on it. You'll soon come to your senses." Grasping her firmly by the elbow and waist, he steered her out to the parking lot. "It's as easy as choosing someone else," he insisted in terse farewell. "There's lots of guys with the agency who need the cash. Who will put up with you for four—"

"Put up with—" She absorbed the blow with indignation, frantically working to keep her balance as they scooted along. He was literally sweeping her off her feet with his heavy-handedness. But it bore no resemblance to the romantic vision the term suggested. She felt like a dustball in the way of a rough, stroking broom.

He halted between the rows, realizing that he'd over-played his hand, not knowing which car was hers. "Here now," he bluffed. "I'll bet this boxy gray sedan is yours. Reliable. Four-door."

"You're wrong."

"Oh, really?"

"This white boxy four-door is mine," she retorted, marching over to a car of similar make. "They were all out of gray ones." She inserted her key in the lock and he stepped up to whisk open the door.

His eyes glinted in the shadows. "It's been grand knowing you."

Jill slipped behind the wheel, fastening her seat belt. "It ain't over till it's over, Travis."

Matt shook his head, folding his sinewy arms over the expanse of his chest. "It's over, copper," he asserted. "It's over."

Chapter Four

To Matt's chagrin, Chet was anxiously awaiting his return to the grill. His father's watchful eyes were on him as he passed the booth formerly occupied by Jill. Two young women in pastel shorts and blouses were seated there now with glasses of beer. Their faces brightened in excitement as he leaned over the booth, then fell again when all he did was scoop up Jill's forgotten sweater and stalk toward the bar.

"So, what's the deal?" Chet asked, moving away from the register.

"It's nothing."

Chet pursed his lips in doubt. "You sure were outside a long time over nothing."

Matt propped a hand on the brass post behind his father, keeping his head and voice low. "She wasn't here officially. She was connected with Harrington."

"Oh! She wanted a husband, did she?"

"Shh!"

Chet shook his gray head. "The poor little thing. I feel sorry for all those ladies who need a service like that."

"It's just your old-fashioned values, Dad. Ladies who can afford the service are independent and usually contentedly single."

"She must've struck a chord with you," Chet surmised. "I can't remember the last time you've been so worked up over a gal."

Matt balked. "I thought she was going to arrest me!"

"That would've taken fifteen seconds to sort out," Chet pressed. "You were gone fifteen minutes."

"I had to explain why I couldn't take the job."

"Why you—" Chet broke off in disgust. "You turned her down?"

"Naturally! She's just not the type I could spend four whole days with." Without putting my hands on. "I couldn't play the part convincingly," he spluttered, "cuddling up to a cop—a narrow-minded authority monger."

"Well, then, I'll just put the monger's sweater in the lost and found," Chet declared brusquely, grabbing for the knit jacket.

Matt held it out of reach with a vigorous, knowing nod. "Oh, sure. And have her accuse me of stealing it."

"I'll protect you, boy," the slight man heartily promised with a clenched fist. "Pow. Boom. Bang."

Matt cleared his throat. "I'll just make sure she gets it back. That'll nip a fuss."

Chet winked, much to Matt's dismay. "You might have sold me with that excuse. If your whiskers weren't flecked with that lipstick."

Matt's fingers flew to his mustache.

"Nip a fuss," Chet repeated in a hoot. "Fuss follows you around like a waggin' tail on a spaniel, son."

"Well, this spaniel is home to the kennel," Matt announced, reaching behind the bar for his key ring. "Papers to correct. Early to bed for tomorrow's track meet."

"Yeah, now there's a wild man's life. Where'd that girl ever get the idea you'd be a match for her?"

"Dad—"

Chet waved him off as he took a waitress's order for two vodka tonics. "Fuss... Get the hell out of here before I call the cops on you myself!"

MATT STORMED the Harrington Agency the following afternoon after school.

The receptionist in the airy outer office nearly toppled off her chair in horror as she scanned his powerful body, exposed in his gray, hacked-off sweats, and worn grass-stained athletic shoes.

"Mr. Travis!" Her hiss echoed up through the high ceiling.

He paused before the woman's ornate desk, his right arm akimbo, his left hand crushing the open book she'd been reading. "Where is she?"

The receptionist glanced at the two young well-dressed women seated on the teal satin sofa, then back to him. "I thought you just spoke to Rachel on the telephone—"

"I did. She told me to come right over."

"I mistakenly assumed you were dressed."

His head snapped up at the sound of his employer's voice. Rachel was standing at a doorway down the hall, an elegant counterpoint to his scruffiness in her red shawl-collared suit, with her brown hair woven in a flawless French braid. She crooked her finger, summoning him forward.

Remembering his manners, he turned to nod at the pair on the sofa. "Ladies."

They rewarded him with brimming smiles as he passed, then tipped forward to watch his progress down the hardwood floor. "He's a husband?" they chorused to the receptionist.

"Ah, yes," the receptionist affirmed uncomfortably.

"We'll take two."

"Just like him!"

Matt absorbed the complimentary remarks, then sauntered into the office after Rachel, shoving the door back into its frame. "Maybe I'm on to something with these rags," he goaded. "They want me out there. Without references. What refreshing clients. Ones who don't peek everywhere but inside my pants!"

"Ooh, aren't we the Neanderthal today," Rachel commented briskly, folding her arms across her chest.

"What are you trying to do to me?" he demanded in a roar, prowling around the sedate sitting room.

"Figure you out, for starters." Rachel shook her head in bewilderment. "I've never seen you so out of sorts. Never known you to shoo off a client—"

"But it can be done, right?"

Rachel winced in his hopeful face. "Jill Ames has to terminate the deal. You see, she made a down payment—"

"On my devotion," he interrupted. "Yes, she told me!"

"You gave me the power to act on your behalf a long time ago," she reminded him. "And I've done so many times without incident."

"I guess you were about due for a mistake," he generously admitted. "The next step will be to turn the screws on her. Get her to renege."

"I might be able to persuade her," she rephrased with a reprimanding look. "But I'd like to have an explanation. She's lovely, Matt. Charming, sweet..." And desperate, in a way only another woman could truly understand. Rachel was touched by Jill plight. How sad, to be totally prepared to confront criminals day after day, yet to feel so helpless with the people who were supposed to care about her. The idea that such a top-notch lady would ever doubt herself seemed a crime in itself! "Perhaps if you had a clearer picture of Jill," she reasoned, "of the job—"

"I understand the job! Four long days with a type A cop. I'm type B, you know," he claimed with a nod.

"To me, you're behaving like type C. And C stands for chicken."

His protesting squawk sounded a little on the fowl side. And it brought a glimmer of comic relief, causing them both to lighten up a fraction.

"What's gotten into you, Matt?" she chided, gesturing to his hairy limbs and tousled head. "You look like a man who didn't sleep a wink last night. Who didn't even comb his hair!"

"The wind is a coach's comb. Aw, maybe I didn't sleep much," he confessed after a pause. "I was overloaded with students' essays on the Revolutionary War." Overloaded with visions of the kiss, too. The lip smack that was supposed to turn her off. He didn't know how it affected her, but it had rocked a traitorous response inside him. His own senses had turned against him, lavishing in her heat and softness. It was a wonder that the papers got corrected at all. Why, every time he picked up her sweater, he couldn't resist drawing it to his face, inhaling her sweet perfume. He finally had to stick it in a drawer about three o'clock in the morning—if he ever hoped to get any work done!

"Can't you see this match was a mistake?" he asked, stalking across the scatter of Persian rugs. "She was no doubt expecting an even-tempered teacher, someone stable enough to make the marriage look authentic to her critics—and diplomatic enough to keep it up for four solid days!"

"That's the Matt Travis I've known for a year," Rachel argued quietly.

He whirled on her so fast, it stirred the papers on the desk. "Huh?"

"Matt, you have always delivered that kind of service in the past, smoothly stepped into awkward, tough situations, wacky predicaments." She lifted her hands in confusion. "Somehow, Jill Ames has drawn out the very worst in you."

There was a silence between them. Matt gave her a guarded look, then peered out a window overlooking the front courtyard to buy some time. She was probing. For the first time in their satisfying arrangement, she had her doubts. He was sinking fast in the deep stuff because he'd unleashed his temper. Rachel didn't know about his teenage skirmishes with the law. Nobody knew, aside from close friends and family.

And nobody had a right to know. An alibi, a half truth, seemed best.

"Look, Rachel," he began on a pleading note, "this Ames woman embarrassed me. Ran an official check on me."

Rachel had the grace to wince. "Oops."

"Oops?" he repeated angrily, charging her desk.

"I'm sure it's a routine thing in her mind," she said with a tap of her pencil. "Can't you look at it with a sense of humor?"

"That's a very good question," a third, feminine voice challenged.

Rachel and Matt fell silent at the sight of Jill in the doorway.

Rachel smoothly stood up, flashing Matt a warning look. "I invited Jill over to settle this matter."

Matt watched as Rachel rounded the desk and shook hands with Jill. Coincidentally, they were both dressed in similar red suits, short tailored jackets with A-line skirts. A fact they paused to discuss in platitudinous tones, as though he wasn't even there. How he fervently wished he was someplace else! He hated his current state of helplessness. Over at the school, he was king. One blow of his whistle and fleets scrambled. Right now he was trapped in a haze of red. Fire engine red. He had to rein in his emotions. He had to sever this agreement now. Take a stand!

He cleared his throat with force. Luckily, it did have the influence of a whistle blow. Both women turned to him in dubious query. "Look, Jill," he began, lines of tension fanning his eyes and mouth.

Jill folded her arms across her chest, her spine stiffening. It appeared that he hadn't mellowed a fraction since last night.

"I—"

"This is the way I see it, Travis," she broke in anxiously. "I don't have the spare time or energy to fight you on this arrangement of ours—"

"Good!"

The new pleasure infusing his voice made her tingle beneath her layers of gabardine and nylon. She couldn't resist openly inspecting him, finding sensuous delight in the fact that he had on the same raggedly revealing clothing he'd worn out on the school field yesterday.

He began to advance with a hopeful, crooked smile. Obviously, he'd felt the chemistry in their kiss, too. Thank heavens for that! He'd do the job and do it well.

As he moved into her space, she couldn't help but relive their encounter, the pressure of his hands in her hair, the driving hardness of his mouth, the tantalizing burn of his whiskers on her skin.

No man had ever dared treat her that way. She never knew why for sure. Perhaps some were put off by her aloof nature or by her job.

Or perhaps it all boiled down to the fact that she'd always been careful to select the right kind of man. The kind she could understand, second-guess.

Matt Travis was the wrong kind of man. Explosive, unpredictable. She never knew what he was going to say or do next. His intensity left a foreign and provocative brand on her.

She inhaled deeply, struggling to keep her voice steady. After all, this was a professional arrangement. "Travis, sometime in the middle of the night, something crept up on me—"

"Burglar?" he asked with a wolfish glint.

Her creamy forehead puckered in discontent. "No, the question of your qualifications for the job."

"Wonderful," he said. "I gave it a good, fair look over-night myself. My pass at you was a bit rough, but I did it to prove how unfit I am."

"What pass?" Rachel demanded impatiently with a tap of her red suede shoe.

"It's all right, Rachel," Jill soothed. "It made everything so clear."

Rachel blinked. Twice.

Jill beamed. "And clarity is so important, because time is of the essence."

Rachel's gaze narrowed. "Exactly what are you saying, Jill?"

"She wants you to fire up that computer over there, Rach," Matt interjected jovially, gesturing to the desk. "Find my replacement, pronto. She already blabbed to somebody about me, so it will have to be a husband who fits my general description, who's willing to use my name—"

Jill raised her slender ivory hands with a squeal of indignation. "Stop right there! I expect you to take on the role of my husband. As agreed!"

"You can't mean it, Detective!" he thundered in correction.

They stared at each other for a long, tense moment of speechless disbelief, each believing the other to be totally insane.

"I know my own mind," Jill eventually said, flaming patches of embarrassment heating her cheeks. Somehow, they were getting their signals crossed here. But hadn't last night's passionate explosion changed the dynamics of things between them? She knew he'd kissed her to drive her away. He'd made that crystal clear. But in her mind, the ploy had backfired. She'd gone home and collapsed! From that moment on, she assumed he'd be more than willing to do the job. And about three o'clock this morning, after hours of tossing and turning, she came to realize that he was just right for it.

Jill was accustomed to dealing with every adversary in a forthright manner. It took all her savvy to tip up her chin, stare deeply into his syrupy dark eyes, searching... Was Matt Travis as unyielding as he seemed?

He met her sky blue gaze with a hammering heart. For the first time in his life he clearly understood raw fear. Not that he hadn't been frightened on occasion. His time in that juvenile halfway house hadn't been pleasant. And there'd been skirmishes at his dad's bar, when he'd played bouncer to some dangerous losers. But the pulsating waves heating his nervous system right now were nothing short of alarming. His libido was humming uncontrollably, with no connection whatsoever to his brain.

Matt pressed his fingers to his temples. He had to relieve the pressure. He considered kissing her again. But then he realized it was a trick his body was playing on his good sense. "Jill," he uttered in perplexity. "I thought you understood. I'm the wrong kind of husband for you."

"Of course you are!" She wholeheartedly agreed. Smart girls didn't marry men like the sort Matt had proven to be, rough, callous, selfish. They held out for the kind of man he had appeared to be on his résumé. But if she was going to play pretend, why not go for the biggest show?

Forget the firecracker romance. Bring in the stick of dynamite.

Men that reached out and grabbed a lady for a kiss—they were the rogues of fanciful dreams. Why not capture her friends' imaginations, bask in their shock over her choice? Be the envy of everyone for a change!

"I can't fool your slick friends with forks and pomp," he complained.

"I admit that was my original intention when I signed you on," she explained with hands clasped at her chin. "But I've concluded that your impossible temperament is even better!"

His strong jawline sagged. It appeared that he could do no wrong with her. No matter what face he revealed, she improvised to make it suit. She was a witch under that conservative veneer. A captivating sorceress determined to make use of him no matter how he struggled. Chet would never believe it of a Bayside cop. Not in a million years.

"Well, it's settled then," Rachel said, hurriedly moving to her chair behind the desk. "We'll just finish up the paperwork."

Matt gulped. "Now?"

"I need you, Matt," Jill declared bluntly, finding such candor comfortable from a business perspective. "We don't have any time to lose. The wedding is two weeks away."

"It's just a case of a few signatures and dates," Rachel told him significantly, "being that I've already committed you."

"Ah, yes, the down payment on my devotion," he couldn't resist murmuring with a trace of mocking. "The important details are already settled."

Jill's face burned hotter despite her reserve. "Well, what else would you call it?"

"Nothing suits me better." He flashed a row of large white teeth beneath his mustache. "You've just bought yourself the big bad wolf, lady."

The lady flinched just a little bit, keeping her voice steady. "Wonderful, Travis. It shouldn't take more than a few hours to mold you into the man of my dreams."

It was Matt's turn to flinch, as he imagined her hands on him . . . like a sculptress manipulating soft clay.

A LESSON IN MATRIMONY, courtesy of the very single Jill Ames. Matt's lean muscular form vibrated with annoyance and anticipation as he jammed his thumb into her apartment doorbell the following night. He'd never had to take pointers from a wife before. On the bright side, though, dinner was included. And there was going to be some tutoring from both sides of the old proverbial desk if he had anything to do with it. At the very least, he was going to challenge the age-old theory that the customer was always right.

Deep inside he knew his attitude was wrong. But he was having trouble reining in his emotions. This whole thing about her being a snoopy police officer had started as a grain of irritation that had now inflated way out of proportion in his mind. He never should've kissed her in an effort to turn her off. Ironically, it had been the flame that had really lit the fuse. He'd come to believe that she probably would've dumped him if he'd kept his distance, allowed her to dig out his secrets on her own.

But in his own defense, he hadn't understood why she was probing. It had made him jittery. Even though he was innocent of any wrongdoing, he'd feared being suspected, misunderstood by the cops all over again.

To top it all off, he now had Rachel Harrington on his case, furious with his unprofessionalism, deaf to his excuses. He'd pointed out that he kissed ladies on the job all the time. But Rachel argued that the meter wasn't running yet with Jill Ames, and it was likely that he'd delivered more than the purse-lipped peck expected of agency men. Rachel's suspicions were correct, of course. He couldn't stop thinking about the wet heat of Jill's mouth, the way her upper lip trembled when he grazed it with his mustache. Or the way her body had eventually involuntarily responded in the hurried moments to follow—before he pushed her away with a curt goodbye. How he longed to feel her softness against him again!

So here he stood, rubbing the back of his neck, corded rigid as a timber. He was contractually bound to play the part of the caged rebel, snagged and put in line by Officer Ames.

Hell, maybe tonight's encounter would cure him of his fever, put the job in a more objective perspective. Maybe she wasn't as pretty as he remembered.

Jill swung the door open, an oven mitt on one hand, a huge two-pronged fork in the other. "Hi."

He groaned inwardly. She was that pretty.

"Sorry it took so long to answer," she went on, with an awkward wave of her fork. "I was cooking."

Matt's gaze slid her length, lingering on her legs. She was nicely outfitted in a pair of new blue jeans. They gloved her small seat in a very appealing way. But they were so stiff looking. He suspected all her jeans had this same brand-new quality. As unbroken in as she herself was. To her credit, however, her loosely woven green sweater with mid-arm sleeves was right in fashion over at the school, and her makeup was far brighter than her regulation coral. He had the feeling that she was trying to loosen up a bit, perhaps make herself more appealing to him so he'd be more comfortable in the role. But a comfort zone seemed hopeless. His thoughts of her could never linger on a professional plane, not when he habitually envisioned her naked.

"Coming in, Travis?" she prodded, openly puzzled by his slack-jawed expression.

"Yeah, sure." He stepped past her, noting with amusement that her fair hair was a bit mussed on one side of her ear. Must've happened while she was poking around at the stove. She'd discover it, fix it. But in the meantime, he'd enjoy the little flaw, hope it was a sign of fragility.

She peeled off her mitt with an impatient gesture, obviously tired of the inspection. He smoothly shifted his gaze to her home. Everything in the cramped little place was off white! Drapes, chairs, walls. With little dashes of navy blue for contrast.

"You don't get much company, do you?" he asked, shoving his hands into the back pockets of his jeans.

"Why do you say that?" she asked in affront. She couldn't believe how this man could so adeptly hit a nerve. With that crooked grin and cocky walk. A walking, talking lady-killer.

"I didn't mean anything," he claimed, with a casual gesture.

Sure you didn't. Jill's gaze narrowed as he began to wander around on her champagne-shaded carpeting. He was vivid masculinity against the pallid canvas of the room, adding strength, presence and color. His glossy brown hair was catching the last rays of the setting sun glinting through the window. His shirt was blue and his denims were a trendy faded black. His shoes were worn brown leather that had traveled many a mile. She hoped the soles were clean.

"I suppose I keep things a little bit too neat for your taste," she wagered, wandering up behind him as he examined a silver-framed sketch of the San Francisco marina.

Sterile was the word that jumped to mind. He was tempted to quip that he would feel more than safe having his appendix removed right there on her satin sofa, but judging from the chipped diamond glitter in her eye, he suspected she might just give it a try with her mitt and megafork, without anesthetic.

"My place is more cluttered," he confessed conversationally, "what, with all my hand-me-down furniture and my printed materials. It's really been over the top since Hill's fund-raiser last fall, when the kids were selling magazine subscriptions." He shook his head and chuckled, "I was quickly pegged as the man who could not say no."

She smiled with open coyness, as though tucking away that secret for future reference. "Well, I like things neat. Places, people. Life."

He looked doubtful. "Sure you do."

"Excuse me?" she challenged with a frown.

"Lies are the messiest of all, Detective," he said. "And you have summoned me over here to concoct a whopper."

"I figure I'm entitled to one whopper in my lifetime," she answered. He had pinched a nerve. "Heaven only knows how many you've told," she added pettily.

He studied his blunt fingernails. "None of my business."

Her temper simmered under his benevolent expression. "You're acting like it's an insult to need an escort!"

He lifted his broad shoulders as though they were feather light. "I just think this isn't your style," he murmured, "playing games with friends and family."

"Well, has it occurred to you that it's liars like me that keep you in business?" she asked.

He threw his head back with a burst of rich masculine laughter. "You want to win this one, fine. You desperately need a husband."

Dark passion flickered in her eyes, darkening them to midnight ink. He was deliberately taunting her, probably out of curiosity. There was so much he didn't understand, about her past, her needs. She was torn between straightening him out and shoving him out the door. Instead, she took the middle road. "C'mon, let's eat."

Matt trailed after her into the kitchen. The bland decor flowed into the tiny nook, right down to her practical ceramic dinnerware. "So what are we having?" he asked, scanning the two place settings on her U shaped counter space.

"Meat loaf."

He inhaled appreciatively. "Smells great."

She bent over to open the oven, catching a look at her reflection in the tempered glass door. She wasted no time smoothing the rough spot in her hair.

He played sentry to the operation, rubbing his hands together with anticipation. "I love a juicy homemade loaf.

My mom uses bread crumbs and basil and a touch of to-mato paste.''

"Oh, this isn't homemade," she quickly corrected, reaching into the oven with her mitted hand.

"But you've got that big old fork," he protested.

"I use it to poke the middle, see if it's still frozen," she explained. He released a groan as she removed an alumi-num pan from the rack.

"It's not so bad," she assured him, sliding it on to a butcher block board near the plates.

"I know what it's like," he lamented. "I make 'em all the time. Granny Goodrite's Gourmet Loaf."

"I'm afraid I don't know much about cooking."

"Well, I know enough about it to make this kind of dis-appointment really hurt."

She stepped around him to the refrigerator, producing deli cartons of cole slaw and potato salad. "It's your own fault for assuming way too much."

"Yeah. I did peg you for the type who ate foods with just the right balance of nutrients and calories. Fresh kale sal-ads and grilled chicken with just a dash of lemon pepper. Steamy popovers from scratch."

"Sounds delicious," she agreed, pouring ice water into two tall frosted glasses. "Know any cooks who deliver?"

He picked up utensils to slice into the loaf, then placed slabs of meat on their plates with an experienced flourish. "There are a couple of Hill High teachers who wouldn't mind. Cooking for me. Or with me," he added with wicked pride, causing her face to scrunch.

"I'll just bet," she said, jabbing serving spoons into the deli cartons.

"Girls looking for—"

"Tarzan the monkey man!"

"Looking for companionship," he smoothly corrected. "A nice guy."

She flashed him a grand smile. "I wish them well in their continued search."

"They're continuing their search because I don't want to settle down," he informed her, affronted.

Jill arched her soft brows. "I'm sure. Hope you went easy on 'em." *Easier than you've been on me.* "Well, dig in," she invited, easing onto one of the stools. "Like you would if we were really married."

"Huh?" It was his turn to make a face.

She lifted her slender shoulders. "That's part of why you're here, of course, so we can practice being together."

"You need practice being with someone?" he demanded in disbelief.

"I'm not used to you," she clarified on a defensive note. Actually, she was accustomed to doing most things alone, but she'd have rather died than admit it. "And married couples are supposed to have a fair amount of rapport while they dine together," she went on to point out.

He slanted her a wary look. "This isn't a test, is it? I mean, you don't want to see if we can chew in sync or anything, because—"

"Just chew, dammit!" she exclaimed in embarrassment, curling her fingers around her water glass. He was deliberately making this hard. It wasn't right. He was the employee!

His gripe with her obviously didn't diminish his appetite. Before Jill could blink, he was scooping large portions of food onto his plate.

"Any tasty dishes waiting for us back home?" he asked, forking some slaw.

"Think you'll be hungry again by then?" she retorted, then took a sip of water.

He ignored the gibe, intent on getting a feel for the trip. "You mentioned something about staying with your aunt yesterday. The one who raised you."

Jill studied her plate. "Yes. It's expected that we will stay there."

"Well, tell me about her."

"She's not much of a cook," she sweetly replied in misdirection. "But you won't have to worry. There will be one party after the other—for the wedding. You can prowl from one buffet to the next."

"You make me sound like a bear on the prowl."

"Not at all," she denied, slicing her meat into cubes. "I'm confident you'll do your job. Be my man."

The fervency in her tone rattled his bones. When it came to his role, she was direct, forward and focused. But she'd swiftly reneged at the mention of her aunt. There undoubtedly was a deep undercurrent involved, probably a motivation behind Jill's charade. But was it enough to intimidate a savvy cop like her into such a tight corner? He already understood the basics of the job—fool her close hometown circle into believing that she was hitched. Why would this beautiful, successful creature bother?

Jill stiffened her spine, toying with her food. He was beginning to dig into things that didn't concern him. A problem, since she intended to reveal only so much and expected him to respond obediently. A sidelong glance to his strong, set jawline cautioned her that he wasn't accustomed to that kind of compliance.

"I'm good at my job, Detective," he eventually assured her in the tense silence.

"Well, you can start by calling me Jill," she suggested. "Detective just won't ring right down in Santa Barbara."

"Yes, you're right. Have any dessert, Jill?"

She sighed hard. He toyed with her name like a naughty word. But how could she voice a complaint that he wouldn't twist around with fiendish delight? "There's a lemon pie in the freezer," she said. "It's nothing fancy. But feel free to dig it out while I go get my notes."

Notes? Matt watched her slip off the stool and disappear through the doorway. Of course she would take notes. He perused the dinner remainders, observing that she really hadn't eaten much of anything herself. She didn't keep a shape like hers without eating sometime. Was it nerves? Over the job? Over him?

It was crazy to care about a client. Much wiser to do his duty. Get it over with. The pay was good and would cover the cost of replacing his old freezer with a new deluxe model. Considering his busy schedule and his lack of a good woman, he was destined to be stocking a variety of Granny Goodrite's products indefinitely.

Chapter Five

They ended up in the living room a short time later, Matt with his wedge of mediocre lemon pie and Jill with her neat little autobiography.

Had she revealed anything that could be used against her? She paced beside her glass-topped coffee table, studying her paper through gold-rimmed reading glasses, sipping ice water. She gazed at Matt, pausing to ask if he was comfortable on the sofa.

He grinned grimly. Of course he wasn't! On his turf the sofas were couches. And if they were slippery and spotless, it was because they were covered in clear protective plastic. So he sat stiffly, with his dessert plate balanced on his knee, alert for any falling crumbs. He felt like taking her for a roll in the crumbs, breaking down her defenses just once for a good long look.

"Okay," she began pensively. "Guess you won't need to review my vital statistics."

"We could review them," he obliged, with a flicking inventory of her curves.

His look burned clear through her. She couldn't help but wonder what he was thinking, if he did like what he was seeing. But it shouldn't matter, she reiterated. He was a temporary employee. An oversexed, overpowering male, a small inner voice taunted. She endured the tingle racing along her spine. But she already knew that, didn't she? It was the reason she was proceeding with him in the role.

He was going to singe the socks off of all her friends. Just as he was doing to her right now. Which was all that mattered. That her friends be impressed.

"I included my stats because I originally planned to mail this report to you," she explained angrily.

"Sure, sure." He swallowed his last bite of soggy crust and imitation lemon freeze, then set his plate and fork on the table with a sigh of relief. The inferior pie was hardly worthy of the balancing act with the plate.

She opened her mouth to press the issue, then clamped it shut. She filled the uncertain moment with a sip of water. As she hovered over this crass excuse for a spouse with her glass poised, she found herself studying his head, rashly tempted to give it a dousing. His hair was rather a nice color of brown—most likely streaked to its shiny caramel shade by the sun. She grew so intent on its rich texture and highlights that she was taken off guard when his hand snaked up for the paper between her fingers.

"Hey! Give that back!"

Matt laughed, his sinewy arm holding the paper just out of her reach as he read. "How many commendations have you gotten? Four? Wowee. Slappin' on the cuffs right and left."

"My friends know all about it, and will expect you to know, too," she said defensively.

"Naturally! I want to know everything. Let's see..." He trailed off, scanning the printed page. "Happy birthday. You just turned thirty last week. And...you love vanilla ice cream, baked potatoes with a dash of salt. Favorite games are Trivial Pursuit and chess." He lifted his broad shoulders a fraction. "No shocking revelations here, Detective. Really nothing to get huffy about."

"Thanks for the ten-second analysis!"

He reared back in amazement. She was truly insulted. She'd made this list for him, and now she didn't want to release the information. A self-chiding reminder about his own penchant for privacy niggled in the back of his brain, but he dismissed it. He wasn't seeking companionship, she was! She wasn't going to impress his friends with her devotion, he was going to impress hers.

"Just trying to cut through the red tape," he explained. "We'd be here all night if you insisted on spoon-feeding me all these details, gauging my reaction to each and every one."

Jill rubbed her delicate jawline in contemplation. He made sense. In an objective way. But the invasion she felt was subjective. She was a private person who knew only too well that information was power. Her aunt had used every weakness she possessed in an effort to control her as a child. She'd sworn to never reveal anything vital to anyone ever again. She knew she had to tell him some things, but they were her facts to give in any way she chose to give them. Her eyes narrowed to slits as she met his snappy ones.

He laced his fingers behind his head, leaning back on the sofa. "Consider me a professional, Ames," he suggested mildly. "I've done this gig many times and pick up on only the information I really need."

"I'll try," she agreed guardedly.

He returned to the sheet, intent on absorbing the rest. She suddenly recalled that she'd penciled in some things at the bottom, single-word reminders of things she considered telling her *faux* husband, about her old boyfriend, Roger, her aunt Wilma's stern disapproval, her lack of centered family life. But that had been way back on Saturday, when she had envisioned Matt Travis to be a caring, sensitive sort. Right now her defensive walls were as high as they'd ever been with anyone. She wanted to reveal absolutely nothing to this man. But at the same time she wanted him to show them all how mad he was for her.

"Hey, what's all this scribbling at the bottom mean?" he wondered, jarring her back to the moment. "Something about a prom?" His thick brown brows crowded over his nose. "What were you planning to do? Case out Hill's prom? See if I can dance? Well, for your information, our prom is after your wedding. A whole week after. And who's Roger? And what's this about Glory Farm wine? Wasn't that popular back in the eighties?"

Jill's blood began to boil over his defensive attitude, his rude probing. Enough was enough. "Some of those notations were for me alone, you nosy jerk!" She peeled off her glasses and made a wild grab for the paper, gasping as she lost her footing between the table and sofa.

"Hey, you're the one who can use some dance lessons." His chuckle quickly turned to a yelp as she fell into him, sloshing the last of her water into the hollow of his throat. A cold surprise, followed by a hot cushy one. It was almost worth the icy sting of the water to feel the supple crush of her body against his. Almost.

"Brr!" He snagged her wrist, rescued the glass, set it on the table with a thump. He liked the feel of her fine bones beneath his fingers, so much so that he snagged the other wrist, as well. For a brief huffing moment he held her arms above his head, enjoying the softness of her soft breasts pressing into his chest. The paper that had caused all the ruckus had drifted to the floor, completely out of their reach.

"You—you can't just take information, Travis," she breathed in rage, trying to twist out of reach. "Information I don't want you to have."

"Ah, chill out, will ya?"

His lazy command sunk in, making her realize that this confrontation was silly. He knew nothing. Not yet. She instantly stopped struggling, opening her eyes to find that their noses were touching, their lashes close enough to brush.

A little squirming verified another fact. They were laid out limb for limb. She applied a questing pressure, taking in his every contour, every muscled twist and plane, eventually realizing that the casualness reflected in his sloe-eyed look didn't quite reach below the belt. Rigid flesh nudged her belly, straining at their barriers of clothing. Lustful yearnings surged through her insides despite her annoyance. She couldn't help but wonder just what it would be like to make love to him. Her heart was beating fiercely in her rib cage. Could he feel it? Could he hear it? Would he figure out just how easily he sent her spinning?

Matt stared up into her blazing features snared in a seductive trap of his own. Lord, she had him nailed, hot, bothered and vulnerable. Luckily, she was too upset to realize what a clever sculptress she was with this hunk of clay. "Pardon me," he crooned in suspect apology. "Happens at the oddest moments."

"Thanks a heap!" She lunged off his length as though he'd turned combustive.

With a huff of relief, he sat up in the center of the pristine sofa, tipping his face up to hers. She was standing at a safe distance, with her arms folded across her chest, vibrating with annoyance. Her hair was really messy now. He exhaled heavily, resting his forearms on his thighs. "If you refuse to give me even basic information, how can I do a good job?"

"You'll manage," she returned, her cold voice doing little to quell the fire banked inside her. She couldn't remember the last time she'd tumbled to the floor that way, or brought so prompt a response to a man. Was it real or, as he claimed, a fluke? He wanted her to see it as a malfunction.

"I won't manage without more facts, Jill," he said impatiently.

Facts. They both shifted their attention across the carpet, back to the paper. Jill was quicker this time. She charged forward, bringing her sandaled foot down on it hard, capturing it, folding it into several pieces. "Just forget all about the extras on here," she advised. Realizing that she had no pockets, she stuffed the paper into the scooped neck of her green top, wedging it into her bra.

"You have a funny way of urging me to forget me to forget all about all the extras," he raved roguishly.

A rap on the door interrupted their duel.

"Expecting anybody?"

Jill's eyes widened. "No." She moved across the carpet, smoothing her hair, tugging at her clothing.

"Better check the peephole," he advised grumpily. "Might be your partner, charging in to protect you."

"What would you like me to do if it is?" she wondered incredulously.

"Secure the chain and get me another piece of pie."

Jill released an audible groan as she checked on her caller through the peephole.

"Anybody I know?"

"Yes." Before he could protest, she swung open the door. "Krista. Amanda. What a surprise."

Matt's stubbled jaw slacked as his seventeen-year-old students crossed the threshold without real invitation.

"Evening, Coach," Krista said with a coy look. The lanky blonde sidled up to the sofa with her petite brunet cohort on her heels. Both girls were dressed in hooded flannel shirts, cotton shorts and black tennis shoes.

Jill swiftly closed the door and joined them with wringing hands. "I wasn't expecting you—"

"Sure you were!" they chorused in affront.

"Not tonight," she clarified firmly. "We talked about Saturday morning."

"Yeah," Krista admitted, tossing her flaxen mane over her shoulder. "But then we spotted Coach's car, and thought, well..."

"What's he doin' here, we thought," Amanda finished with shining hazel eyes.

"Krista lives in the building, two floors below," Jill explained for Matt's benefit.

His mouth curled discontentedly. "I know."

Jill rolled her eyes. "Nothing gets by you, does it?"

"You guys having a fight about something?" Amanda asked eagerly.

"Hey, I bet you came over here to find out why Jill was spying on you over at the school," Krista deduced with a snap of her fingers. "Why were you doing that, Jill?"

"I wasn't spying," Jill denied with just the right dash of acrimony. "Not on him. I was just..."

"Checking out the school's security," Matt supplied, feeling a sudden overwhelming urge to conceal their circumstance from these young, prying, judgmental eyes. It wasn't a protective gesture toward a cop more than capable of taking care of herself, no way. No matter how limpid and stricken those blue eyes of hers happened to be right now. It was a self-preserving move, pure and simple. He had to face these girls every day. And they didn't know about his moonlighting at the Harrington Agency. No matter how you sliced it, his visit was none of their business. A fact he told them with characteristic directness.

"We didn't come over here to see you, anyway," Krista staunchly assured him with a sniff.

"Not really," Amanda agreed, with a bob of her curls. "Just because we saw your Jeep in Jill's guest parking slot and figured it was weird doesn't mean we don't have a real reason to be here. Our own real reason."

Matt rose to his full height, looming over them like a thundercloud. "Okay," he said sternly. "Give it to me."

"Why don't you girls come back on Saturday," Jill hastily intervened. She grasped them by their respective hoods and frantically tried to shepherd them toward the door. She had to turn this around! Before he saw her inventory. Clearly understood what a loser she was.

"Let us look at your collection now," Krista pleaded, with hands clasped for prayer. "Please. We'll make it quick."

"This was supposed to be between the three of us," Jill said with a meaningful glare, stiffly aware of Matt's keen observation. He would like to have something more on her right now. And this revelation was the key to everything, taking a quick front seat to the sheet of paper they'd been tussling over.

"Ah, don't worry," Amanda advised in breezy misunderstanding. "Nobody at school knows about your legendary collection. Not that we wouldn't like to set you up with a little rental business—"

Jill pushed a silencing finger to the girl's lips. "I already told you I don't care to rent anything out to anyone!"

"We'd only take ten percent," Krista coaxed.

Jill's mouth sagged open. She was amazed at their persistence. "No!"

"What is going on?" Matt erupted, edging out from behind the coffee table.

"Nothing!" Jill cried out. "Really, it's nothing."

Matt squinted in confusion. She was behaving as though she had a dead body hidden in a closet someplace!

"Oh, don't be so modest," Krista admonished.

To Matt's amazement, the girls broke free of Jill and headed across the living room to the only visible closet, a large one spanning the long wall near the entrance.

Jill was rooted helplessly to the carpet as they pulled the mirrored bi-fold doors back to reveal her secret.

"Dresses?" Matt squinted and advanced for a closer look.

"What were you expecting?" she flared. "A row of skeletons?"

"Well . . . not dresses."

Not just any dresses, she thought, agonized. The sturdy wooden eight-foot rod was heavy with hangers straining from the weight of sumptuous formalwear. Gaudy, pricy, formal gowns in a spectrum of colors, fabrics and styles.

Jill sagged against the wall just inside the hallway as the girls rummaged through the garments. She stole glances at Matt, who was fingering through the hangers himself.

"This is quite a collection," he said with awed interest. "I didn't realize women kept a jazzy wardrobe like this."

"Not just any woman does," Krista boasted, tapping his arm. "It takes time, cash and a whole bunch of pals lucky enough to find—" She faltered, realizing that she'd crossed the line.

"Find what?" Matt demanded, puzzled.

"Well, a man," Krista supplied on a feeble note, busying herself at the jammed rack, peeling out a lemony halter knit with a sheer bolero jacket. She held it up to herself, exchanging opinions with Amanda, who had stumbled upon a purple crepe culotte with matching gold belt.

Matt was dumbstruck. Did Jill have a man for each dress? Twenty plus men? If so, what did she need him for? He stroked his jaw, querying her with a measuring stare. She tucked her silken hair behind her ears, averting his gaze. She was really uncomfortable. What was the deal here? Was she a secret party girl? Someone who played the straight cop by day and roamed the clubs at night dressed to the teeth? He pondered the idea, envisioned her on the prowl. What an enticing stretch of the imagination.

"You go out a lot or something?" he finally blurted out. "Is it for work?"

"Work?" she repeated reprovingly. He had to be stringing her along again. He seemed to enjoy doing that a lot.

Her anger wiped away his smile. "I only mean... Well, it seems extravagant on a cop's salary—which is something like a teacher's pay, isn't it?"

A pink tint crept across her cheeks. He'd been closer with his skeleton-in-the-closet theory. To her, each gown represented another secret letdown, to be hidden away, forgotten. Defeat coated her reply. "Matt, they are bridesmaid dresses."

He balked. "All of 'em?"

"Yes," she assured him with a hiss.

"She's sure popular, isn't she?" Amanda chirped, slinging a shimmery green strapless over her arm.

"Hey, come over here, Mandy," Krista squealed from the opposite end of the rack. "You've got to see this sleeveless cocktail dress."

Jill inhaled sharply as pain sliced her heart in two. Of all the garments in the closet, Krista had produced her senior prom dream dress. Her precious sapphire damask, with a flirty petaled skirt that swirled as she twirled. Jill pressed her lips together and squeezed her eyes shut. Oh, how she'd twirled. Around and around in her old bedroom at Aunt Wilma's house, dizzy with anticipation and excitement, only to be let down by her boyfriend, Roger Bannon, in the end.

How time flew. The memories and the dress would be twelve years old this spring. It seemed unfair that the old feelings, old wounds, remained so fresh inside her. If anything, her efforts of suppression over time had heightened their clarity. Thank goodness Roger wouldn't be dropping back home for Penny's wedding. As a tabloid journalist, he hadn't made any of the nuptials in years, only stopping by to see the old crowd intermittently. Self-absorbed and devastatingly charming, he always managed to have things on his own terms.

"This looks like it's never been worn," Amanda noted in undertone, her brown head nodding with Krista's yellow one.

So true. The price tag was still hooked to the inside label. Jill thought her heart would burst from the emotional pressure pulsing through her system. She surveyed Matt, standing by with his thumbs hooked in his belt loops, openly curious, then strayed back to the girls, just discovering the tag.

She pressed her fingers to her temples. Everything was happening so fast. Penny's marriage, confessing her plight to Rachel Harrington, her passion-charged conflicts with this stranger who was to play her husband. It frightened her to deal with emotions on a deep, shattering level. She was long out of the habit, and intended to stay that way.

Maybe Bob Williams was right. Maybe it would be wise to simply return home as the single cop she was. Endure being last for the final time, never to return again.

But the embarrassment would be compounded now. She'd already told Penny she was married to Matt Travis, teacher, coach, husband extraordinaire, and Penny in turn would've told everybody. How could Jill ever explain that move and still manage to save face? They would know then how much it bothered her to be the only one in the crowd who couldn't survive in a nurturing relationship.

With forced nonchalance she strolled over to her teenage visitors and gently took the blue dress from Krista. "Why don't you girls take your selections into my bedroom," she lightly suggested. "You can try them on."

"What about that one?" Krista demanded on a frantic note.

"It's the only one that's off limits," Jill replied evenly, her fingers tightening around the wooden hanger.

Krista's young face crumpled. "Oh, gee, I wish I'd never seen it!"

"If you had come on Saturday as planned, you wouldn't have," Jill admitted. "Go on now, it's getting late."

They charged off down the short hall in a giggling flurry, slamming her bedroom door shut behind them.

Jill marched over to the closet without looking at Matt. She didn't want to see his sardonic expression, endure his gleeful gibes. She slung the dress over her shoulder, freeing her cold fingers to straighten and realign the inventory. Within seconds she could feel the weighty hanger slipping down her backbone. Before she could act, Matt had moved up behind her, scooping up the garment.

"It goes right here," she said coolly, pushing aside the crush of fabric to make room at the very end of the rod. She waited for him to wedge the dress in, but he kept a step back.

"Travis—"

He scanned the dress, then her. "Hmm, this must be a new one."

"Why?"

His mouth twitched. "Because of the tag, because it would fit like a glove."

"Oh, you don't know anything," she scoffed.

Matt reached past her and closed one of the doors. Jill whirled back, only to be confronted with their reflection. She stared at the man hovering in the background, wearing that sloe-eyed look again. Did he really still hope to frighten her off? Was that the motive for his persistent proximity? Capturing her from behind, he curled his arm around her throat, draping the formal over her front, as though dressing a paper doll.

"Yeah..." His croon was hot in the curve of her ear, his expression appreciative in the mirror. "Just like I thought. A perfect match for your eyes."

She dropped her sweeping pale lashes against the sight, against the trip back to a happier time when she had ticked off the minutes until she would wear the dress, capture the attention that had always just eluded her all through school.

"Take it off me," she ordered tightly.

He watched her thoughtfully, aware that her body was stiffening against his. "This for the trip home? Or are you saving it for something else?"

She parted her lips, struggling for a terse comeback. But then it hit her. He really didn't get it. Had no way of knowing how much this hurt her. He was actually trying to flirt—had to be with those dancing eyes and quirky grins of his. Why, the whole evening had probably been his clumsy attempt at dalliance. But she'd been too wrapped up in her misery to comprehend.

"You have to bring this along," he said.

"I don't think so, Travis," she demurred.

His free hand was at her waist suddenly, causing her to flinch. "You know, it really isn't a good idea for me to play your man," he reiterated.

Her face crumpled in lament. "Not this again!"

"Jill, you make me nuts," he confessed in candor.

"How professional of you. I'll bet Rachel—"

"Rachel would fire my tail if she knew—saw us this way." The arm propping up the dress curled deeply into her collarbone. "You bring out the fool in me, as quick as you bring out my temper. How the hell do you do that?"

Jill died a little as the coarse hair of his arm grazed the tender column of her throat. Died and zoomed straight to heaven. She had to admit that she enjoyed his touch. It was tantalizing and different. Men weren't ever bold with her this way. She swayed back against his solid length, giving in just a little bit, anxious for a little taste of intimacy. The dress slipped through his fingers and pooled at her feet. His fingers slipped down to the curve of her breast as his mouth dropped to the side of her neck.

Jill quivered with electricity. Keeping a sultry eye on their reflection, she drew her hands back to his legs, squeezing his muscled thighs through his soft black denim. She delighted in his muffled moan of approval.

"I never should've kissed you," he uttered plaintively.

"I know, Travis."

"Fire me before I really mess this up."

Her stare was steady and stubborn in the reflection. "No. You're perfect."

"Impossible woman."

"Impossible man."

His hand weighed the softness of her breast and skimmed to her belly.

The creak of a door and a spurt of high voices interrupted their play. Travis broke away quickly, stumbling toward the sofa. He was going nuts to pull a stunt like this. Absolutely insane!

The girls appeared in the hallway, instantly realizing something had transpired between the adults.

"What's up?" Krista asked.

"Matt was trying to talk me into wearing this dress," Jill explained truthfully, stooping to retrieve it.

"Hey, yeah," Amanda squealed. "To the prom!"

Jill shot up to full height with a flash of panic. "What do you mean?"

"Our prom," Krista clarified. "We'd have to get you there somehow, though."

The girls pondered the problem.

"Never mind," Jill awkwardly insisted.

"Hey, I got it," Krista rejoiced moments later. "Haven't you already thought of it, Coach?"

He was far too busy trying to bow out of their other engagement!

"We are not dating," Jill declared flatly.

"Of course you aren't," Krista cajoled matter-of-factly. "You don't have anything in common at all! But it would do you good to get out more. Anyway, that's what my mom says. I was thinking that maybe you could be hired as an off-duty security person. That way you could show off the dress, have some fun with us."

"Well . . ." Matt shifted from one foot to another.

"I don't think so, girls," Jill quickly replied. "Did you find something to wear?"

It was ten minutes before Jill could usher her guests and their formal wear out the door. She didn't think Matt was ready to leave, but she couldn't take any more. He'd looked absolutely mortified over the thought of her attending his prom! Again, he didn't know how much that particular rejection could and did still hurt her. The caution signs were flashing over and over in front of her eyes. He could tap into her secret places without even realizing, wound her, please her. What a dangerous capacity.

Maybe she should be paying closer attention to his protests. Maybe he was too wrong to be right for her. He had a troubled past. Granted, so did she. But he'd broken the law!

The phone rang just as she was securing her dead bolt lock. She hurried to the kitchen, fearful that something was happening at the station.

"Ames."

"Is that how you answer the telephone now?"

Jill rolled her eyes, leaning against the refrigerator. "Aunt Wilma."

"Hello to you, too."

"Sorry," she said with a sigh. "I was expecting a call from work."

"I daresay. I was expecting a call about your marriage."

"Oh. Yes."

"I heard all about it in the grocer's today," she complained. "You can only imagine how humiliating that was, young lady. Why, I..."

Jill half listened to her aunt's long-winded chastisement, wondering if Wilma would even bother to congratulate her. She didn't. Naturally, if she had really gotten married, she would've called, despite their strained relationship. But as it was, she'd been putting it off. Telling Wilma had been the final step to making it all a reality.

"I was planning to surprise all of you," Jill said placatingly. "Then Penny called with her news and I blurted out mine...."

"Yes, Penny's made a lovely match. A charming man."

"Have you met him?" she asked doubtfully.

"Well, no. But I daresay he's charming. The Richmans, with their real estate business, are pillars of the community, and Penny is an idol with her children's program."

"Yes, Aunt Wilma." Jill knew better than to ever perceive herself as an idol, to make a match half as charming as Penny's. By the time Jill hung up the telephone on the tail end of Wilma's abrasive lecture, any temptation to tell the truth had evaporated.

A ring on her finger and a man in her bed. The two things Wilma had always admired most in any woman. Jill planned to flaunt both these status symbols to the maximum. At that moment she remembered that she hadn't discussed the sleeping arrangements with Travis. She'd honestly intended to prepare him, give him the chance to absorb the idea. But then the girls had shown up, and the night had orbited into other areas.

What would he say when he discovered that she expected him to sleep in her old bedroom, in her compact bed? Maybe it was a twist of fate that she hadn't told him. Maybe it would've been the final straw, the one that would've sent him charging off for the last time. She just couldn't have that. In his own way he'd niggled into the role, making it his alone. So, it was settled.

The bedroom secret...would be one best kept for the bedroom.

Chapter Six

"I figured you'd show up." Matt flashed Detective Bob Williams a knowing look from behind the bar at the Green Door the following Friday night. He'd been counting down the days until his job for Jill. They hadn't communicated directly since the night of their dinner at her place. They'd played telephone tag instead. She left a message on his answering machine, outlining her plan to pick him up tonight for the drive down to Santa Barbara. He, in turn, had called her machine with the message that he'd be at the grill, helping Chet out for few hours because of the Memorial Day weekend rush.

In these final hours before the marital blastoff he'd figured maybe Williams would let things be.

Bob smiled, setting his green mug on the bar. "Just relaxing with some of my cronies."

Matt gazed through the milling crowd to a booth in the front, where a few of Bayside Station's finest were sharing two large pizzas and three pots of coffee. Those guys were always in here. Without Williams.

Bob was smiling, but there was hard glitter to his gray eyes that could only be described as resolute. A man out for a few laughs with his buddies didn't wear that kind of determination so openly.

"I hope you're just out of coffee over there. But somehow, I doubt it."

Bob heaved his barrel-shaped chest. "Okay, you've got me pegged. I wasn't planning to do this. But in the end, guess I couldn't resist."

Matt lined up empty glasses on the bar, scooping ice into each one. "If you didn't want Jill to hire me on, you should've discouraged her."

A glimmer of humor reached Bob's eyes, as he slid onto a padded stool to his left. "Nobody tells Jill what to do."

"So I noticed!"

Bob turned a square napkin in his fingers. "Sometimes, however, she doesn't know what's good for her."

Matt lifted a heavy dark brow. "Meaning?"

"Meaning that Jill's alone too much."

"Oh." Matt felt a begrudging wave of relief. He knew it shouldn't matter what Bob or anybody else thought of him, but nobody had the right to tell him he wasn't toeing the line. Not any more, they didn't. "She seems to know where she's headed," Matt disagreed. "Like a lovely steamroller."

"But to try to fool friends about such an important event."

Matt squirted cola into all the glasses, followed by shots of dark rum. "We all have our pride. Jill seems to have way more than her share."

"You don't sound like a doting husband to me," Bob accused.

Matt produced a plastic box of lime slices and began shoving them in the drinks. "When the meter kicks in, I'm the best damn hubby you can imagine. Exactly what they've ordered. I'm even bonded now, you know," he added grandly.

Bob's large features clouded, but he gritted his teeth in restraint. "I'm not against you, Travis, I'm just concerned about Jill. She's normally so rational, so predictable. This farce is the craziest thing she's ever done."

Matt paused for a moment, his good sense kicking in. Bob Williams was an irritant, no question. But it appeared that he genuinely cared for Jill, had somehow managed to edge close enough for a relationship. So it was possible to do! Suddenly this cop was worth knowing, after all these years. He was his pipeline to the real Jill Ames. As the days passed since their dinner at her place, Matt's desire to figure her out had mounted to heights nearly matching his physical desires. He closed his eyes briefly, reliving the moment when he'd held that jazzy blue dress up to her in front of the closet mirror. The softness of her backside grazing his thighs, the clean scent of her shampoo filling his nostrils. He had originally believed she was trembling. But now, he wasn't so sure. She was so tight, after all, from her pressed lips to her solid rear end, with both feet planted firmly on the ground. The quake inside him may have been rumbling them both!

"Look, Matt, I just want to make sure that your animosity for the police—"

"For you especially," Matt said.

"Well, yeah," Bob conceded. "My point is, this wouldn't be a good time to get even with the Bayside Station. You could really hurt Jill without knowing it. And she hasn't done anything to you."

If only it was true! "This is just another job to me, Williams," he lied. "And I've never had a complaint yet." Bob Williams didn't deserve to know that Jill was already in the driver's seat with their arrangement. That he felt she had the power to hurt him. Her restraint, though annoying, was a challenge that intrigued him.

"She ever been married?"

"No," Bob replied. "I don't think she's even taken the time to look for a husband. Too stubborn to even realize she might like to have one," he muttered half to himself, rubbing his chin.

"She probably just hasn't met the right man yet," Matt wagered.

"Not many women make detective by twenty-seven. That's when she did it. A lady has to get pretty tough to fight crime and City Hall."

"You worried about me?" Matt asked in a syrupy tone.

Bob pinched the handle of his coffee mug. "You'd be damn lucky for the chance to even carry her wedding veil up the aisle if she did find Mr. Right."

"I thought they carried trains up the aisle," Matt countered thoughtfully.

"Sometimes it's veils, too," Bob insisted with a slow nod.

"So you think the right man could tap into her tender side, then?"

"What the hell are you up to, kid?"

Matt grimaced into Bob's large blazing face. He'd gone too far, aroused the detective's ire and suspicion. "I'm just trying to understand her for the role," he claimed evenly, shifting his gaze to the row of amber lanterns above the bar. "Most of my clients give me more to go on, help me hone my part."

"Oh." Williams absorbed the explanation, grudgingly buying it. "Well, make sure you come through."

Chet stepped up between them, refilling Bob's empty coffee cup. "Hello, Bob. Haven't seen you in here lately."

Bob lifted the green mug to his mouth for a sip. "Nothing is wrong, Chet."

"I already know that," Chet said mildly, his gaze shifting to his steaming son. "Matt's done the family real proud. Just came over to tell you that Jill Ames is out back in the parking lot, Matt. Caught a glimpse of her on the security camera back in the stockroom."

To Chet's obvious surprise, Bob was the one who was stricken.

"I gotta get outta here!"

"You aren't afraid of your little partner, are you?" Matt queried in suprise.

"She's just like a third daughter," Bob rapidly clarified, slipping off the stool. "Which gives me the excuse to interfere and the good sense to evaporate afterward."

Matt shook his head with a grin as he loaded his drinks on a round tray. Bob's fondness for Jill, his protective demeanor were an impressive endorsement. Matt was on the right track, all right. Jill was worth a little trouble, a little risk. This cranky old fossil not only trusted her on the job, but considered her a surrogate daughter. As much as Matt appreciated the insight, however, it wasn't going to stop him from giving Williams some farewell static. Just for old times' sake.

"Hey, hold on," he drawled as the detective turned to get his bearings in the crowd. "You owe us for the brew and the pizza. Wouldn't want anybody to think you'd walk out on a debt to so-ci-ety," he enunciated.

"Jerk." Bob reached to the back pocket of his worn slacks and extracted his wallet. "Here's enough for everybody over there," he said, tipping his shiny head toward the booth holding his pals.

Matt took the bills from the bar. "What about a tip?"

"Tip?" He paused, then leveled a finger in his face. "Okay, hotshot. Bring Jill back the happiest girl in the world or you're in major crap." With that he spun on the heels of his scuffed shoes and zoomed toward the green front door.

Jill was just entering the grill from the back, wincing against the sting of the smoke and the din of voices. The figure bounding out the front entrance in a rumpled brown suit looked a whole lot like her partner. But that was impossible. Friday nights were slotted for Bob's favorite comedies. Nothing but an emergency would tear him away from the television.

Did he still give Matt Travis that kind of priority? Had he committed a crime that made him suspect, even now? Bob would've told her, of course. She wanted to trust Matt. He was just right for the job. Sexy in a natural, reckless way. As much as her fears troubled her, the wish to surprise and impress the folks back home overpowered everything else.

She moved into the crowd, unaware of all the male heads that turned to watch her body's graceful glide. She was dressed for comfort with a dash of style in white leggings and a hip-length magenta top. The knit fabric of both pieces clung to her slender curves like a second skin, giving her a catlike quality. Her hair topped off the kittenish look, fluffed around her face, softening her set features.

She caught sight of Matt just rounding the bar with a tray of drinks balanced at ear level. He looked extremely busy, hardly on alert for her. She tilted her wrist to study the face of her silver watch, noting that she was punctual to the minute. It was exactly eight o'clock. Did he get the message? Was he prepared to go?

Answering machine communication was never ideal. But she couldn't bring herself to speak to him directly. It had been so easy to leave the message, then receive his acknowledgment in the same way. There was a formality involved with recorded communications, a comfortable distance. It was easier for her to think when Travis wasn't purring his thoughts into her ear on a heated breath, closing his hairy arm across her slender throat.

She continued to clock his progress to a round table at the far wall, where he passed out the glasses with a practiced flair. He moved easily in the cramped space, tucking the tray under his arm as he spun round. When he did lift his eyes, they slid in her direction, revealing no surprise at all. He was playing games with her! And she knew just the game—claim and tame the naughty Neanderthal—if you dare! She took pleasure in matching his lazy, knowing look.

He beckoned her forward. "I'll be ready in a minute. My suitcase is back here," he explained, rounding the bar.

"I'll wait outside then," she said, noting the Bayside Station people at the front table.

"No, don't, please," he said. "I want to introduce you to my dad."

"Oh," she said in surprise, trying to keep out of the officers' range.

"Hey, Dad! C'mere a minute."

A shorter man dressed in baggy twill pants and T-shirt bearing the grill's Green Door logo ambled his way down from the cash register, extending his hand.

"Jill, this is Chet Travis. Dad, Detective Jill Ames."

"Nice to meet you, Jill."

Jill smiled at the gray-haired man with the sloping shoulders and pale dancing eyes. She sensed he was an extremely nice man. "I've heard a lot about you and this place," she said on a complimentary note. "It's awfully popular."

"Sounds like she did a check on you, Dad," Matt observed fiendishly.

"Maybe she was wondering what the odds were of getting her sweater back," Chet speculated, throwing some of the heat on him.

"My sweater?" she demanded in surprise, pinning a glare on Matt. "You saw my sweater?"

"See it?" Chet hooted. "He took it over. I tried to put it in the lost and found here. But the boy insisted on delivering it to you personally. So you wouldn't accuse him of theft."

Jill gasped indignantly. "Why, I assumed a patron took it—when you didn't say anything."

Matt frowned. Damn Chet and his sense of humor. He'd kept the sweater so he'd have some string leading back to her if he needed one. How uncomfortable to be caught doing it!

"Let's go before Chet has me in the slammer," he said, giving his father a scowl as he reached into a cupboard for his suitcase. "See you Tuesday, Dad."

"Not if I see you first," Chet teased, waving them off.

Matt followed Jill outside to where she'd parked her Lumina, quietly watching as she opened the trunk to accommodate his soft nylon tote. He dropped it inside beside her tony blue luggage. There was a case of Glory Farms wine stowed way in back, as well, he noted, remembering the penciled scribble concerning the sweet fizzy beverage on her notes right beside the name Roger. There were so many things he wanted to ask about, but her stoic expression discouraged him.

"Watch those sticky fingers," she advised, abruptly dropping the lid in place with a flourish.

"I'll get my own door, if you don't mind," he said, keeping his fingers to himself as she inserted the key in the passenger side. She nodded, proceeding to the driver's door. He could've sworn there was a wicked curl to her mouth in the shadowed light. Surely she didn't think he'd stolen her sweater, did she? He had, but he hadn't! Not really.

The interior of the car smelled brand-new to Matt, despite the fact that the Lumina was the '93 model. Brand-new with a hint of vanilla cologne. His Jeep was a rummage sale on wheels, the backseat piled high with textbooks, weights, shoes, jackets. He had no intention of shoveling through the rubble, either. He liked having gear handy. Generally speaking, he knew where everything was, even the things that were spread out among his friends, students and fellow teachers. His policies on such things were in stark contrast to his client's. As were his driving habits, it appeared. Why did serious people always get behind the wheel and bullet around like maniacs? He was adjusting his seat back as she peeled onto the steep street fronting the grill, nearly knocking him into the dashboard.

"Watch it!"

"You should be wearing your seat belt," she scolded without remorse.

"I didn't have time—"

"It's the law."

One law he heartily approved of! He swiftly adjusted the belt with a click, staring out at the blur of buildings along the city blocks. So his latest spouse was quick to redirect the blame for things. Boy, was he going to earn his salary on this gig.

A stifling silence pervaded the car, making Matt fidgety. They had a long drive ahead of them down the freeway. He knew from experience that they should be establishing a rapport.

"Go home much?" he asked conversationally, turning to her profile. He couldn't help but notice the way her fingers tightened around the steering wheel as she took a hairpin turn onto a narrow downtown alley.

"Weddings and funerals, mostly," she returned distantly.

"Weddings and funerals," he mused. "The checkpoints of life, really. Always make you take pause and wonder if you're all you can be."

"I am all I can be!"

"I was speaking in general terms. About the human race."

"Oh, yeah, sure." She braked for a stop sign, dwelling on the fine line drawn between those two ceremonies, how they affected her life. Each one brought her in contact with those who made her feel small. Laughter and tears always intermingled, reflecting her confusion. It always felt better here in San Francisco, where she knew the course, a direction she'd set up to suit herself. "Well, we're going to have a good time at this wedding. A real good time."

Matt lifted a dubious brow, gazing out the passenger window at the blur of city lights.

"Was that Bob Williams leaving the grill when I arrived?" she abruptly asked a short time later.

They were just whizzing onto the freeway entrance ramp at the speed of light, so Matt didn't have the endurance to tell a lie. "Yeah. He stopped by to have pizza with his friends."

"Not likely," she emphatically denied. "Not on a Friday."

"That was his excuse," he clarified, his head spinning back to gauge the headlight beams of the oncoming traffic. "He's worried about you."

"Oh. He really shouldn't," she said self-consciously, gunning the engine.

Matt sighed. They were properly eased into the right lane. Thank God! "You make caring seem like a crime. Williams means well. In his own irritating way."

Jill bit her lip. "Matt?"

His head snapped to her in wonder. "Do you realize that's the first time you've called me by my first name?"

Jill pursed her lips. He would call attention to the fact. But she needed the practice. This was another last chance, to add to all the other lasts involved. "Did you get my bio in the mail?"

"Yeah," he swiftly replied with a yawn. "The info's bound to help me through those sticky moments." He felt he was being generous. In truth, it was the same old list they'd tumbled over in her living room, minus the pencil scratches at the bottom. She certainly monitored unconscious revelations. She liked to feed facts by the measured spoonful. But in all fairness, he felt she was trying to do the right thing, fashioning the report after his own Harrington one. And it was all he should need. All he usually expected.

She took her eyes off the black ribbon of highway to give him an impatient look. "Is there anything else you want me to know?"

He stroked his chin. "Well, I didn't mean to steal."

She nearly pounced across the seat with the opening. "When you were a kid?"

"No, dammit. I meant the other day, with the sweater." He pulled a tight smile in the darkness of the car. "It's eating you up. My record."

"No! I . . . just thought you were making a confession."

"I hate people who hold the past against someone."

"So do I." Despite her hearty agreement, Jill was wrestling with an internal conflict. The tiny frightened girl of yesterday called out to the methodical cop of today. Together they wanted to know everything about Matt Travis. It was an unreasonable expectation, but a pressing one.

Matt regarded her with a mixture of exasperation and sympathy. "I suppose you'll need some extra info to pad your conversations. Let's see here..." He adjusted his legs under the dashboard. "I went to Lindale High downtown. Scraped my way through to a diploma. Then down to college in San Diego—"

"Must've straightened out in between," she ventured hopefully.

He shot her a groggy grin, his head lolling back on the cushioned seat. "Not really. I messed around down there, too. It wasn't until my junior year that I really buckled down for some grades. And it wasn't until I began teaching that I came to an understanding about putting something back in this world."

"You're falling asleep, you crumb!"

His eyes remained closed. "I'm sorry, Mrs. T, but I've been up since five a.m."

"But we need a story!" she lamented with a toss of her head. "About our wedding, our honeymoon. Where we met in the first place! Penny already asked me about that."

He wrinkled his brows. "Make something up. I'm listening."

She nodded soundly, gripping the wheel like a vise. "Okay, okay. Let me think. I suppose we might've gotten married aboard a cruise ship, or up in a hot air balloon."

He groaned with a weary wave. "Hey. Slow down, Ames. First of all, you aren't the type to do either. You'd be on steady dry ground if you took the plunge."

"How do you know?"

"I know. And your friends will be doubly sure, strongly suspicious."

"I just want everything to have been nice for us."

"It was." He drew a lopsided grin as though replaying the memory. "Small wedding. A few friends at Dad's grill. My mom made the food."

Her mouth curved fondly. "Oh? What did she serve?"

"Ham, potato salad, great big pickles and baked beans." He inhaled appreciatively. "The best beans you've ever had."

"She really make them?"

"Uh-huh."

"You have a wedding planned in advance for yourself?"

"Naw. It's the meal she made the day I got out of juvenile hall. Mom put on a feast then." He could hear a hiss of breath in the silence that followed, and cracked an eye open to find her paralyzed with affront, her profile locked in ivory as she whizzed along at seventy miles an hour. "Just kidding about the party, Ames. The truth is, I really would like those foods at my reception, when the time comes."

She slanted him a scathing look. "Do all your clients hate you, Travis?"

"I think you're the first one."

"This isn't going to work," she said.

"You want some friendly advice, Mrs. Travis?"

She swallowed hard. "Drop you off at the next gas station?"

Matt felt a stab of remorse. She didn't deserve a hard time on top of her other stresses. "I won't let you down. Just concentrate on keeping the story simple. Saint Stevens is right down the street from Hill High. Let's say we were married there. The good father's name is Mahoney. Small, real facts. Stick to my agency bio as closely as you can when speaking of me. Trust me, I'm a pro at this. Improvisation is my specialty."

She released a conceding sigh. "All right. And I guess we don't need to know everything yet because we had a whirlwind courtship."

"Now you're getting the idea. Anything else?"

"I think you should know about my friends. The ones in the wedding."

He made a noise between a yawn and a roar. "Can't it wait till morning?"

"I like to be prepared." She made a sharp lane change to jolt him.

His head rolled into the window. "Watch it!"

"Penny Richman is the one getting hitched," she began briskly, as though making a report to her officers. "She has the children's program on public broadcasting. Next in line is Rebecca Lambert. She's the career homemaker, with two kids and a doctor for a husband. Then there's Alison Sherwood. She's a flight attendant with a pilot husband. The last one is Gayle Fairchild. She and her husband operate a restaurant out in wine country. They have a baby under a year."

Jill was impressed with his rapt attention, so she continued with information about the husbands. It wasn't until he erupted with a loud snore that she realized he was only behaving because he was sleeping.

THEY REACHED Santa Barbara around midnight. Once back in her old neighborhood, Jill opted for a narrow seaside road, opening her window to indulge her senses. There was an invigorating breeze, cool, tangy with salt. The moon shimmered over the black waters, making them glisten. She and her friends had spent many happy hours out there on the sand, in the frothy waves. Daydreaming, boy-chasing, stretching curfews, with only their impetuosity as an excuse. This setting, a feast for the senses, always brought everything back with an untarnished focus, allowing Jill to reminisce about the best of times.

A disoriented groan rose in the car. Matt was waking up, rubbing the length of his face, raking into his clipped brown hair. "Where are we?"

"Home."

He shivered and grumbled. "Why's the window open?"

"To wake you up," she lied softly.

"Your aunt have a beach place?" he asked in awe.

"No, but it's a nice neighborhood, several blocks from here. Rebecca Lambert and her family have a sumptuous beachfront home, though, about a mile up this road."

Rebecca Lambert? Matt wobbled his jaw, summoning his thoughts. By her tone, he was supposed to know who she was. He remembered the beginnings of a rundown, but he'd drifted off without absorbing any of it. He was on the verge of confessing, then nixed the idea. She was already as taut as a bowstring. She would be so angry with him, right before they hit auntie's. Aunt Wilma, who was bound to have a cushy place to sleep. This was not the time for a review, or a lecture. He would bluff his way through it, own up in the morning over a cup of strong coffee.

Jill maneuvered through her old neighborhood with new caution. It gave Matt a chance to get his bearings. Everything was so neatly spaced on the winding roads. Sprawling homes set in impressive yards full of trees and shrubbery. Spanish and mission style structures glowed in the moonlight.

"People certainly aren't on top of one another the way they are back in San Francisco," he remarked, pointing out a particularly large estate with a sweeping driveway and bricked security wall.

"It's all really a state of mind, though," she said with a philosophical sigh. "A person can suffocate anyplace. When it gets stuffy enough."

Matt weighed the remark as he stared out the windshield, sensing her distress in the close quarters of the car. She seemed more vulnerable now that she was weary. If only she'd just open up and lay it all out for him! But he knew she couldn't be pushed. Tonight would not be the night for any revelations.

They drove a few more blocks, to a straight street where the homes were relatively smaller and a couple of decades older. The yards were still generous by California standards and the boulevard was lined with tall palm trees. Jill pulled into the driveway of one of the smaller ranch-style houses with a garage and a carport positioned on the right. She came to a stop just outside the port and killed the engine. She cracked her door open to provide some light.

They needed that light, Matt realized, looking past her to inspect the property. The front of the house was drenched in blackness. No welcome glow at all, inside or out, aside from the illumination of the moon. And it hurt her. He could see it in her sluggish moves as she hauled her purse on her lap, digging inside for a comb, tugging it through her hair.

"Jill?"

"Don't make a crack about being expected, Travis," she cautioned with forced lightness. "The meter is running now. No more gibes."

"I only wanted the keys," he explained quietly, opening his palm. "Thought I'd take the cases out of the trunk."

"Thanks." She tucked her chin to her breastbone, drawing even breaths. She'd foolishly let this lack of a brass-band welcome openly bother her. Even a small clang of cymbals would've been nice. But as everyone in town knew, Wilma Ames never clanged.

In an unexpected move, he reached for her instead of the key ring, hooking her chin with his finger, drawing her closer. "I'm on the Frisco team, remember?" he crooned with a stroke to her downy cheek. "Us against them, and all that."

She searched his face for an electric moment. The longing in his tone was a tantalizing match for the passion in his eyes, making her quiver. He was so strong, so wonderful, just the sort of ladykiller she'd always dreamed of springing on them.

Always dreamed of capturing for her very own.

But it was hazardous to confuse the personal and professional issues. Matt was playing a part. Period.

"You believe me, don't you?" he asked earnestly. "I'll be the man you want."

"Yes." Her voice was a soft rasp of relief. He could make her believe anything when he moved in this close, scraped her with his fingertips.

His eyes were full of intent as he moved closer for a kiss.

"What are you doing?" she squeaked against his mouth.

"An old lady in a bathrobe is coming down the front steps," he explained. "Pucker up like you mean it."

"Oh."

Matt eased his hand beneath her tide of hair to her warm neck, delivering a potent but restrained version of their last kiss. All the while, he pondered her mood swing. Her "yes" and "oh" replies had been degrees apart, plummeting from a cozy hot zone to way below zero. He couldn't help but wonder if the drop was strictly due to the news of her aunt's appearance, or because she hoped his motives were more personal and spontaneous. Maybe she was falling for him. Just a little bit.

She was falling for him, all right, like a ton of bricks off the face of a coastline cliff! His kiss was nothing more than a tentative taste, and she wanted more.

"Say, I meant to ask you," he mumbled against her mouth.

"Hmm?" she asked dazedly.

"Where do you stand with Aunt Wilma? If you're going to confide in her, we don't have to give her the deluxe show."

Her breath hit his face like a blast of forced air. "No, Travis! Kiss me again. Like you mean it. Like I'm the sexiest woman on earth."

No problem there. He was beginning to perceive her as just that. Stubborn, proud, irritating. But sexy. Yeah, man . . . With a groan he accepted the invitation, crushing his mouth to hers for a deep, delicious taste.

She weathered the full force of his hunger like a fragile flower, swept up into his own private tornado. Her body went languid in his arms as he kissed her on and on with dark, demanding purpose.

When he did lighten the pressure, she opened her eyes to find his lids hooded with bedroom intent. It reminded her of the final-hour confession she had to make. "Matt?"

"Yeah, honey?" he crooned.

"Since we're getting along so well," she began haltingly, "I'm sure you won't mind at all that we have to sleep together."

"Huh?" His single syllable of protest exploded through the car. "It's the very reason we shouldn't sleep together, Jill! It's not the Harrington way!"

"I know. That's why I didn't say something sooner. But I simply cannot tell Wilma that we're faking it," she beseeched, cupping his furious face in her hands. "Oh, please don't give the game away."

They stiffened as the woman jerked open the dislodged driver's door all the way. "I thought it was robbers!" she scolded. "Scared me half to death the way you sat out here!"

As she stepped back on the grass, her arms folded across her chest, her mouth set in a grumpy line, Matt couldn't help but think that she thought nothing of the sort.

"I'm on the other side of the law, Aunt Wilma," Jill joked woodenly, easing out of the car. "And you had to be expecting us."

"Not at this hour!"

Matt exited the passenger side, watching as Jill moved up to give her aunt a hug. It was a brief and awkward reunion, with Wilma Ames offering a single pat on the back before edging away, nearly bouncing into the hedge.

"It's my fault we got a late start." Matt intervened with a charming smile.

"Ah, the husband, Matt Travis. I'm Wilma Ames."

"Pleased to meet you," he returned graciously.

Wilma was a case, Matt decided behind his professionally composed front. Not only did she put a regal emphasis on her own name, but her inflection on the word *husband* bordered on sardonicism. He took the withered hand she offered, giving her fingers a short terse squeeze to match the hug she'd offered Jill.

She was also a picture of severity, dressed in a blue wraparound bathrobe, with a head of black brush curlers. The robe was the bulkiest terry cloth he'd ever seen, cinched snug at her waist to give nothing away, and the curlers were set in pinched, precise rows against her pale skull, banked with two plastic pins each. Even though she was surveying Matt, she obviously didn't like the same treatment. She sniffed, tucking her shawl collar deeper into the wrinkled hollow of her throat. The suppressive gesture reminded him of Jill. But that was the only similarity. Aunt and niece were standing only a foot or so apart, and he promptly understood that the subtler story was told in their eyes. The moonlight did wild and crazy things to Jill's blue ones. They glowed like precious gems, full of fire and desperation, unfulfillment. The moonlight did just plain crazy things to Wilma's. They flinted like steel as they flicked in judgment and annoyance.

Even though Matt didn't really know Wilma yet, he knew of her kind. She dominated her closest circle with negative games. Logic told him that she not only was expecting them, but was watching for them behind one of the blackened windows. They weren't in the driveway two minutes before he noted the tiny yellow light by the front door popping on over Jill's shoulder, and she was storming the steps.

"Well, let's collect your bags and go inside," Wilma directed on a huff. "Don't want to give the neighbors a show."

"I'm sure Jill has kissed a fella or two out here in the night," Matt said with twinge of good humor.

Wilma's mouth thinned with suspect sympathy. "Not many, have you, Jill?" With that she wheeled on her hard-soled slippers and stalked for the house.

Matt joined Jill at the trunk as she struggled with the bags, setting his hand over hers. "She's lying to you, Jill," he intoned, mocking. "She does like a show."

Jill laughed mirthlessly, stepping back as he hoisted the bags out of the compartment and onto the concrete between them. "It would serve her right if we turned on all the yard lights and wrestled on the grass like a couple of randy pups. How's that for a honeymoon to follow your imaginary reception?"

Couldn't she see what this kind of temptation was doing to him? Matt bit his lip with a steadying breath, trailing after her with most of the luggage. Whether they dived into the flower bed or her bed, he was going to have a hell of a time keeping his hands off her.

Jill double-checked with Wilma to make sure they were to use her old bedroom, then swiftly led Matt, baggage and all, through the one-floor house.

Wilma's idea of hostessing was to flip on the light switches in Jill's old bedroom and the bathroom before proceeding down the hallway to her own room, securing the door with a good-night and a thud.

The first thing Matt noticed about Jill's room was that the bed was a double. He was accustomed to stretching out on a king-size mattress. Alone and in the nude. He was bound to bump into her on that little square of spring, wishing that she was the naked one!

Jill watched him saunter over to the bed with a critical eye. "If you think we'll be cramped—"

"We will," he cautioned.

"You can sleep in my beanbag chair over—"

"We won't," he swiftly amended.

"We will," she admitted as she dropped her tote bag on her vanity. "I'm so sorry, Travis. Are you very mad?"

"A crazy kind of mad more than anything else, I guess," he admonished. "I told you back at your apartment that you drive me nuts, and you stood there, not making a peep about these sleeping arrangements."

She remembered the moment well. He was wedged into her back like a contour chair, holding the column of her throat captive with his sinewy arm. And if that wasn't enough, he was draping her old prom dress down her front, bringing back a flood of adolescent memories she still had no control over. The notion that she was supposed to be thinking at all at that point was ridiculous! "Would you have come if I'd told you?" she dared to ask in a small voice, openly acknowledging the full depth of her guilt.

"I really don't know," he confessed laboriously, plowing a hand through his short brown hair. "It would've been a very tough call, considering that Rachel had guaranteed me, and you, in turn, had told your friend already. But I think it's fair to say, this move would've been a breach of contract, giving me a justifiable out."

She met his smoldering eyes with a tentative twinkle. "Then in a way, I did you a favor, took the burden of choice out of your hands."

He bowed deeply at the waist. "Thank you very much, Mrs. Travis!"

She blushed, busying herself with her tote. She couldn't help but breathe a sigh of relief as he hauled his own bag onto the bed, rifling through it for his toothbrush. He was going to stay! At least for the night. "Feel free to use the bathroom first," she invited shyly.

"Guess I can't get into much trouble doing that," he flared, stalking for the door.

Matt stood before the medicine cabinet mirror in the pink tile bath, polishing his teeth with the care and vigor usually reserved for waxing his car. Did she think him made of stone? he wondered with a full body shudder. What a sneak she was, coming on as the ice princess, only to spring this bedtime buddy thing on him. In all fairness, there were some meltdown moments in between. And amazingly, he couldn't help but perceive her as sincere with every surprising turn.

He pulled a rueful grin in the mirror as he rinsed his mouth with water. Rachel would have a heart attack if she discovered what he was up to under the Harrington Husband umbrella. Surely he couldn't be bonded for this kind of hazardous duty.

But duty this time around was intermingled with some very personal exemptions. He and Jill were courting in their own bumbling way. She was far too wrapped up in this trip to acknowledge all the signs yet, so he would have to play the waiting game.

Play it cool, while squeezed against her softness on a
minuscule mattress.

He knew he was risking his job and his heart, all in the
name of a whole lot of maybes. He wasn't even sure Jill was
capable of committing to anyone. And even if she was, the
commitment itself was bound to lead to a lot more frustration. He'd be a naive fool not to recognize that, with her
secretiveness, her stubbornness, her position of authority,
she would be even more of a challenge after the lovin'.

Lovin' was the last thing he dare think about tonight, he
schooled himself ten minutes later, as he tossed and turned
in bed to the whir of Jill's shower. He'd come to suspect
that her casual offer of first dibs on the bathroom was more
calculated than polite. She wanted him asleep before she
crawled in beside him.

In a twisted way it was further encouragement. She, too,
was scared stiff of bumper-to-bumper closeness.

He gritted his teeth as she eased under the covers a short
time later, feigning sleep for her sake. The give of the mattress and her springtime fragrance sent a torturous pulsation straight to his groin. He could only tell himself over
and over again that if he really wanted her, he would have
to wait for her to catch up. That the sweetest conquest
would be the one she initiated. It didn't prove to be much
comfort as she burrowed into the opposite edge of the bed,
inescapably nudging him with every move.

Lost in her scent and softness, it was a long while before
he managed to escape through sleep.

Chapter Seven

So much for gallant acts. Matt awoke to find Jill curled up behind him, squeezing him to her soft curves like a prize teddy bear.

He blinked in dismay, desire snaking through his system all over again. Her long slender fingers had slipped between the buttons of his brand-new striped pajamas and into the crisp hair around his navel. Suddenly the stiff cotton fabric was binding him everywhere.

How did men stand these confining pjs anyway?

He'd incinerate them the minute he got home.

But there was a more clear and present smoldering to deal with right now. The one caused by the friction of her fingernails, the pressure of her palms, scraping, squeezing, exploring... Spontaneous combustion to deal with and douse.

One of them had to be dreaming.

He eased up on his elbow, twisting to gaze at her. Sure enough, she was. Her sweeping pale lashes were tight against her cheeks and her mouth was pursed in a cute little pout. Her hair spilled like liquid gold against her pillow. Some temptress, buttoned up tight in a flannel nightie, breathing in soft, even puffs, like a newborn babe. Jill had so many facets to her personality. Every one was an intriguing surprise to him.

Matt sank back down on the mattress with a bewildered breath. Would he ever understand women? Jill didn't trust him with her sweater, but she trusted him here. Like this.

But how much was a man supposed to take, even when the come-on was an unconscious one? His fingers were shaking over the prospect of wandering over the smooth slope of her hip. It suddenly occurred to him that whether or not he touched her wasn't the most urgent issue here. It was Jill's interpretation of what was happening. She would be horrified to wake up in this position. And she would promptly blame him. Even with her patties in his shirt, she would accuse him of instigating arousal, making it a crime! Such a confrontation would shatter the bond they had begun to forge.

Matt hastily hopped out of bed, digging around in his tote for some fresh clothes and his shaving kit, intent on a swift retreat to the bathroom. Escape was his only option, even though he knew what was in store for him—breakfast with Wilma.

The first thing Matt heard when he moved through the house a short time later was Wilma's laughter. It was an alien noise, but probably genuine. A second, more musical murmur followed, warning him that she already had female company at eight o'clock. He grimaced in the hallway. A pair of them looking him over, fielding questions. He should've waited for Jill. It was up to the client to take the lead. But he couldn't wait, could he? At least he'd formulated a plan while washing up. A light meal of some kind, then off to the street for his daily run. That was his ace in the hole if the going got tough at any given moment—he could always sprint off, at a speed that nobody over twenty could match. With a fortifying sigh and a tug to his Hill High regulation T-shirt and shorts, he launched ahead.

"Good morning." It was a polite blanket greeting that Matt offered as he absorbed the kitchen scene. He was good at sizing up a situation like this swiftly and sedately. It was a requirement of the job.

"Good morning!" the pair chorused.

Wilma was seated at the small round table with a contemporary of Jill's. The older woman was still outfitted in the same robe and rollers, but was definitely putting on a front of cordiality. She either had separate personalities for night and day, or this visitor brought out the very best in her, in a way that Jill obviously could not do. Considering Jill's need for his services, he suspected the latter.

"Matt, I'd, like you to meet Jill's closest friend, Penny Richman."

"My pleasure," he intoned, extending his hand. She was a good-looking woman, very approachable. Petite, with short curly red hair. Her round face was pretty, with twin dimples in her cheeks and wide-set green eyes that twinkled in genuine merriment. She was dressed for comfort in a yellow blouse and white shorts, her demeanor relaxed and nonthreatening.

Why was Jill lying to this charming woman?

"Shame on you for not inviting us to your wedding," Penny scolded on a teasing note.

"I imagine Jill told you all about Penny's job on television," Wilma cued, obviously expecting him to automatically match her gush.

Matt sat down at the table, reining in his temper. What pleasure such a welcome would've given Jill last night. But it wasn't Penny Richman's fault that Wilma was behaving like an imbecile. "You have the children's program on public television," he supplied with a gracious smile. "As a teacher, I can appreciate the good you're doing."

"Thank you very much," Penny said, sipping from the bone china cup full of coffee before her. "This man deserves some breakfast, Wilma."

"Of course. I have some pancakes warming in the oven." When he nodded she rose from her chair. "Coffee, er, ah, Matt?"

She was struggling to make an appearance of fond familiarity, Matt realized cynically. "No, thanks. Any kind of juice would be appreciated, though." While Wilma bustled back and forth between the old gold appliances, Matt turned to Penny. "Congratulations on your upcoming wedding."

"Thanks. I suppose Jill's told you all about the game we've played between us through the years."

His heavy brows rose in perplexity and genuine curiosity.

"Oh, it's nothing really," she said, taking a blueberry muffin from the basket in the center of the table.

"Let me get you a plate for that," Wilma suggested.

"Oh, no," Penny declined, slipping out her saucer to serve as a dish. "It's bad enough to be the only one using your good china. We were considered the permanently single pair of the neighborhood," she explained to Matt, "putting our careers first. We've always had a good time as bridesmaids for everybody else, joking about the dresses we were forced to wear. I can only imagine Jill's shock when I called to make fun of my own dress—" She paused, nibbling on the edge of her muffin.

New understanding flickered in his eyes as he mentally slid another piece into the complicated puzzle of Jill Ames. He'd realized that the dresses made her uncomfortable, but it had to be a painful closure in her eyes. To be the only single left. Even if she liked being single, it had to hurt being last. He had the feeling that Jill had been the unchosen one her whole life through, at least on the home front. No wonder she forged a fresh start away from here. No wonder she hid her feelings, for fear that they would be loaded in a mouth like Wilma's and bulleted back at her.

"The real shock's been ours, to discover that Jill has married herself," Wilma said tartly, setting down a plate of pancakes in front of him. He met Penny's sheepish expression. The plate was plastic. Everything on the table was, aside from Penny's china service. "Not a word to anybody. Not a chance to adjust. Orange juice all right, Matt?"

He bared his teeth, surprised she wasn't pushing sour grape. "Perfect, Mrs. Ames."

"Why, I thought I'd find a second husband before Jill ever found her first," Wilma confided.

Penny wrinkled her nose and shook her head as the old woman dipped her head behind the refrigerator door. Matt liked the perky television personality more and more with every passing minute.

"How glorious that Jill and I both land men within weeks of each other!" Penny marveled as Wilma closed in to top off her coffee.

Everyone turned to the doorway as Jill marched into the kitchen, dressed in a red blouse and madras shorts. "The bride herself!" she exclaimed with open delight, rushing toward Penny.

Matt couldn't help but note that Jill could expose her heart, impetuously, joyfully. The charade signified that she cared what her friend thought, but her loving expression reflected a deeper caring for who Penny was.

Penny jumped up and they exchanged hugs and compliments. "You know, you shouldn't have bothered to even get dressed," Penny said with a sly look that brought a flush to Matt's cheeks. He cleared his throat as the pair noted his discomfort.

"Don't get nervous," Penny teased, tweaking his ear. "I just mean that I have Jill's bridesmaid dress with me. We need to do a fitting."

"I knew that." He jabbed his fork in the direction of the plastic garment bag hanging on a hook by the back door, then used the utensil to stuff pancake into his mouth. Wilma was a rotten cook, but anything probably would've tasted like paste right now. Jill and Penny were behaving like his students, and making him feel like an awkward teenager again himself!

Jill gazed at Wilma, fussing by the sink, uneasy with the lighthearted exchange. Her aunt wasn't known for her sense of humor and frequently distanced herself from laughter. Wilma turned to redirect the tone. "Jill, you must see Penny's engagement ring. It's absolutely stunning!"

Penny rather reluctantly extended her hand to display a huge diamond solitaire set in a circle of rubies. Jill swallowed hard. Wilma had no doubt noticed Jill's plain gold band last night. It had been the best Jill could do. Her budget was already stretched to the limit with her payment to the Harrington Agency. She'd purchased her band at a pawnshop while tracking down an elusive fence working the Bay Area. She'd spotted the secondhand ring at a rock-bottom price and snatched it up.

"I know it's rather gawdy," Penny confided with a nervous giggle as she spotted Jill's ring. "But the press will expect something showy."

"It's glorious, Penny," Jill raved.

"We got married in such a hurry that I didn't have time to do any real shopping," Matt said, annoyed with the way the scene was unfolding. The widowed Wilma didn't have much of a rock on her finger, yet she felt compelled to rub Jill's face in a third party's good fortune.

"Let's do the dress fitting now," Jill suggested. "That is, if Matt doesn't mind."

He drained his drink with a shake of his brown head. "No, I'll just take my morning jog." Jill bit back a grin as he broke into a run right in the kitchen, thanking Wilma for the meal on his way out.

Wilma frowned at the bouncing screen door. "Jumpy, isn't he?"

"Not at all," Jill argued. "He's very relaxed. Has to be, to control hundreds of kids every day."

Wilma made a humphing sound. "I just can't imagine Penny's Lieutenant Bruce Kildare acting like butter on a griddle."

Jill edged past her to get the dress. "C'mon, Penny."

"Just like the old days," Penny remarked once they were shut away in Jill's bedroom.

Jill's eyes crinkled. "Another bridesmaid dress?"

"I meant dodging Wilma, shutting her out," Penny corrected bluntly, rolling her eyes.

"I don't miss her negativity, Pen," Jill said sadly. "It's a shame she couldn't believe in me just a little bit."

"Well, she has always been impressed by the wealthy of this town. She was proud that you ran with a more moneyed crowd."

Jill pondered the thought, gazing at her old bare dresser. There was not a trace of her identity left in this room. Wilma had long ago removed the bits and pieces of her childhood. Even her delicate mint green curtains had been replaced with starched white shades from some discount mart. "Yes, I think that about the only thing I've ever done right in her eyes."

"Unfortunately," Penny commented without argument.

"And the showiness of your job, of course, was bound to put you even farther ahead as we enter our thirties," Jill couldn't help saying.

"It's too weird to comprehend," Penny soothed, slipping her hand around her taller pal's waist. "But now you've bloomed. Not only do you have a good job, but you have a good man."

Yeah, sure. The best husband money could buy. Jill sighed wistfully, smoothing the white chenille spread over the mattress as Penny laid the gown on it. She was in the habit of making her bed the moment she popped out of it.

Today had been no exception. It had taken longer than usual, though. Sleeping with Matt had left the covers in a tangle. She'd been exhausted, never moved a muscle all night long. Or so she thought, anyway. They'd done some kind of tango to make such a rumple. But he hadn't tried anything, she assured herself. He wasn't that kind of man.

"Jill?"

"Huh?" Jill's head snapped up to look at Penny, who was patiently standing beside her with a smirk.

"Can you get your mind off that bed for one minute?"

Jill gulped, realizing what she was insinuating. "Very funny."

Penny laughed with dancing green eyes. "Don't get huffy. Newlyweds are supposed to dwell on sex, sex and only sex."

"As you, too, will soon discover," Jill teased, deliberately tossing the spotlight back at the real bride.

Penny unzipped the plastic garment bag and gently removed the dress with a rustle of taffeta.

Jill gasped in wonder at the sleek, deep orange gown. "Tangerine dream lives up to its name. It's stunning, Pen." Penny eased it off the hanger as Jill stripped her shorts and blouse off. Clad only in her panties, bra and sneakers, she held up her arms so Penny could slip the dress over her head. The slippery fabric fell over her shape, the hem falling to mid-thigh. She moved over to the freestanding mirror near the closet.

"Hold still a minute!" Penny complained. "I have to zip you up."

They both wheeled to the door as it swung open.

"Travis!" Jill cried out in amazement.

"Who else, Travis," he returned with a meaningful look. She should be calling him Matt. And be damn glad to see him.

"You guys call each other by your last name?" Penny quipped, sizing them up with her hands on her hips. "Hey, that's cute."

Jill cleared her throat. "What are you doing back, honey?"

"Forgot my baseball cap. Can't run without my cap."

"Well, good thing you showed," Penny said, pulling at his arm. "I was just about to do your job."

His jaw sagged. "Huh?"

"Zip up the bride."

He balked. "You're the bride."

"I'm still a bride, too, Matt," Jill reminded him.

Her voice was feeble, and he knew why. Her dress was hanging open to reveal her bare back, striped only with her tiny pink panties and bra. He felt a fleeting trace of mercy, but it was gone like a bird in flight. An anxious greed set in as he closed the space between them. He already had a taste of dressing this beautiful doll and he couldn't resist indulging in the process all over again.

"I just need a zip," she murmured over her shoulder.

"I know all of your needs, Travis," he crooned in her ear.

She frowned slightly at his reflection. He responded with a crooked, boyish smile. She sighed with relief when the zipper began to move. But her breathing became rapid as she felt Matt's knuckle forging ahead of it, leaving a scraping tingle along her spine.

"It isn't stuck, is it?" Penny fretted.

"It's nothing a little WD-40 wouldn't cure," Matt replied blithely.

Jill rolled her eyes. "Ha, ha." She fully expected him to back away as Penny moved in, but he did not. He hovered right behind her, his huge hands closing around her waist. The organza bodice of the dress was tight and smooth against her rib cage, with a deep scooped neckline and off-the-shoulder capped sleeves.

"It's a look that's meant to accentuate the bust and shoulders," Penny explained to Matt.

He nodded with an approving, "Uh-huh."

Jill shivered as his fingers glided up and down her waistline over the etched rose pattern on the fabric, pressing into the soft undersides of her breasts. "Matt..."

"Don't worry, it's just right," he assured her, deliberately misinterpreting her meaning.

Penny inspected her keenly. "Of course that pink bra will have to go, Jilly."

"Uh-huh," Matt repeated wolfishly. There was no way to misunderstand that message. Before Jill could react, Matt's hands were on her collarbone, pulling her pink straps down the gentle slope of her shoulders and beneath the half-sleeves on her arms. "How does that look, ladies?"

"Perfect!" Penny declared. "Now, how's that hemline? It should be two inches above the knee."

Jill could feel Travis slipping down her back. "Don't you dare," she warned between gritted teeth. "Worry about it," she added on a softer note. "It's just right, too."

"Okay." He reluctantly straightened up, giving his hands a dust off.

Jill scanned the room, spying his cap on the bedpost. She promptly retrieved it. "Here's your hat."

He sighed hard with a pouty look. "Be that way. Give me my hat. Play dress up without me."

Jill squinted, surprised as laughter bubbled up her throat. "Get going, or I'll give you the boot, too!"

He turned back at the door one last time. Jill and Penny waved goodbye.

"He makes things fun, doesn't he?" Penny observed as Jill glided toward the mirror.

Jill paused in thought. "Yes, he does," she admitted honestly.

"And seems extremely possessive," Penny went on.

"I don't imagine he'll be leaving me alone much this weekend," she predicted wryly.

"Somehow, we girls—" Penny stumbled over her words. "We figured you'd end up with somebody more polished. Like Roger Bannon, for instance."

Jill stiffened. "Well, that makes sense," she said lightly. "Considering that everyone assumed that I would be marrying Roger right out of school."

"Speaking of Roger," Penny ventured slowly, studying her manicured nails.

Jill turned to give her a sharp look. "Why are we speaking of him at a time like this at all, Penny? He left California years ago. It's my understanding that he's on the staff of some newspaper up in New York."

They both knew the paper was a supermarket tabloid, that he was one of their most seasoned, highly paid correspondents, but there was no reason to elaborate.

Penny exhaled. "This is the deal, kid. When I decided to get married, I thought I'd be doing you a favor by inviting Roger back—"

"So what?" Jill interrupted with relief. "I doubt he'll show."

Penny's lips pursed. "He's going to show."

"Oh?" Jill made a dismissive gesture. "Well, I'll be busy with my husband."

Penny made an aggravated sound. "You don't understand. I tried to play matchmaker, Jill. I heard through the grapevine that he's still single. I partnered the two of you in the wedding."

"What!" Jill's blue eyes widened to saucer size.

"It's the surprise I was going to spring on you during our phone call, remember? Then you blurted out that you got married." She shook her head in apology. "I lost my nerve at that point. Thought if I told you about Roger, you might not come back."

"It might have changed things," she admitted softly. Of course it would've changed everything! Given her second thoughts about whether she needed to tell the big lie, needed Matt at all. But how quickly he had gotten under her skin. It was almost impossible to erase him from the picture, even for a brief, experimental moment.

"Roger doesn't matter either way anymore, does he?" Penny queried confidently. "You can go through the motions of the ceremony with him and be done with it. Please try to understand. I was just hoping to heal that old hurt—"

But it didn't seem all that old to Jill. Not even now. Roger had scalded her good once, after a fight shortly before the prom, choosing to take someone else rather than making up. It had been a tough one to swallow. They'd tried to make a go of it again that last summer after graduation, but the magic was gone. But to her frustration, the memories of him still lingered.

"At least, it should be rather satisfying to show off your new man to him," Penny said in response to her sulky look. "I'm sure he's still too cocky for his own good."

Yes! Matt would come in handy for that, she inwardly agreed with relief and tingling anticipation. He'd snowed Penny already, plowed her right under with his sexy overtures, creating an aura of intimate sensuality around the two of them.

The look in his brown eyes, when he realized there was another dress fitting in his future... She shivered slightly at a mental replay.

"So, are you okay with the situation?" Penny asked, accurately reading Jill's blissful look.

Jill adjusted the sleeves on her bare shoulders with a wink. "Couldn't be better."

MATT RETURNED from his run an hour later. He'd spent some time touring the neighborhood, strolling along the public stretch of beach. He liked to get his bearings in new places, and he admittedly needed to think about Jill and their latest encounter. He'd pushed the envelope a bit by checking the fit on that dress. But he knew that first impressions were so important in these charades. Because of the intimate exchange, Penny, best friend and bride-to-be, was sold.

Of course it had been risky, way beyond the call of duty. Luckily Jill herself had responded with an involuntary pleasure quite separate from their roles. He was now totally convinced that the voltage between them, as far back as their parking lot encounter, was the real thing. But would she dig deep enough inside herself to check it out? Discover why she'd been so set on him for the job?

He entered the kitchen to find Jill right there, standing at the ironing board, pressing every stitch of clothing he brought along.

"Hey, what are you doing?" He clomped across the scuffed gold linoleum, surveying the scene. His suit, his dress shirts, sport shirts, were all pressed, and hanging all over the place, on the fridge handle, the doorjambs and knobs. Even a crummier shirt that he only wore in privacy was billowing by an open window. Suddenly all the warm romantic fuzzies tickling his brain surged into steely annoyance. He felt exposed to the world.

"Sh!" she cautioned, spritzing water on his jeans as she moved the iron around the zipper. "There's nothing wrong with a wife tending to her husband's things."

"But to go through my stuff, without permission!" he objected, leveling a finger in her face. "You've been a cop too long, if you think that's okay to do."

"Hey, it's tougher on the job," she retorted, leaning away from him. "I need a warrant." She was secretly glad the board was between them. He'd developed a disconcerting habit of grazing into her whenever he wanted to make a point. Wasn't that a more intimate move than unpacking a tote of clothing for pressing?

He shook his head. "Don't try and kid your way out of this."

"It's just for the sake of appearances, like everything else," she said quietly. "I'd be doing it even if I was a plumber or a meter reader. You lean too much on your resentment of the police," she scolded. "Can't blame us cops for everything."

"I don't," he scoffed, pacing around the cramped kitchen. "It's just that I've been ironing my own clothes for years," he offered in explanation, drawing a glass of water at the sink.

Her brilliant sapphire eyes gleamed shrewdly. "Every Christmas and Valentine's Day, whether they need them or not."

"Maybe not even that often," he professed with a frown. "I don't like everything neat and in place. Life is a wrinkled affair."

"Not my life," she informed him succinctly.

He reached out a huge hand, planning to muss her hair. She held up the iron like a weapon. "Freeze, sucker."

He stepped back with his hands raised. "Don't press me along with everything else. Please, Officer."

She sighed hard at his mocking expression. "Haven't any of your other wives ever done any of the little things for you?"

"You don't do things for me, Travis. You do things to me." He edged closer with a low sensuous growl that made her squeal.

Jill quickly clamped a hand over her mouth. But it was too late. Just as she feared, it drew Wilma to the back of the house. She breezed in with a bottle of glass cleaner in one hand and a rag in the other. Jill noted that Wilma's gray curls were glistening with spray and her regular puttering clothes were replaced by a newer floral housedress. Probably on the chance that Penny might return with her beau.

"Is there trouble?" Wilma asked crisply, expectantly.

"Of course not," Jill murmured absently, busily urging the iron down a pants leg.

"But I heard some very strange noises."

Matt swallowed a laugh. "We were just sparring a bit, Wilma. I just feel that Jill works way too hard. I'm accustomed to doing my own housework."

"Good thing." Wilma chortled, nodding at Matt. "I don't recall Jill doing much of anything around here."

Jill bit her lip as she flipped the pants over on the board. Wilma didn't know what she was talking about. Her late husband, Jill's uncle Art, did the bulk of the housework during Jill's youth, while Wilma attended club meetings and luncheons. And Jill always helped him. It was deliberate timing on her part. She was finished and out the door before Wilma returned, spitting fire over the incompetents of the town. But it didn't matter anymore, she reminded herself. She had a new, rewarding life of her own.

Matt watched her carefully as he began to collect the hangers holding his clothing. She was struggling with what had to be an unfair observation from Wilma. Somehow, she must've done her share around here. Duty was ingrained in her every pore. "So what's on for this afternoon?" he asked brightly.

Wilma inhaled as though the question included her.

Jill swiftly spoke as she unplugged the iron. "You and I are having lunch with Penny and Bruce. She's at the studio right now, taping back-to-back episodes of her program. We're meeting them there."

"Great." Matt slipped his free arm around her as she scooted out from behind the board, giving her a kind peck on the cheek. "Thanks for spoiling me." He stole a look at Wilma as they started down the hall with their clothing. She was disappointed. Really disappointed. It disgusted Matt more than he could say.

Chapter Eight

Matt suggested that Jill might be tired of driving after their trip down the coast and offered to take the wheel for the afternoon. Jill conceded, despite the fact that she was sure it was for the duration of their stay. There was a distinct air of finality in the way he adjusted the driver's seat to accommodate his long legs, and a huff of relief escaped his lips as he shoved the key in the ignition. Could the complaints about her intense driving be true? she wondered.

The trip downtown to the studio was a pensive one for both of them, only directions and small talk exchanged. To her surprise, Jill found that she was really enjoying their time together, the team spirit evolving between them.

The local television studio where Penny taped her "Kid Konnection" program was located on the fringes of downtown in a revamped warehouse. It was a three-story structure of whitewashed brick. Jill had been there a couple of times, and explained their presence to the guard at the security station inside the entrance. He made a call and within minutes the elevator behind the station dropped, the doors swishing open. A short, rotund man with black, slicked back hair, stuffed into a sinfully expensive brown cashmere suit, exited the car. Jill recognized him to be Wayne Smeed, Penny's manager.

"Welcome, folks!" he boomed grandly, anxiously scuttling past the guard, as though reuniting with beloved old friends. Penny had cautioned her years ago, at an awards dinner in her honor, that exaggerated greetings were the show biz way. Jill had spoken to Wayne exactly three times in all the years that he'd represented Penny. But the smile she offered him was genuine. He understood the celebrity jungle and took good care of the creative, all too whimsical Penny.

"Hello, Wayne," Jill greeted him warmly. "I'd like you to meet my husband, Matt Travis."

Matt shook his hand, blinking against Smeed's gaudy fingers heavy with gold. As he extended his arms to envelop Jill in a hug, Matt noted that the manager's glitter climbed up his wrists to a Swiss watch and large square ruby cuff links. This guy was an operator who liked to advertise himself as stylish and prosperous, the kind Matt often met on Harrington assignments. The flashy Smeeds moved in an entirely different world. One that didn't interest Matt in the least.

They whisked up to the third floor by elevator, then through a maze of beige hallways broken with a series of office doorways.

"Penny's just about to wrap up the second segment of the second show," he explained over his shoulder to the couple marching behind him, breezily waving to people as he passed by the doorways. "Then she'll be all yours."

Smeed ushered them through a huge steel door to a soundstage. The hushed office atmosphere was replaced with concrete and steel, high-ceilinged openness. There was an energy in the room. Many people, most of them in their twenties, were bustling around in sportswear, donning headsets. Some had clipboards, others had files. The threesome worked their way through the wires and cameras to a blaze of lights around a colorful set. It was an exaggerated version of a playroom, with oversize chairs, tables, counters. Accessible, cheery, yet simple in design.

"The home of 'Kid Konnection,'" Jill told Matt, an unmistakable note of pride in her voice. Penny was seated on a large blue stool, dressed in a yellow and white dress, in the gingham fabric that was her television trademark. A technician was holding a meter near her forehead, measuring the lighting, and a stylist was fluffing her short red hair with a pick. She waved when she spotted them. "We'll get this on the first take, I promise!"

"She's been relying heavily on the teleprompter today," Wayne whispered with disapproval.

"She's getting married in a couple of days!" Jill objected, swiftly jumping to her friend's defense.

Wayne's suntanned, pan-shaped face tightened. "Yes. I know."

Jill's features furrowed in concern. "You don't seem thrilled, Wayne."

"I am," he instantly assured her. "It's just that the timing of everything—" He broke off, obviously struggling for the right words. "We're filming an extra show today to make up for the week she intends to take off. But this is a very crucial crossroad in her career. There is going to be a Penny doll out just in time for next Christmas, miniature replicas right down to the gingham. Momentum is necessary. Everything has to be handled carefully." His voice fell off, as though he felt he'd said enough. But there was an unmistakable undercurrent of things left unsaid. Jill wondered if he was so selfish as to expect Penny to be on every minute of every day.

"She deserves a personal life," she said pointedly.

"Yeah, but she isn't going to ever have much of one," Smeed bluntly predicted. "The tabloid reporters watch her like hawks, waiting for her to slip up, tarnish her squeaky-clean reputation. The children who make up her audience adore her and want in on every detail of her existence." His stones winked in the lights as he swiped his brow. "It's a lot of pressure."

The set was ordered to silence soon thereafter, and Jill and Matt sat with Smeed on canvas chairs off to the side.

The show proved to be magic. Matt made the judgment as a teacher who tried to weave his own spells every school day of the year. The focus of the segment was bike safety. Penny outlined rules and tips incorporated into a very catchy song, dancing around the set with a few oversize animal puppets. She was captivating in delivery, vivid in appearance.

Jill matched his pleasure, with an added dash of pride, tapping her fingers on her thighs in time with the music.

A man appeared behind Wayne's chair just as the director was calling the program a wrap. Jill turned slightly to her left to give him a once-over without being overly obvious. He was dressed in civilian clothes, tan slacks and pale green knit shirt, but he fit the description of Penny's lieutenant. His butternut colored hair was trimmed to a crew cut and his eyes were a "dreamy hazel."

Penny joined them with a flounce of her gingham skirt, affirming the man's identity by enveloping herself in his arms for a long, passionate kiss. The trio looked on in silence. Jill felt that even sharpie Wayne felt a little bit uncomfortable as the moment stretched on. But Penny did like center stage, for all audiences. It was a compulsion their high school crowd had come to accept.

"So you've met Bruce," Penny eventually said breathlessly, bracing her hands against his chest.

"We haven't had a chance," Jill admonished teasingly. "Nice to meet you, Bruce." Jill couldn't help but note that Bruce was quick on the uptake with introductions, for someone who'd just singed the lips off of somebody for several hot minutes.

But he did prove to have a motive. "Hang on, everyone. I want to take your picture."

Penny flashed him an endearing look. "Oh, Bruce, you think of everything."

"Well, I noticed your camera in the dressing room, and I thought, hey, might as well do you the favor of taking some shots for our personal album."

Wayne tried to edge his way out of focus, but Penny held him near. "Bruce is so thoughtful," she said, motioning Jill and Matt closer. They posed and Bruce took two pictures. Before anyone could move, Bruce switched places with Matt, who took two more shots.

"I am famished," Penny announced, glancing at her watch. "What do you say we get better acquainted over lunch?"

"If I tagged along, we could go over some business matters, as well," Wayne added.

"Not on your life," Penny said poutily with a tap to his nose. "I have a reservation at Gayle's place, for just the four of us. Do you know about Gayle?" she turned to ask Matt.

Matt swallowed hard under Jill's strained smile. He was supposed to know this Gayle.

"Remember, hon?" Jill prompted. "I told you all about her on the way down? She and her husband, Ray, have the restaurant in the Santa Ynez Valley?"

"Ah, yes, that Gayle," he said with contrived recollection. He hadn't meant to fall asleep during their en route conversation, but he'd been so blasted tired. She had a right to be angry. He should've confessed earlier.

"They operate the Cozy Kitchen and have a baby daughter who must be going on five months..." Jill trailed off in sheepish uncertainty about the child's age.

"She's nine months now," Penny corrected.

"Maybe I should come along," Wayne persisted.

"We don't need you," Penny insisted with growing annoyance.

"Or want you," Bruce said with finality, squeezing Penny's shoulders. "Just let us be, Wayne. We're getting married in two days."

"All right!" Wayne clicked his polished shoes together and hustled off.

"Can we ride with you, Jill?" Penny wondered. "I rode over with Wayne, and Bruce's rental car is rather small."

"Yes, of course," Jill said, her pale brows lifting a fraction.

Matt had seen that expression before. Jill's eyebrows were like feelers that rose with the first sign of static. He ought to know, after all the doubts she expressed about him. But it wasn't a crime to drive a rental, he reasoned. It might seem odd that any man in California did not own a car, but Bruce Kildare was Navy. Maybe he had no place to store a vehicle. Maybe he was at sea a lot. Hell, he didn't know. And it was something he'd never bother to question. But to his own frustration, he found himself questioning it, solely because she was doubting it!

He scratched his head. The process was scary, first reading her thoughts, then turning over the same suspicion to decide if it had validity. He didn't want to slip into that kind of thought pattern. If anything, Jill could strive to be more like him, more accepting of people at face value, at least during her off-duty hours. But he suspected that she wasn't going to turn a new leaf with this lieutenant. She was going to delve into his personal business, satisfy herself that he was good enough for her best friend.

The thirty-mile drive into wine country began on a friendly and relaxing note. Conversation focused mainly on the area. Penny was well versed in the companies and families who owned the vineyards, the wines they specialized in. Matt slanted a look to the passenger side more than once, to find Jill's teeth planted in her lush lower lip. She wanted real hard facts on Bruce, and the small talk was killing her. She'd tried a couple of times to veer off in more personal directions, but to her open chagrin, Penny controlled the conversation with firm vivaciousness.

Matt suspected this was rote for their relationship, Penny—and perhaps the others in their clique—leading with a confidence built from years spent in supportive, affluent families. The theory was still conjecture, but it made some sense. Their neighborhood was moneyed. From what Matt managed to piece together through Jill and Wilma, Art Ames had been an investment banker of moderate means. Apparently they just scraped by enough to live in one of the neighborhood's smallest homes. And it was obvious that Wilma Ames had been a nightmare parent, worshipping Penny—and perhaps the other girls—while downplaying Jill at every turn. It wouldn't take much for Jill's pals to have a better support system at home.

Loving relationships with subtle conflicts. He'd figured there had to be sensible reasons for practical Jill believing she needed a husband. Somehow, unearthing one or two gave him a sense of accomplishment, brought him closer to understanding her urgent need to appear fulfilled. It certainly was more than plain old pride, as he'd first thought. Jill was hurting, nursing the wounds of the past. He was compelled to give her a stern talking to, insist that it wasn't worth it. But how could he do so when he was guilty of doing the same thing in his own life, wallowing in the troubles of yesterday. Maybe it was time to start looking at things with a fresh eye himself.

"Isn't that just wild, Matt?"

"What?" He flashed Penny a polite smile over his shoulder, hoping it was warm enough to compensate for his pensive lapse.

"I mean about the wine," she repeated with a huff, obviously not accustomed to being overlooked. "All this wonderful vino at our fingertips and we used to drink Glory Farms. Can you believe it?"

"Ah—" Matt was about to mention the case of the cheap fizzy stuff in the trunk behind them, but Jill was suddenly holding his thigh hostage in a very painful clench. He shot his bogus bride a glint of understanding. The Glory was a surprise. "Girls will be girls, I guess," he said between his teeth, unclamping Jill's fingers from his leg. To his relief she soon shifted on the car seat for another crack at the groom.

"So, Bruce," she began on a firm note. "I've always been intrigued by military men."

Jill had turned full face on the seat in order to face the lieutenant, resting her arm and chin on the back of the seat. She'd noted the quirky grin forming on Matt's face, but she didn't care. She loved Penny and felt it absolutely necessary to play the inquisitive cop. This guy was so out of whack with the type Penny went for her whole life through. Penny never cared for men with conservative policies, Spartan habits. She liked her males wild, rough-edged and free, the sort Jill had goaded Matt into playing. It didn't make sense to Jill and she was determined to understand.

Bruce ran a hand through his oddly shaded hair, meeting her expectant stare with clear hazel eyes. "Well, I'm flattered by your interest," he calmly claimed.

"Penny tells me you met at some charity function," she prompted.

"Yes. The Navy was raising money for a hospital in downtown San Diego and Penny was on hand to provide the entertainment."

"You're stationed at the Point Loma, right?"

"Yes, that's right."

"I imagine a lot of you guys rent cars rather than own them," Matt said in his defense. He fully expected the keen look Jill slanted him, but despite his loyalty to her, he felt the man should be given the benefit of the doubt. Jill was a cop with a hunch and he didn't like the setup.

"Well, it's a lease really," Bruce casually explained. "Penny used the wrong term. Rent implies a shorter length of time, a matter of days. I lease by the month, in sync with my schedule. I don't have real roots right now—"

"But you soon will," Jill pointed out.

"Right. Sure," he said, easily accepting the correction.

"I intend to get him a new car as a wedding gift," Penny confided.

"You mean it?" Bruce exclaimed joyously.

"Of course," Penny said, casting him a strange look. "Haven't I always been generous?"

"I really could use a car of my own," he told her earnestly, as though trying to reassure her.

"Okay," Penny said abruptly. "We'll iron out the details."

Jill frowned slightly. He didn't seem to need a car. Until she was willing to pay for it.

"His work is a huge passion to him, takes him away quite frequently," Penny went on conversationally, patting his knee. "He's with the Navy Oceanography Command."

"Yes, the reason for the rushed ceremony," Jill recalled from their phone conversation.

"There's bound to be a lot of travel involved in a unit like that one," Matt wagered. "Do I need any directions, Travis? A navigator facing the windshield?" When Jill didn't move, he nudged her with his elbow. "I'm talkin' to you."

"Keep going straight," she directed, keeping a steady bead on the backseat.

His fingers curled around the steering wheel. "Yes, dear."

"So exactly what do you do?" Jill asked. "Where do you travel?"

"Well, I do hydrographic and oceanographic surveys," Bruce replied patiently. "On the high seas, in foreign waters. That's about as specific as I'm allowed to be."

"It all takes too much time," Penny said. She nuzzled his neck with a cooing sound. "I'm going to hate those separations."

"It'll be tough," Jill sympathized. "You really like a close, sharing relationship, Penny, always have."

"We'll make it work somehow," Penny said with certainty.

"Of course you will," Jill soothed, realizing it was time to back off. From the grim set of Matt's profile as she twisted forward on the seat, he obviously felt she'd gone too far already. But it just didn't feel right. A most obvious mismatch. One she couldn't really accept just yet.

The conversation grew light once again, Bruce offering some history on Point Loma. Jill almost felt like it was out of a textbook, but sought to keep an open mind.

Before long it was time to direct the driver to veer off into one of the sleepy-looking towns off the main road. The western-style buildings were in stark counterpoint to California chic, with a down-home touristy feel along the one block long main street. The Cozy Kitchen proved to be a gray frame structure set between a red schoolhouse and a white steepled church.

"Maybe Matt should pull around back to the lot," Jill suggested.

"No, no," Penny blurted out, pointing to an open space at the curb marked with a reserved sign. "I called Gayle this morning to let her know we were coming and she's holding that spot." Penny abruptly bounced out of the backseat after they rolled to a stop.

Jill watched her bound up the Kitchen's porch ahead of them and inside the door with a measure of bewildered annoyance. Back at the studio Penny had seamed herself against Bruce, in the car she'd cooed over him. Now she was miles ahead of him. He seemed in no hurry to chase her, falling into step with Matt, questioning him about his work at the high school.

A burst of laughter filtered through the screen door, and Penny's red head came into view. "Get a move on," she prodded impatiently.

Jill shook her head knowingly. Despite the fact that Penny had traded her gingham for a more subdued striped blouse and pale blue skirt, she was just as perky as she'd been on the set, calling the shots as though they were her life-size puppets. "As always, it's your show," Jill joked, stepping over the threshold.

"Not this time!" Penny excitedly exclaimed, clapping her hands together. "Surprise!"

Chapter Nine

Jill stopped dead in her tracks in the center of the pine-paneled room. Penny had launched ahead to make sure things were ready—for what appeared to be Jill's surprise party! There was a congratulations banner emblazoned with her and Matt's names flanking the arched entrance to the main dining room.

"Now you can see why I didn't want you in the back lot," Penny told her. "You might have recognized some of the cars."

The same old pattern between them, Jill bemusedly realized, wagging a finger at her. The moment she was at her wit's end with Penny, her rambunctious pal turned around and did something downright generous, like gathering people together in her honor. Thank heavens she and Matt both had chosen appropriate clothing for the so-called lunch. She'd looked at her blue jeans twice before settling on a copper-colored culotte dress, and Matt had surveyed his jeans three times before opting for khaki slacks and a plaid shirt.

A quick accounting confirmed to Jill that everyone from the old crowd was on hand. Their hosts, Gayle and Ray Fairchild, stood out in their matching white oxford shirts and black slacks worn by the Kitchen staff. They were currently passing their baby, Suzy, between them. Rebecca

Lambert was standing by in a peach suit, minus her physician husband. Alison and Tom Sherwood, the tall, striking flight attendant and pilot team, were inspecting a canape tray. Even Aunt Wilma was hovering near the reservations podium with Penny's petite parents, dressed in one of her best dresses, an eggshell A-line polyester.

"Gotcha!" Gayle rejoiced, aiming a finger at her like a pistol as she approached with her child.

If only they knew, Matt fretted, sidling up beside Jill in a supportive gesture. She cast him an anxious, helpless look, swiftly ticking off their names for his benefit. He understood her transformation from grand inquisitor to uneasy newlywed. She hadn't expected any fanfare concerning her own nuptials, a retroactive reception complete with gifts. A small gasp escaped her lips as Jill spied the table stacked with wrapped boxes inside the dining room.

Most important in Matt's mind was that their goodwill was undoubtedly sincere. Lanky, raven-haired Gayle was thrusting baby Suzy into Jill's arms. Mother and daughter offered her deep dimpled smiles. Plump, raven-haired Rebecca joined in the circle, complimenting Jill's hairstyle, explaining that her hubby, Charles, was busy with his family practice today, but would be the perfect host for Penny's barbecue at their place tomorrow night.

Jill exchanged hugs and kisses with everyone, with Matt standing by with a smile and a kind word. Even Wilma knew when to shine, stepping up behind the Sherwoods to squeeze Jill's hand. But the prune-faced aunt couldn't resist pointing out to Matt that Alison Sherwood was considered to be a Cindy Crawford lookalike among her flight attendant coworkers and that little Suzy was the image of Gayle as a baby, the most beautiful and well-behaved of the neighborhood kids back then.

Matt's mouth tightened as his worst fears were confirmed. Wilma's praise flowed over the women like the seawater so common to the area. Warm, comforting, innocuous—unless it came in contact with an open wound, like the one festering in Jill's heart. It was no wonder that she avoided these old ties, was so openly tired of being last. It made him so angry that he wanted to offer Jill extra unsolicited support that she might be too unnerved or embarrassed to ask for.

Waiters were moving through the crowd of well wishers now with trays of fluted glasses of champagne and club soda. Penny supplied Jill and Matt with glasses of the bubbly, then reached for the last glass on the tray, a soda. "To the hunky groom, Matt Travis, and his naughty bride, Jill," she toasted in her lyrical voice. "Who tried to pull a fast one, only to be caught by the nearest and dearest of friends."

Cheers and applause followed. Matt felt it was his cue to kiss the bride. He felt Jill's spine stiffen slightly as his free hand slid down her back. "Darling..." He sought her attention in a seductive murmur.

His voice was a silken caress in the curve of her ear, an invitation. This was their first moment of improvisation for a real crowd. Jill's stomach fluttered as she tentatively tipped her china blue eyes to his simmering brown ones. Their hot little history was reflected back at her, their kisses, the dress fitting.

She felt like a real bride just then. Fulfilled, radiant and desired. It was indescribably wonderful. And was about to get even better...

Her lashes lowered as his lips closed overs. His firm lips heated hers, making her pulse pound. Keeping a steady hold on her glass, she wound her free hand up around his neck, scraping the short hairs on his neck. He emitted a soft, hungry groan, urging her mouth wider for a moist taste.

Jill tipped her head back farther, drawing in his masculine scent and unique flavor. Exciting, frightening urges tempted her. It would be so satisfying to lose herself in this man for real.

She hadn't felt this kind of fireworks since her teenage days with Roger Bannon. Whether or not that had been a strictly hormonal surge or something more was a mystery to this day.

A mystery that might well soon be solved. Leave it to audacious Penny to orchestrate a reunion between them— after all these years! Jill's practical stance had always been that if Roger wanted her, he'd have come looking. Her phone number was listed.

Matt's kiss went on and on. Jill's senses lavished in the pleasures, but her mind began to tug free to examine her position. She was about to be trapped between the only two males who had ever really set her heart to pumping with a simple kiss. And neither one was really bound to stake a claim. Matt, because he was so new. Roger be- cause . . . well, he would assume she was taken, for starters.

Wilma cleared her throat moments later to bring them out of their spell. Jill blushed profusely when everyone ap- plauded again. "You two don't even do that at home." She tipped her gray head close to whisper for their benefit alone.

"An oversight I'll make sure to correct," Matt returned evenly, causing the prim Wilma to flush before wheeling out of range.

The crowd began to buzz again, people clustering for conversation.

"This is a really nice surprise," Matt remarked to Jill, taking a draw from his fluted glass.

"Yes, but so unexpected," she confided on a whisper. Despite the false pretenses, she couldn't resist reveling in the celebration, accepting the good wishes of everyone.

"You're doing just fine, Jill," he assured her breezily under his breath. "Your biggest problem is that you're ac- customed to mapping out your future inch by inch."

"That isn't wrong!" she retorted saucily.

"It's pretty confining, though, when you're trying to pull a fast one."

She made a face at his wink, then waved to a couple just walking in the door. "I don't think I could ever make a habit of this kind of subterfuge."

His grin grew crooked. "Good thing. You make a rotten liar, honey. I, on the other hand, am pretty good at slinging the bull in a jam. Feel free to lean on me if it gets sticky."

"A company man to rely on," she teased.

He gave her upturned nose a tap and turned to shake hands with Roy Fairchild.

Penny snagged her arm, drawing her into the dining room. "So what do you think?"

"I think you're nuts," Jill assured her with a blend of affection and disgust. She gestured to the linen-covered table of gifts. "I really wish you wouldn't have encouraged this."

"Why?" Penny asked with the same mixture of emotion, as though they were still a couple of schoolgirls. "It's your due, your turn."

Jill sighed hard into Penny's indignant freckled face. "It's just not right. It's just not—"

"Give it up, Jill," Penny insisted.

Jill toyed with the flaxen strands of hair grazing her cheekbone, feeling naughty and frivolous and more like a real bride by the minute. Penny and Matt were both right in their own ways. It really wouldn't hurt anyone if Jill took center stage for the afternoon, pretending to be the blushing bride. She could always ship the gifts back after a few months, with a note of explanation about a sudden divorce. The word divorce made her heart lurch, though. Could she bear to part from Matt when this was all over?

"Gads, I'm starved!" Penny proclaimed, steering Jill toward the buffet table set up beneath windows facing the street. Two uniformed waitresses were busily arranging a vast array of foods. "Cold salads, steaming pans of meats, potatoes and rice." She inhaled appreciatively. "Perfect, ladies. Everything is just right."

The young pair nodded and headed for the kitchen door.

Jill's jaw sagged as she scrutinized the situation. This was far more than a surprise party, it was a banquet. "You are paying for all of this, aren't you?"

Penny popped a green olive in her mouth. "It's okay. I'm rich, remember?"

"Oh, Pen..." Jill averted her friend's impish face, staring off at the enormous stone fireplace across the room.

"Hey, I understand, kiddo," Penny murmured, tipping her bright red head into Jill's arm. "Wilma should've taken on the task. But I did it with a joyous heart, honest."

Jill's painted lips compressed. Wilma should've done it. She'd been so busy building her house of lies, she hadn't even noticed the oversight. "I owe you one, kid."

"Oh, shut up!" Penny hooted.

"All right!" Jill helped herself to a pink dinner mint from a cut glass bowl. "Any word from Roger yet?" she asked as casually as possible.

Penny's russet brows scrunched. "No, not a word since his original telegram, agreeing to come. Guess it doesn't really matter. Matt can pinch-hit for him."

"Yes, of course," she agreed haltingly.

Penny eyed her shrewdly and wagged a finger. "I think you're more disappointed than I am!"

"No," Jill denied lightly. "Roger is history. Though I churn a little whenever I look at my unused prom dress," she confided with a shrug.

"Oh, sweetie," Penny moaned, "do you think it's been a good idea? I mean, to keep a museum piece like that?"

Jill inhaled to respond, only to be interrupted by Matt and Bruce.

"So here you are!" Matt said with mock lament. "I need you," he said pointedly.

Jill could only imagine. What with all the questions doubtless being fired at him. "Just look at this spread, Travis," she invited with an expansive sweep of her hand. "Homemade food, straight from the kitchen to you."

"We all know Wilma isn't much of a cook," Penny intimated with a playful look at Matt.

"Jill and I are guilty of the same flaw," Matt confessed with feigned sorrow.

"None of us were much for home economics back in school," Jill recalled with a far-off smile.

"Hey, speak for yourself!" Gayle interrupted. The owner of the restaurant glared as she waltzed by with a platter of sliced bread. "I made these loaves with my own two hands, wheat, rye and white!"

"I cook, too," Rebecca protested, sidling closer. The physician's wife appeared at Jill's side, a hand planted on her rounded hip. "Day and night. Night and day and night!"

"You must be a wizard to run such a full household, Rebecca." Matt's voice rang out clearly above the rest. He'd turned her way, attentiveness on his lean features. "I heard you have three children as well as a husband on call."

"Pretty good for the homecoming queen of our class," Jill added with pride. She also felt a rush of warmth for her *faux* hubby. He'd accurately sensed that Rebecca might be overlooked now at functions, with her thickened shape and homemaker identity. Rebecca was grounded and confident, but fragile in her own way like everyone else. She blushed with pleasure, launching into a typical day at the Lambert beachfront home, full of carpooling, scout meetings and school sports. Her face glowed to a shade similar to her peach suit.

"She's hosting the groom's dinner for Penny and Bruce tomorrow," Jill informed Matt. "Why, Bruce must be—"

She stopped herself when she realized that he'd taken a few steps away to speak to a young server bringing in a stack of china.

"Never mind, Jill," Rebecca murmured, seeing her stormy expression. "I don't expect gratitude from the lieutenant."

"Maybe he's just overwhelmed by everything," Matt said placatingly. "Sometimes men don't understand all that goes into these things."

"But you certainly seem to be in touch with what's important," Rebecca marveled. A beeper suddenly went off in the handbag on her arm. "Oh, that must be Charles at the office. Excuse me, please."

Jill tugged at Matt's arm until they were down at the end of the buffet near the punch bowl. "You learn anything juicy about the groom?"

"Hell, no," he said incredulously. "Not even if he likes juice!"

"It wouldn't hurt you to think like a cop just a little bit," she wheedled.

"That would be a torture way beyond the call of duty," he argued, with a stubborn set to his jaw.

"All I know is that I ordered every woman's dream man, and I expect him to emerge, full blown."

He leaned closer, until his nose was grazing hers. "Give me a fresh rundown."

She released a shaky breath, pulling back. "Okay. Ninety percent grizzly bear with a dash of warm fuzzy. Plus, an additional inquisitive streak to make you wonder about Bruce."

Matt released a frustrated growl, beginning to feel every bit the Neanderthal she'd ordered. He broke away to capture a glass of champagne from a waiter near the arched entrance of the dining room. He leaned against a glass-doored cabinet full of curios, sipping, watching Penny glide in from the alcove to Jill, her small arms flying in animation as she reported something. There was a sudden flash of excitement in Jill's eyes. Matt realized it was a look he'd seen once before, out in the parking lot of the Green Door after he'd planted his mouth on hers.

A stirring in the doorway drew Matt's attention to the left. To his surprise, Wayne Smeed had come after all, despite the rebuff he received at the station by both Penny and Bruce. He began conversing with Penny's parents, who he presumably knew quite well. Matt wandered closer, planning to join the conversation. Wayne noticed his proximity and hailed him over.

"Ah, Mr. Travis," he intoned, adjusting the lapels of his cashmere suit jacket. "I had no idea this was to be a party for you—a gathering for anybody."

"Yeah, guess we're all surprised," Matt concurred.

Smeed cleared his throat. "I want to explain something if I may."

Matt raised his brows in surprise. What? That the manager had crashed a luncheon he'd mistakenly assumed was for his client? "Why not join in the fun?" he invited. "Plenty of food. And you must know some of the guests."

Smeed smoothed his glossed hair with a jerky motion. "I'm not here for lunch. I've found myself acting as a chauffeur for somebody who showed up at the studio. He's combing his hair in the men's room as we speak."

Matt's forehead puckered in bewilderment. "I really don't understand why you're telling me—"

Suddenly a blond giant of a man in crisp white trousers and a navy cotton shirt breezed past them, giving Smeed a slap on the back that nearly sent him reeling.

The room watched in wonder as he advanced on Jill from behind. He whirled her around, clamped his hands around her waist and lifted her clear off the floor.

"Roger!" Jill squealed, grasping his shoulders for leverage. "Please!"

Despite her protest, Roger began to twirl her around and around overhead. Matt watched in shock and envy. This guy looked and behaved like a lumberjack, but he was far from the woods in Calvin Klein clothing. His hair was shaggy, and close in shade to Jill's. Her tresses had fallen over the top of his, shielding their faces from view. It was difficult to tell where he ended and she began under the blond curtain. What was happening? he wondered in fury. Were they kissing?

Smeed glanced soberly at Matt's clenched fists. "Apparently he's the old boyfriend."

Matt's features smoldered, revealing the burn rising from his belly. Naturally Smeed assumed he knew Roger existed. Roger... Wasn't that the name scribbled in the margin of her bio? She should've told him everything way back when he asked!

If only Jill wasn't so damn secretive, he griped, shifting the blame to her alone. Every scrap of information had to be pried out of her. Had she staged this "other man" confrontation on purpose to steal the spotlight from Penny? Make it look like she was not only hitched, but desired by two men rather than only one?

"Sorry I was the one to deliver him," Smeed ventured in apology as he realized just how angry Matt was. "But he was insistent on tracking you down. He's in the wedding, after all—"

"He's in the wedding!" Matt growled, taking the blow without grace.

"Yes," Smeed said in low tones.

"I don't know a damn thing about him," Matt confessed.

Smeed sighed hard. "Then you're on even ground, Matt. He doesn't know a damn thing about you, either."

"What!"

"He's set on rekindling his affair with your wife," Smeed persisted. "Went on and on about her. I didn't wish to interfere, you understand. Not my business. . . ."

And in truth, it wasn't Matt's business, either. This was Jill's show. Her life. Another possibility crowded his brain. Maybe hiring him was all about Roger Bannon from start to finish, for the ex-boyfriend's benefit alone.

Matt tried to brush it off with a visible shrug. So what? If she wanted this lumberjack as her man, hell, it was none of his business. If she'd been working up to a flashy reunion with this guy, she had a right.

Matt ground his teeth over the unpleasant possibilities. It would be agonizingly interesting to see if this whole deal had been set up just to make Roger sit up and take notice, work to win her back. It would take a strong stomach and a razor cunning on Jill's part to have come this far without revealing her manhunting motives, to cross personal lines with him just far enough to keep real desire aflame in his manner.

DESPITE THE twelve-year lapse, Jill's senses instantly sprang to life as Roger's mouth pressed against hers. The same old tingle, same old sensations pulsed through her, transporting her back to a more innocent time of newness, of pleasurable discovery. Stolen kisses in school hallways. Embraces in the backseat of his old Chevy. The warm fuzzy feelings of truly belonging to somebody. And ultimately, their first and only sexual encounter the summer after high school graduation.

The whole trip down memory lane and back took about twelve seconds, a heartbeat for each year gone by. There hadn't been enough time to comprehend it all before she was back on her feet again. Jill snapped her head up, smoothing her tumbled flaxen hair, catching her breath on a nervous laugh.

Everyone was watching, of course. But a pull of energy came from the doorway where Matt was standing. His coffee brown eyes were snapping for her complete and utter attention. She searched his face to gauge his reaction. Surely he didn't think she'd planned for this to happen! But that's just what he thought, she realized. Her body began to hum beneath her dress as he drilled her with a betrayed look.

What kind of man let another handle his bride so intimately?

Not this kind of man, she concluded with trepidation.

"What's the matter with everybody?" Roger demanded, wheeling around to scan the buffet, then the archway. He, too, was riveted to Matt for a long, measuring exchange. Roger was the first to break contact. "Hey, Jilly, am I missing something here?" he murmured, perplexity in his wide-set blue eyes. "Penny said you'd be glad to see me. Ripe, tasty... Said it would be worth my while to pluck—"

"Roger!" Penny complained. "I didn't refer to Jill as a tempting grape on the vine. You're twisting my words."

That did it. Matt stalked across the room, the heels of his shoes making a resounding clomp in the silence of the room. He had this guy's number. He was the overgrown boy who could say and do anything and get away with it. The self-absorbed charmer who expected the world to revolve around him. Matt had known the type back in school and could easily spot them in his classroom today. They caused trouble, then sought absolution with flimsy excuses and plastic smiles. They oozed their way out of a jam with a story and a little preening. They never went to juvy hall.

Matt edged up beside Jill, his fingers curling around her upper arm in a possessive gesture. "Introduce me."

The command held a silkiness, Jill decided. Not the cordial kind, but a dangerous smoothness bordering on vehemence. But she'd asked for a caveman only moments ago, hadn't she?

She inhaled, launching into a lilting overture. "Uh, Roger, this is my husband, Matt Travis. Matt, this is Roger Bannon, an old friend."

"Husband? That can't be!"

Roger had a couple of inches and thirty pounds on Matt, but the strength in their handshake was an equal balance. Roger could hold his own in a tussle, Matt decided, gauging him as he gauged all the men he met. It took strength and prowess to pick up Jill, hold her over his face the way he had. But Matt couldn't help noting that some of Roger's extra weight came from the good life—thickness around his middle, a sagging under the chin, traces of puffiness around the eyes. But it didn't stop him from being attractive to women still, Matt was certain. Phony charisma had a timeless quality that blurred minor flaws.

"You are simply awful," Penny said, scooting up to tweak Roger's chin. There was a real fondness in her expression, Matt noted. Roger was obviously the perpetual adolescent of their crowd, despite his expensive clothing and a ruby ring, the one they made allowances for, forgave over and over again. It was likely that Jill had something to forgive him for. Would she do it?

"I tried to reach you with the news, Roger," Penny continued with a defensive huff of apology. "But one of the clerks at the magazine claimed you were totally incommunicado through this weekend. Roger's a reporter for *Celebrity Circuit*," she put in for Matt's benefit.

Roger absorbed the logic of Penny's explanation, simmering down a little. "I don't check in much on assignment. I was staked out in London. There were rumors that some of members of the Royal Family were entertaining some of the Kennedy clan. False alarm, unfortunately. And then, of course, I didn't want to be disturbed this weekend while flirting my tail off with Jill here.'' He flashed a boyish grin as he wound an arm around her.

Jill flinched as she found herself sandwiched between the two men. For the first time in her life! She couldn't help but bask in the power a little.

"So tell me, Jill, just how did you manage to get hitched without anybody finding out?" Roger complained. "And just who the hell is this guy?" he demanded with a playful poke to Matt's solid chest.

Jill fluttered her lashes in a silent plea for Matt's understanding. "It all started during a safety meeting at the school where Matt teaches."

"And coaches track," Matt inserted, placing his hand well below Roger's on her back. "Nothing like a good run in the morning around the track for fitness, is there, Roger?" he asked, knowing full well that the other man didn't run much with his softened waistline.

"When I jog," Roger confided on a low, conspiratorial note, "it's usually at night in a tangle of streets. Many an irate star or angry husband would like to catch up with me after I've invaded their turf...." He trailed off with a far-off look that brought a round of knowing chuckles.

Matt shook his head in disbelief. Everyone had a first love stowed away someplace. But never in a million years would he have guessed this jerk to be Jill's choice!

Chapter Ten

"I thought you didn't cook." Matt blurted out the remark later on that afternoon when he stumbled across Jill in Wilma's kitchen, gathering together ingredients and utensils on the table. Judging from the huge bowl, pans, canisters of sugar, flour and eggs, he figured the project was cookies.

"And I thought we weren't speaking," she declared flatly, cracking three eggs on the edge of a brown ceramic bowl. The fragile shells nearly crumbled to pieces in her iron fist. It was no wonder, as the tension had grown incredibly taut between them since Roger showed up, reaching a snapping pinnacle after the forty minute drive home with Wilma and Roger in the back seat of the Lumina. If her aunt had been a few decades younger, she'd have been all over Jill's ex-boyfriend like a second skin. Instead she'd been all over him like a pouty parent, denied the desired link between the Ameses and the Bannons. Jill's relationship with Roger was one of the few accomplishments that Wilma acknowledged with open admiration. Roger's father ran a very lucrative accounting firm in town, and his mother was first cousin to the Santa Barbara social giants, the DeBaults. Roger had always been showy on his own, as well, the class catch back then, football halfback, editor of the school paper. Wilma brought up all his past glories during the trip home.

Matt watched the deep emotional play on her features. He'd probably interrupted some gooey thought about that old flame of hers. The only person at the luncheon who seemed to view Roger Bannon with a practical eye was Rebecca. She'd given Matt the scoop on Jill's track record with Roger, even explaining how Jill had spent her savings on a pretty blue cocktail dress for the prom, only to be shoved aside for a richer, prettier girl. A painful lightning bolt of understanding had shafted through him. That dress at her apartment with the price tag, the one that Krista had wanted to wear, the one he'd held up to Jill himself, was her prom dress. She'd saved it all these years, like a captured dream in a bottle, hoping it would someday be realized.

Matt achingly wondered what Roger would do next, and just how Jill would respond.

"We didn't say we weren't going to speak to each other," he said stubbornly. "We just sort of stopped doing it."

A fourth egg exploded in her hand. She moved to the sink to rinse off.

"Chocolate chip?" he persisted, sauntering closer to the table, making it necessary for her to make contact if she wanted to continue with the project.

She edged past him with a bullying budge, wiping her hands on the small terry apron cinched at her waist over her faded T-shirt and cutoffs.

The body collision set him off unexpectedly. He couldn't resist grabbing her firmly by the upper arms. "What's really going on?" he demanded roughly.

"Sugar, big shot," she said saucily. "The cookies are sugar."

"You know what I mean," he prodded, with a shake to match his tone. "I came into this job with the best intentions—"

"You came kicking and screaming," she corrected tersely.

"But I've done you right," he insisted. "So, if you've been hoping to use me to settle the score with your ex-jock boyfriend, I think you should have the guts to admit it!"

To his amazement, she began to laugh. "Do you seriously believe this was deliberate? That I knew he was coming?" She wrenched out of his reach, tossed her towel on the table and tackled another egg. She was careful this time, landing it in the bowl without mishap.

His dark gaze followed her. "We need to talk about Roger."

"I'd prefer not to talk about him right now, if you don't mind," she said briskly, beating the yolks with a wire whisk.

"Not talk—" He broke off in gaping frustration.

"You ever try not talking, Travis?" she challenged meanly.

"No."

"I don't cook much, so I do like to concentrate when I'm making the effort," she announced with a toss of her blond head. "That means no spectators in the kitchen."

He arched a suspicious brow. "Who are these cookies for?"

"They're for Penny's bridal shower tonight. Sort of an old delicacy, like the Glory Farms wine." She couldn't help but enjoy the relief flooding his features. "Satisfied?"

"Set aside a dozen for me and I'll help," he bartered, struggling to keep his cool.

"Let me be and I'll make it two dozen," she countered hopefully.

"I'll start sifting your dry ingredients," he announced, reaching for the measuring cup. "Where's your recipe?"

"Up here," she replied with a smirk and a tap to her temple.

"Good lord, no man's ever going to get up there to get the whole story," he lamented.

She nodded with a satisfied gleam. "Damn straight."

"But I do expect some answers for the here and now," he said firmly.

"Two cups flour and one cup sugar."

"Smart ass." He opened the metal canisters and began to scoop out the proper amounts of each, pouring them into a smaller bowl.

"Can't you just be satisfied with the fact that I did not deliberately lay this trap with the other man?" she wondered on a pleading note.

"No."

She was watching him with huge soft blue eyes. "Please, for now, just do your job."

He pursed his lips, deciding it was his turn to deliberately misunderstand. "I'm trying. How much baking soda?"

"Two teaspoons," she said softly.

He picked up the soda box and jabbed the spoon inside. "I don't play the chump for anyone."

"You're not—I'm not—" She made an exasperated sound.

"I'm going to walk if you don't answer my questions," he announced abruptly.

She whirled with blazing eyes. "I'd sue!"

"And call attention to this little make-believe marriage?" he asked. "I don't think so."

"Okay, Travis." She set her whisk against the bowl with a clank. "What's the problem? Exactly, without games. Wilma's shopping, but she won't be gone more than another hour. If you're bowing out, I want you gone before she comes back."

He grimaced at her cold approach. But he'd initiated the bluff. She was only calling him on it. He exhaled, folding his arms across his expansive chest. "Would you have considered me obsolete if you'd known sooner that he was coming?''

A tingle raced her spine. As if anyone could ever perceive this masculine wit as obsolete! He was so strong in identity, in will and muscle power. And so alarmingly unforgettable. She stared at her shoes. ''What do you mean by sooner?''

''I mean after the meat loaf,'' he stated. ''Granny Goodrite's loaf!''

''I'd say by then we had our story pretty well sewed up,'' she blurted out.

He backed up a bit in time. ''How about after the parking lot deal?''

''Maybe!'' she exploded. ''You were trying to ditch me then, remember? All I know is that I might have settled for Roger along the way had I known he was going to be my partner in the wedding,'' she begrudgingly admitted. ''It would've been convenient.'' She lowered her eyes, fingering the measuring spoons on the table. ''Just for the record, I believe that if Roger desired me, he'd have looked me up a long time ago.''

''That, at least, makes some sense,'' he murmured in relief.

She bristled at his attitude. ''This little confession is tough on me. But I'm willing to make it, because it makes my stomach turn to think that you feel set up as the other man in a triangle. That's not my style. And you should know it by now!''

''I do know it, Travis.'' He encapsulated her in his arms, relief surging his system. She hadn't come back to harpoon that dandy. And they were really beginning to communicate. His threat to walk away had been a cheap trick, but it had gotten her talking.

Jill didn't protest when Matt pushed her head against the softness of his gray sweatshirt, stroking her smooth tide of hair with a huge palm. She lost herself in his comfort zone, enjoying the intimacy of sharing his last name with no audience to please. He eventually cupped her cheek, guiding her gaze to his. "Let's make a deal," he proposed softly.

"What?"

"Let's handle Roger together, as a team, just as we're doing with everyone else."

"Sure, Travis, that's a good idea," she promptly agreed. "It might get a little annoying," she warned. "Everybody looks to Roger as a hometown celeb, even though he certainly doesn't deserve it. He's bound to steal the show away from all of us!"

Roger's irritating ego wasn't Matt's main gripe at all. It was Bannon's open interest in Jill that had him worried. He certainly had all the signs of a man on a seductive mission. How vulnerable she still was to his charms was the big question. High school crushes died hard—if at all. Often the memories grew vivid and ideal over time. He faced seedlings of adolescent infatuation every day on the job. And he remembered the hot passions of his own youth. But he'd moved on, as most people did.

"So we're okay with everything then?" she coaxed.

He forced a gleam of confidence. "Very okay."

"Good. Now let me get back to my baking." She stepped to her project, scooping shortening into a measuring cup.

Matt made a noise of protest when she unexpectedly plopped it into his flour with a big spoon. Flour dust flew from the bowl, causing him to cough.

"That isn't the way you mix," he scolded, grabbing the big wooden utensil.

She rolled her eyes. "I've done this dozens of times."

"Done it wrong." He gently began to knead the ingredients with a steady hand. "Let me show you."

It took all her self-control, but she allowed him to assist her with the project, right through to pressing the cookies on sheets with a glass dipped in sugar, then baking them toasty.

"The girls will love these," she enthused, sinking her teeth into one hot out of the oven. "Here, Travis, taste."

He snagged the hand holding the cookie, bypassing it for her face. He flicked some crumbs from her chin with his tongue, then sucked the sugar off of her lower lip. "Mmm . . . yummy."

Pleasure bubbled up her throat in a husky laugh. "I never knew cooking could be this fun."

"Me, neither," he growled. "Maybe our frozen meat loaf days are over."

Matt's moves sent Jill's pulse galloping, but she fought to keep her mind focused. "Have you thought about tonight?" she wondered aloud.

"Have I!"

His spontaneous bedroom-centered reply sent a shiver of longing rippling through her. "No, not that, Travis," she scoffed, blushing. "I'm wondering if you plan to make a showing at Bruce's bachelor party while I'm at the shower? I heard him ask you at the luncheon. And I heard you stall. It shouldn't be too bad," she wheedled, fingering the neckline of his shirt, "just a small get-together courtesy of Wayne Smeed."

"Sure, sure," he acquiesced, softly blowing at the short fine hair at her temple. "It's part of the job. Would seem odd if I didn't go."

"Lieutenant Bruce Kildare is the one who strikes me as odd," she confided, nibbling on her cookie.

"Yeah, I noticed that," he said in exasperation. "Look, you can't condemn a guy for not owning his own car."

She lifted her hands in concession. "I admit that it would take more than that to mean anything. It's a case of building up a lot of oddities, piecing them all together. That's how we do it."

"I admire your loyalty to your friends," he began.

"Penny is a bigger concern than the rest were," she interjected. "She's prey to any fortune hunter who's got a smooth line. She's always been a fool for men. She likes the chatty, amorous ones who fuel her ego."

Matt pulled a chair away from the Formica table and sank down. "Kildare strikes me as another huge ego, who's wise enough to realize that he has to pump up Penny, too. I don't know how many snapshots he took of her at our luncheon—had to be a thirty-six roll in that camera. He finagled himself into many of them, hoisting the camera into other people's hands."

"Penny seemed appreciative on that score," she mused. "But did you notice how he never really listens to anyone, like Rebecca for instance, when she was talking about herself? You'd think if he wanted a solid foundation with Penny's friends, he would have made an effort."

"I can't argue that Rebecca was a bit uncomfortable. But again, it doesn't mean much on its own."

"His hair is an unnatural butternut color," she added. "They encourage dye jobs in the service?"

"No, but maybe he's self-conscious because the press will be there."

"Penny has never been the least bit interested in being married to military, either," Jill went on, a glint of triumph in her eyes. "She hates any kind of rigidity. Just for example," she said, pacing around the table like a prosecuting attorney at the jury box, "Penny never makes her bed."

"Which means?" He prompted her with the wave of a cookie.

"Bruce must tuck in the covers on a mattress with a precision—"

"Like yours," he dourly inserted.

"Well, yeah!"

"I don't make my bed, either," he argued after he swallowed. "But I have the feeling that won't stop us from making it together sometime soon."

Jill flushed over the sexy pun that mirrored her own thoughts. "Only you'd try to line up a rendezvous while I'm talking about something else."

"I can't help it," he purred with a grin.

"This is important, Travis!"

He leaned back on the creaky wooden chair, extending his legs across the gold flooring. "Sounds to me like it's her habits that make you wonder, as well as his."

"I just can't see them together, all right?" She went to the cupboard and brought two Ziploc bags to the table. Matt helped her load the cookies into them, squirreling away a pile for himself in the process.

"And doesn't it seem weird that Bruce has no buddies throwing him a party?" she demanded, pinning him with an accusatory look.

"Maybe he already had that kind of party," Matt guessed. "They probably wouldn't let outsiders in to a military bash. You have to admit that none of your friends seem to know him very well yet. Whether that's his fault alone I don't know."

Her fair hair rippled on a firm nod. "Another suspicious piece of puzzle."

"But nothing to condemn," he argued. "It's that cop brain of yours ticking out of control. Bruce may be a bit less comfortable with Penny's crowd because they are civilians. It stands to reason that he wouldn't want to be rowdy around them yet."

"How rowdy do things get at these bashes?"

"It depends," he hedged, closing the bag. "Hey, don't look at me like I'm some kind of masher! Dad hosts lots of them at the Green Door. Basically, it's a lot of guys drinking beer and telling stupid stories."

She placed her palms on the table in front of him. "Well, I have every confidence in you."

"To tell the stupidest story?" he guessed hopefully.

"To spy," she clarified with a glower.

His brows jumped in mocking fear. "Please don't make me."

"Who's the boss around here?" she grilled with slitted eyes.

He hauled her into his lap for a deep discussion on the subject, easing his fingers beneath her top to touch the satin skin of her back. She gasped in glorious affront as his thumbs strayed to explore the undersides of her breasts.

They didn't even hear the back screen door creak open moments later.

"Lands!" Wilma exclaimed in reproval. "You two better schedule a proper honeymoon—as soon as possible!"

Matt's chuckling response was velvet promise against the curve of Jill's ear. "I couldn't agree more."

Chapter Eleven

The bridal shower at Alison Sherwood's apartment and the bachelor party at Papa's Italian Eatery were on opposite ends of town, so Jill arranged for Bruce Kildare to pick up Matt in his rental car. Matt entered the living room later that evening to find her peering through the front curtains for a sign of headlights.

He knew the choice of driver was a deliberate ploy to draw him closer to the groom, but he didn't argue. He was determined to prove Jill wrong about her suspicions concerning the lieutenant. It was nuts the way she got working on a lead, gnawing at it like a terrier on a pants leg. If it was possible to ease her out of the habit, he'd like to begin without delay.

"He never did say exactly what kind of car he was driving, did he?" she murmured.

"No, honey," Matt replied with a patient sigh. "But I think anything downsize that swings in the driveway will be the one."

She offered him a prune look over her shoulder. "I just like to know."

"I know."

"Now here's a surprise!" she exclaimed moments later.

"A bicycle," he guessed.

"No, Wayne Smeed's black town car." Jill pulled back from the pane as a pair of strong beams illuminated a portion of the front yard. "Hmm, how odd that Wayne always seems to be around the groom," she mused as Matt pulled on his lightweight canvas jacket. "Now, this afternoon."

"Wayne showed up at lunch because he was delivering your old beau," Matt gibed with swift sharpness. He paused by a gold sunburst-shaped mirror near the door to run a comb through his short brown hair, straighten the collar of his green twill shirt.

"Yeah, but he sure wanted to come along in the first place, remember," Jill reminded him, quickly skimming over the subject of Roger like a champion skater on thin ice. "I wonder if he's trying to get to know the lieutenant a little better, too. It did seem like Penny was trying to ditch Wayne today, didn't it?"

Matt slid his comb into the back pocket of his wheat-colored jeans with a patient smile. "Is that what you cops do all day long, bend facts like rubber to fit your theories?"

"No, we try to stay one step ahead of the perps with shrewd second-guessing," she saucily corrected.

The honk of the car's horn echoed through an open window.

"Well, that's for me." He kissed her on the tip of her upturned nose. "Don't wait up."

"I may be the one who's late," she warned, opening the door for him.

"What do ya say we both make an effort to be back at a reasonable hour?" With a wink he was off across the lawn.

Matt climbed into the back seat of the luxurious vehicle, greeting both Wayne and Bruce. Wayne seemed edgy. His slicked-back hair bounced and gleamed under the ceiling light. Bruce's broad shoulders seemed stiff under his dark knit shirt. They both chorused a hello in unison, but Matt didn't think there was any togetherness between the two. It wasn't difficult to believe they'd been having an argument. Perhaps Penny's time and attention were at issue. Longtime manager versus new eager husband. Maybe their relationship still needed some fine tuning. Maybe he was beginning to think like one loopy cop! He wasn't going to do that, he vowed silently as they rolled down the driveway.

"These cars must run like a dream," Matt remarked conversationally several blocks on as they paused at a four-way stop.

"I suppose you wonder why I'm driving," Wayne surmised briskly.

Matt's jaw sagged in the shadows as the entertainment guru surveyed him in the rearview mirror. "Well, not really, Wayne."

"Wayne wants to control my hours, make sure I don't party on too late," Bruce shifted on seat to inform him with a chuckle. "Might spoil me for the other festivities."

"Penny's always found my advice beneficial," Wayne pointed out.

"Seems like a good idea to save your energy for the big day," Matt agreed.

"This is supposed to be the happiest weekend of your life, Bruce!" Wayne snapped, taking a sharp turn at a corner.

"It is!"

"Then I suggest you just play along without a fuss," Wayne strongly cautioned. "I'll be informing the press soon. Then the whole world will be watching how you behave."

"Look, Wayne, you aren't my manager. Never have—"

"Just watch your step!" Wayne cut in. "I've been shaping and grooming Penny's wholesome television image for years. I won't have anyone tampering with it. You are marrying the finest girl on earth—"

"Then maybe you should've just married her a long time ago," Bruce suggested angrily.

"I would have, given the smallest encouragement. But there are some things that even I can't completely manage."

A silence fell over the vehicle after that, leaving nothing more to say.

JILL WAS just approaching the door of Alison's apartment with her case of Glory Farms wine in her arms, sugar cookies and shower gift tucked inside the black tote slung over her shoulder. The heavy case was pressed against her chest, wrinkling the front of her white eyelet blouse, and the tote was set precariously on her frozen shoulder. She ended up ringing the doorbell with her elbow. Rebecca Lambert answered the door.

"Finally! The wine is here!"

"Hey, what about..." Jill shot her a forlorn look.

"Oh, yeah, the cookies, too," she teased, peeking into the tote. "Our favorite combination!"

Jill laughingly allowed Rebecca to wrestle away the heavy box, glad to see that the wife and mother looked far more playful and radiant than she had this afternoon. Jill moved inside to acknowledge the others, all lounging around the living room in blue jeans and blouses. The tall, willowy Alison was at the table setting out stemmed glasses. Gayle Fairchild was unwrapping what were presumably leftovers from the luncheon buffet at her restaurant. And Penny was taking candid shots of the group with the ever familiar camera passed between herself and Bruce.

All of Jill's cares evaporated as she stepped into the comfort of her old clique. The time spent alone with her pals in a relaxed setting was still precious. And the chemistry between all of them was still right. This was the good part about coming home, losing oneself in the same old feelings of belonging.

Jill joined Rebecca at the table and began to open the cardboard case. She noted, not for the first time, that the layout of their place was not unlike her own in San Francisco. Alison and Tom Sherwood preferred apartment living just as Jill did, because like her, their careers at the airline didn't spare them time to putter around with household maintenance. Unlike Jill's, theirs was full of expensive items, reflecting their hefty double income. Heavy Dutch furniture, fine plush carpeting and several abstract prints on the walls all added up to investments beyond a cop's budget.

"Jill, are you listening to us?" Alison demanded.

Jill focused on their beautiful hostess with wide eyes. "No, guess I wasn't."

"Start filling these flutes with the Glory," she instructed, lining several glasses up in a row on the table.

"Won't be hard to tackle this kind of stopper," Jill retorted, grabbing one of the green bottles by the neck and unscrewing the cap. She filled the glasses with the fizzy apple-flavored poplike beverage and Alison passed them out.

"To our two last brides, our two last maids," Alison toasted. "May you both be as happily married as the rest of us are!"

Everyone pressed the rims of their glasses to their mouths. Jill stole a glimpse at Penny. Penny's freckled face was bright, but Jill detected a surprising glint of uncertainty in her best friend's green eyes, and Penny really didn't seem interested in the wine. Jill felt genuinely radiant, and she wasn't even the one getting married!

Jill couldn't ignore the strong instinctive signals of caution flashing neon in her head. If this marriage was wrong for Penny, she shouldn't be going through with it. But why would her headstrong friend feel the urge to marry anyone but the very best? Penny was a celebrity. Loved by millions world round. True, like Jill herself, she might have been having second thoughts on her confirmed bachelorette position. But even under those circumstances, there was no reason to rush into anything!

"Jill, why are you staring at me?" Penny wondered, shifting to tuck her small legs up on the olive green sofa. "I feel as though you can read my mind, even after all these years!"

"I can still read your behavior," Jill saucily claimed, sauntering over to a small striped chair beside the sofa. "As always."

Penny scrunched her brows together in frustration.

"Hey, remember those beach parties after high school graduation?" Rebecca chirped with a bob of her dark permed head. "Barbecues and romance in the sand."

It was Jill's turn to shift uncomfortably on her cushion. They all knew that was the phase when she and Roger tried to patch things up after the prom. Went as far as to make love for the first time in a secluded cove. The roar of the waves had made sweet talk impossible to hear, but looking back, Jill was sure she hadn't missed much. Roger didn't mean a word he said anyway. No matter how hard they'd tried to recapture what they had before the prom incident, they could not. That passionate sizzle seemed gone forever.

It was Matt who turned her on now, sending a thread of fire down her spine with his dangerous dark eyes. One burning look singed away all thoughts of Roger and his motives, making their past fling kid stuff.

"Now I can read your mind," Penny claimed triumphantly.

"We all can," Alison added, her flawless model's face full of satisfaction. "Jill's got two men in the snare and she's squirming!"

A round of giggles filled the air as Jill flushed. "Roger's only true love is Roger, and we all know it!"

"I never would have invited him at all if I'd known about Matt," Penny said contritely. "I mean, if you really have something, you don't want anything or anyone to stand in your way.''

"Hear, hear," Gayle proclaimed.

Penny set her glass down on the end table to her right. Everyone openly noted that she was the only one who hadn't touched a drop of wine. Jill, seated to her right, reached over the armrests dividing the sofa and the chair to pat Penny's hand. "Something isn't right, Pen," she urged. "We are here for you, whatever it is."

"Leave it to you to notice that Bruce isn't my dream lover," she told all of them, centering especially on Jill.

"Well, the whole deal has seemed odd," Rebecca pointed out. "We never saw this man until recently. You say you've been dating several months, but you never even mentioned him."

"It's tough being in the spotlight," Penny complained. "My reputation is so fragile. I didn't want to say anything until I was sure about everything."

"You've never been drawn to a military man before," Jill said. "Bound to be steeped in rigid routine."

"Maybe she likes him because he will be shipping out," Gayle teased.

Jill noted a flash of panic in Penny's eyes. Had Gayle hit a nerve?

"He's not very polite," Rebecca said with an apologetic pout. "Treated me as though I was invisible."

Penny sighed hard, smoothing her pink blouse. "Before you get too gung-ho on this critique, I may as well tell you I'm pregnant."

"Pregnant?" The term made the rounds in gasps of awe and hoots.

"How could you keep that from us?" Gayle chided.

"I'm trying to keep it from the world for the sake of my image," Penny replied in defense. "Squeaky-clean hostess of 'Kid Konnection' having a baby out of wedlock might just ruin my career."

"So that's the reason for the rush-rush wedding," Jill murmured. "The reason you're not drinking wine."

"And the reason I'm marrying a man you think is not quite suited to me," Penny told them. Their telltale looks confirmed her statement. "Hey, don't worry about me," she coaxed on a lighter note. "I know exactly what I'm doing."

"Is Bruce really shipping out after the wedding, like you said?" Alison wondered as she refilled glasses with Glory. Rebecca the nurturer followed with a plate of Jill's cookies.

Penny nodded her clipped red head vigorously. "Yes, that much is absolutely true. I don't know exactly when I'll see him again." A chorus of sympathetic groans filled the room. "Stop the moaning sympathy!" Penny ordered with a slap to her denim-clad knee. "All I want from you is your trust. I'm doing what I have to do. Legitimizing my child for a hypocritical world. Bruce and I will work things out, I assure you. We both know the score and this is what we want."

"Well . . ." Gayle trailed off with a shrug. "If you have your sights on what you really want—"

"I do!"

"Of course we'll back you up," Jill said.

"Without doubts or questions," Penny clarified.

The crowd reluctantly agreed.

"Good," Penny proclaimed, popping off the sofa. "Let's dig into those leftovers from lunch. I'm absolutely starved, kids. Famished!"

Penny did most of the eating, while everyone else moved around, producing their shower gifts.

"This is a personal shower," Gayle announced to Penny, steering her and her brimming plate back to the sofa. "Hopefully, you'll get some use out of these items before you balloon."

"At the rate she's munching, she may not make it through the doorway tonight!" Alison joked, forever concentrating on her own svelte flight-attendant figure.

"I am barely pregnant, for your information," Penny reported between swallows of cola. "To the general public, it hasn't even happened yet. Remember that!"

Once they were all seated, Jill handed Penny a weighty rectangular box. "This is from my aunt Wilma," she reported, rolling her eyes. "You may as well get it out of the way."

Everyone knew what Wilma Ames's standard shower gift was. A rolling pin, along with a clever handwritten note about keeping the husband in line—with many apple pies, of course. Ha, ha.

"Some things never change," Jill said with a false note of gaiety.

"But you got away," Gayle said practically. They all understood the depth of Jill's situation with the disapproving old woman.

"And you've found a happy ending with Matt," Rebecca added, quite fond of happy endings in the tales she read her children every night.

Penny opened the other gifts, a nice variety of flimsy lingerie and scented toiletries. They were examining the loot when the doorbell chimed.

"Who could that be?" Alison asked in surprise, uncrossing her legs, rising from the floor. "All the guys are at the bachelor party."

Jill noted that whoever it was was testing the knob to find it locked. She rapidly rose from her chair to follow Alison.

Alison opened the door, gasping with indignation. "What are you doing here?"

Jill's stomach did a cartwheel as Roger pushed his way inside. "Evening, girls," he greeted. "The other bash was a crashing bore, so I decided to cut out and join you." He grasped Jill's hand in his. Her eyes scanned his length with involuntary appreciation. He was still attractive with his devilish grin and stylish arrogance, cutting a nice figure in his tailored leather jacket, pressed blue dress shirt and creased navy slacks. Despite the camouflaging clothing, though, he hadn't kept himself in peak condition as Matt had. Matt, if provoked, could take him down with one punch.

So where the hell did that thought come from? she wondered.

"Take care of me, Jilly," he demanded abruptly. "Lead me through this jungle of female predators." Before she could protest, he was dragging her toward the table. "Ah, man, Glory Farms wine. Cool." He released Jill and poured himself a glassful. "Remember all those great beach parties? Remember..." He halted in midsentence as he began to remember everything. His expression grew pleased and wolfish. He gulped the glass of wine and poured another. "It's been a while since I've had sand in my trunks. Was the best of times, wasn't it, Jilly? Me, you, frothy water all over us."

Jill stiffened as the sensations of their first time flooded back.

"Gee, this wine hasn't improved a bit with age," he complained, clacking his tongue with disgust.

"Nor have your manners," Penny halfheartedly chided. "Hasn't it occurred to you that you might not be welcome at our hen party? That Jill might not care to relive intimate details of her past with you in public?"

"Aw, c'mon," he grumbled. "In my line of work there's no such thing as a secret." He gazed at Jill with a wink. "Right, Jilly?"

Jill melted under his boyish plea for understanding. None of them could stay really mad at him and he knew it.

His roving eyes landed on the boxes heaped with bright silks and nylons. "Man. You have a shower like this one back in Frisco, Jilly?"

"Uh, no." She could feel his hand pressing against her back. Her eyelet blouse was designed more for flair than cover-up. She could feel the graze of his fingers all too well on her skin.

"I can only imagine—"

"Imagine what, Roger?" she squealed, jerking out of reach.

"How happy you and Matt are," Gayle inserted snidely.

He reared back in affront. "You girls just like to torture me. What you owe me is a little pampering. Came all the way here from Europe, hoping to win back the best girl in the world, only to find her hitched to a teacher. A teacher," he repeated in disbelief.

"Matt is a wonderful man," Jill admonished, gulping some wine.

"Baby, baby, I could show you the world—on my expense account."

"And I could show you the entrance by way of the balcony," a rough masculine voice said nastily.

"Matt!" Jill wheeled toward the door to find her hired husband looking creditably mad. Raving mad, with a lethal look and a ramrod stiff stance. She imagined him as a young man with that same kind of smoldering temper and wondered if he'd learned to control himself under this kind of stress. She hoped he could cope.

"Oh, Travis." Roger managed to chuckle. "Didn't know you followed me."

"We all followed you." Tom Sherwood, Alison's husband, wedged his way inside with the other male guests. "Matt figured out where you were headed, and I supplied the shortcut home."

"I didn't want to miss a thing," Matt said, striding over to stand beside Jill. He angled his arm around her shoulders in a possessive gesture.

"It's all okay, Travis," she said with forced brightness. "Roger is such a kidder."

But everyone there had to know that he wasn't kidding at all. Even Matt, a stranger, could tell. "Well, I'm sure you're up to picking the man you really want."

Jill's nerve endings tingled, partly from the wine and partly from Matt's proximity. He was searching her eyes now and she knew what he was looking for—her real choice. This was her second and perhaps final chance to give Roger another try. All she had to do was make the announcement that she was still single.

What a bullhead Matt was! How many times, in countless ways, did she have to spell out her choice? "Everything's okay, Matt," she murmured tenderly. "Relax, have something to eat."

Matt's expression brightened. He understood her message. He was being an idiot. And he was so happy to know it! "We stuffed ourselves with spaghetti," he confessed, but he did approach the table for a couple of cookies.

The room began to hum with party sounds. Matt took Jill by the elbow and steered her to a corner near an old German grandfather clock.

"Did Bannon try anything, Jill?" he asked intently.

"Let me handle him," she whispered in pleading exasperation, her voice a little slurred.

"Okay," he conceded heavily.

"Let's not call attention to ourselves," she suggested with a giggle.

"You're the one who's had a little too much Glory," he chided gently, very much liking this giddy side to her. Too bad he had to deliver some bad news.

She tried to pull back, but he kept hold of her arm. "This isn't the best time to admit defeat, but I think you're onto something with your suspicions concerning Bruce Kildare," he uttered under his breath.

"Oh, no!" she huffed in indignation.

Their host, Tom Sherwood was watching them, so Matt began to rub her upper arms in an intimate gesture to fend him off. "You know, he hasn't been acting like any groom tonight that I've ever known."

Jill pressed her fingers to his mouth to shush him. "I've changed my mind about their marriage. If Penny wants him—"

"But I think you're on to something," he elucidated. "I figured you'd be thrilled."

"No, Matt," she said adamantly. "We girls had a long talk about trust, about everything—"

"You didn't tell them about us, though," he challenged.

"Well, no, I wasn't feeling all that thorough," she admitted. "But Penny chose to confide and we've all chosen to support her. I'll tell you more about it once we—"

"I caught him in the bar pinching the bottom of a dishy little server in a wench costume," Matt remarked with regret.

She gasped in dismay, turning to locate Bruce among the guests. He was seated on the arm of a chair, reloading Penny's camera with film. Penny was standing over him, massaging his shoulders. "I've never seen him more content than he is right now."

"Maybe wenches agree with him."

Jill and Matt dropped the issue reluctantly and circulated as a couple, making light conversation. Jill made a marked effort not to cast worried looks to Penny. She seemed just fine, taking pictures, doing some of her "Kid Konnection" routines.

Shortly after midnight, Jill suggested they head for home. Matt trailed after her as she hunted down her black tote bag, which Alison had stowed in her bedroom. An intense conversation in a dark spare room enticed them to a halt halfway down the hall. The exchange was between Wayne Smeed and Penny.

"Bruce likes the girls, all right." Penny snorted.

"Well, I don't think anyone saw him," Wayne said.

"I'm sure it was harmless flirting," Penny said dismissively. "So how much was the dinner?"

"I'll pay," Wayne insisted.

"No, no," Penny objected. "Everything is on me. I'm determined to pick up the entire tab for the weekend. Even most of the food tonight is from the luncheon I sponsored for Jilly."

Jill scowled at Matt. Wasn't Bruce Kildare contributing a thing?

"Look, I charged everything," Wayne said.

"So, show me the receipt. I'll give you cash. Wait here while I get my purse."

Jill was rooted in indecision, so Matt snagged her by the waist and pulled her into the kitchen. As Penny passed by, he dipped his mouth to Jill's for a thorough, hungry kiss. Jill could see Penny out of the corner of her eye. There seemed to be a trace of envy on Penny's perky face as she paused in midstep at the sight of them. For the first time ever, Jill felt sorry for her successful friend.

Chapter Twelve

"Whew, what a night!"

Matt made the proclamation an hour later as they shut themselves away in her old bedroom. They'd escaped the shower only to come home to one of Wilma's performances. She supposedly hadn't been waiting up for them, but would be obliged to listen to the details of their evening if they pressed them on her. Matt had left the explaining to Jill, who'd glossed over the night's events despite her tipsy condition. He lifted a brow at the news that the old lady had sent along a rolling pin to a personal shower, but he ultimately decided it was just right.

As much as he wanted to seduce his *faux* bride, Matt couldn't believe the turnabout in Jill's attitude toward the questions on Lieutenant Bruce Kildare. Surely she didn't perceive him as a better man after tonight! And it bothered him. He couldn't rest until he understood.

"Jill, honey..." he began, roaming the room with his pants riding low on his lean hips without his belt. He'd begun to strip, removing not only his belt and shoes, but his shirt, too, revealing his bare, suntanned chest in all its sinewy glory. It looked so brown in contrast with his pale-colored jeans. Jill wanted to stroke the contours of his body, fuse with his heat.

They both knew they were going to make love tonight, she thought with an impatient wince. So what was he prowling and mumbling about?

"Jill," he began again, moving up behind her as she brushed her hair in front of the dresser mirror. "I really do think there's something fishy going on."

She stared at their reflection, her brush freezing in mid-air as he grazed her collarbone with his forearm. The excitement she'd felt back in her apartment when he held that old blue formal up to her charged her system again. But this time Roger had no place in the picture. His memory—of a decade ago, or an hour ago—wasn't welcome.

"Let's just forget about everybody else," she beseeched softly, tipping her head back against his breastbone. Matt's eyes fell to her breasts jutting up through her eyelet blouse.

"You've made me into a snoop, and I think I deserve a say."

She giggled, tipping her head back and forth, causing her flaxen hair to fall in her vision.

"Time is closing in for Penny," he cautioned, whirling her around to face him. "That guy is up to something. He and Wayne were at war in the car. Wayne doesn't think much of their marriage, and Bruce doesn't seem all that excited himself."

Jill breathed deeply, winding her arms around his neck. "Just forget about it, Travis."

He scowled into her luminous eyes. "You always want to be right. I'm trying to tell you, you are!"

"I know," she crooned, kissing his throat. "But I am wrong sometimes. In this case, I'd say, I'm kind of right and kind of wrong."

He shuddered as she drew her tongue under his chin. "Do you believe Penny cares for him?" he pressed.

"Not like a dream lover," Jill decided with a shrug. "Not like I do for you," she cooed with a flutter of lash.

"That's nice, Jill," he murmured, burying his face in her scented hair. "But I just can't understand your change of heart."

Jill drew a finger to her lips. "Shh. Shecret. I shouldn't tell."

"Tell me what?"

"That Penny is pregnant," she blurted with a conspiratorial smile. "She is marrying Bruce because she's having his child." She closed her eyes, tipping a little bit. Matt kept his hands splayed across her waist so she wouldn't topple over. "So you see, it explains why everything is rush-rush-rush."

"I'd never thought I'd say this, Jill, but if there was ever a time for you to be a pure and logical cop, this is it!"

"Want me to arrest ya?" she teased throatily. "Slap the old cuffs to the bedpost?"

"No, you little fool."

Jill exhaled, summoning patience. "Look at it this way. This trip, I'm a friend first and a cop second. Travis, Penny confided in us as friends, asked for our trust. I intend to keep the bargain."

"Ha! I see you as a classic buttinski when you think somebody needs you!"

She drew a pouty look. "I trust Penny to make the right decisions. I trust you to make some, too."

The effects of the wine made Jill just dizzy enough to do what she'd wanted to do all along, forge her fingers through the mat of hair on his chest, just loose enough to let go and behave as she really wanted to. "Just love me, Travis. Forget all about Bruce and Roger and our marriage, pretend you're courting me."

"You sure you want to do this tonight, Jill?" he asked in a hoarse whisper. It was the answer to his prayers, for sure, but he didn't want to catch her at vulnerable moment. "Being dizzy..."

"Positive, darling," she cooed, skimming the waistline of his jeans. "You make me dizzy in an incurable way that isn't about to change anytime in the future."

He sucked in air as she wedged her fingers behind his zipper, urging it open, pushing his pants to the floor. He could feel his manhood growing, hardening, as her hands explored, slipping around on his cotton briefs, teasing for entry at the legs and waistline. He tugged her blouse loose from her jeans, reaching up beneath the eyelet fabric, touching her bra. It was hooked in the front, making it simple to pop open.

Jill gasped in pleasure as he invaded her lacy lingerie, grabbed hold of her breasts for a brief gentle squeeze. Before she could take another breath, his hands were on the outside again. Rather than just peeling off her blouse, he pressed the fabric against her exposed nipples, toying with the dark circles of skin until they hardened.

"What are you doing, Travis?" she gasped in wonder.

"Playing," he rasped. "Something you must learn to do more of." No sooner were the words out of his mouth than he felt her hands plunging into his briefs to clamp his solid buttocks. He made a guttural noise as a hard shudder shook him. "That feels so...good. You're right. Tonight there is nobody else in the whole wide world...."

Matt gazed dazedly at the top of her blond head. It was really happening to him. The ice-princess cop was stooping to pull off his briefs—with unbridled excitement. There was something so marvelous about watching her heat up, loosen up, all for him. Exposed and quaking in anticipation, he raised his hands to her blouse, fumbling with the tiny pearl buttons.

She laughed softly at his clumsiness. "Bras must be your specialty."

He growled in her ear as she took over the task. "My specialties will amaze you." He had no trouble discarding her jeans and panties. A few breathless moments later he was easing her onto the smooth white sheets, into the cushy little mattress. Her sleek slender limbs were so soft against his hair-roughened body, the friction like a raging forest fire on his skin. He couldn't help but scrape himself over and over her length, lose himself in the delicious burn.

Matt eventually eased up on his elbow to watch her play of expression. To his satisfaction her dreamy, set features matched her moans of yearning. He never felt so wanted by any woman. The fact that he fought his desires for so long only escalated them to a seam-bursting tension.

They lost themselves in languid foreplay, teasing, tempting, tasting. She explored his body with open appreciation, gliding her fingers and mouth over the rigid muscled planes of his shoulders and chest, dipping her tongue into his navel, spreading his thighs with her hands for more intimate contact.

Matt lavished in her attention, glorying in the pulsation, allowing it to overtake his system. When he felt on the brink of a meltdown, he grasped Jill by the arms and flipped her snugly beneath him.

Ever so carefully, ever so slowly, he kissed every inch of her silken skin, taking a silent inventory of every luscious curve and every creamy niche, until she was shivering on the brink of need.

It was with a coy smile and dancing eyes that Jill eventually wound her legs around his waist, guiding him inside her.

Matt bore down hard, sliding into her moist tunnel with a swift gliding motion. She arched her back in response to the thrusts that followed, convulsively clinging to his shoulders as they soared to new heights on groans and murmurs. The sensations peaked and exploded around them with an ear-pounding clarity.

Jill lavished in the ebbing sensations, astonished and exhausted. "I never knew it could be like that," she confided huskily.

He smiled down at her spent form, burying his face in her disheveled tide of hair on the pillow. "I have a feeling it could be even better," he rasped. "Back at home. In our own beds."

She skittered his spine with her fingertips. "Yeah.... Something to look forward to."

"Hey, there's a lot to look forward to," he objected, rolling on his side. "I want us to be together, honey. For real."

"I want that, too, Travis. But if you don't mind, I'd like to save any real heart-to-heart decisions for back home. This trip is so full of surprises. And I think you know I don't appreciate unexpected twists in my personal life. I like to be prepared, see the course way ahead."

He released a huge sigh, punching his pillow into place behind him. He knew this was going to take some patience. He knew it from the onset. If only that stupid Roger Bannon wasn't around, threatening to confuse her, tempt her back to a simpler time in her life! He wanted a full-fledged promise, and he wanted it now! But it wasn't her nature and he knew better than to push her.

As Jill snuggled into place, he bounced around on his side of the mattress, failing miserably to find a comfortable position. He knew he couldn't sleep a wink unless he tried to stake his claim for her all over again in the tried and true way.

"Jill, you asleep?" he queried silkily, rolling to his side to face her.

"Huh?" she asked groggily. Her eyes soon snapped open with a gasp as his hand stole to her creamy bottom, wedging their bellies flush. "You want to do it again?" she peeped in surprise. "Already? We have a million tomorrows waiting for us."

He couldn't bring himself to admit that he was afraid the magic might be snatched away from them without warning once the world closed in again. "Please, honey," he rasped. "Just one more time."

"All right, grizzly bear," she agreed, nipping at his mustache. "But it's my turn to be on top. . . ."

"YOU CALLED Bob Williams? Without my permission? Without my blessing?" Jill was both irritated and flabbergasted Sunday morning when she awoke around ten o'clock to find Matt seated at the kitchen table with a notepad and pencil before him, dressed in some of his hacked-off sweats. She cinched her terry robe tighter around her waist and snatched the pad for a look. "You hate him! Still, you called him!"

"I called him because he has access to Bayside's computer bank," he explained. "We need some information on Bruce Kildare, and fast."

"But Bob, of all people! When that grill of your father's is crawling with cops you like much better."

"Well, I figure he can't be all bad if you like him," Matt explained, sipping from his coffee mug.

Jill was effused with warmth over his obvious effort to give Bob a fresh chance. He had to be doing it for her, to bridge their worlds back home. But that didn't change the fact that he was sneaky. She eyed him keenly. "What happened to our teamwork pact, our vow to trust?"

"I would've checked with you, had you been awake. But as it was," he crooned with dancing eyes, "you were in a deep exhausted sleep."

"That is a flimsy excuse, from Mr. One More Time."

"Jill, to be perfectly honest, I think you've buried your trusty radar in a sea of orange blossoms," he accused without rancor. "I'm one of the few people around here with no prejudiced ties to the past who can see that Bruce should be investigated even if Penny's set to marry him."

"You've even made a list of suspicions," she noted, inspecting the top sheet. "How notoriously policemanlike of you. Leased car. Benign attitude. Static with Wayne Smeed. Dyed hair. Wench pinch. Hey, what's this one mean?''

Matt automatically knew which one her manicured finger was lodged on. ''I was going to tell you all about it last night before you pulled down my zipper.''

''Granny?'' she queried with a wrinkled nose. ''As in Granny Goodrite's meat loaf?''

He chuckled with pleasure. ''No, silly girl. Bruce bent down to tie his shoe and made a granny instead of a square knot. Seems strange for a sailor to do. And a separate issue from his romance with Penny, by the way. Another angle entirely.''

Her mouth sagged open as she absorbed the shock. ''Oh. No. You mean he might not even be a sailor?'' She dropped the pad on the table and poured herself a cup of coffee.

''You know how it is with us investigators,'' he said expansively. ''We get all these puzzle pieces, then try to fit them together.''

She couldn't help beaming with pride. ''You just might make a decent detective.''

''I'll settle for a decent partner,'' he amended.

She moved to the table to top off his cup. ''So when is Bob going to get back to us?''

''Soon. He needs some time to adjust to my calling, and a little more time to investigate.''

Jill, in true meticulous form, was tempted to call Bob, reiterate everything. But she held back, not wanting to spoil the new truce forging between the men.

''I told him time is of the essence,'' he added over the rim of his coffee cup, ''with the wedding tomorrow and all.''

''Oh, no,'' Jill lamented, pressing a hand to her cheek. ''What if he's not who he says he is? What if he's a fortune hunter?''

He reached across the Formica tabletop to squeeze her hand. ''Let's just play out one card at a time. See where it leads us.''

A rap at the back screen door interrupted them. Jill was delighted to spy a uniformed man on the doorstep holding a bouquet of flowers. She flew over to accept the delivery, tipping him from Wilma's stash of bills in the cupboard by the sink.

"Oh, Matt, you shouldn't have!" she raved in pleasure. The arrangement was absolutely gorgeous, an assortment of wildflowers already set in an etched glass vase.

"I didn't," he flatly confessed, stooping to pick up the white card that fluttered to the gold flooring.

"You read it for me," she suggested lightly, turning to the tap to add an inch of water to the vase.

"Not only flowers grow up wild," he recited sourly. "Roger."

Jill inhaled between her teeth, gingerly setting the vase in the center of the table.

Matt closed his eyes, summoned fortitude. "Jill, I understand your wish to be popular around here, but I do think this could get a little out of hand. This man obviously doesn't mind playing the adulterer! Or playing the village idiot by testing my temper!"

"That darn Roger is so spoiled, so accustomed to getting his way, that's all. I'll make it more than clear that any future with me is impossible." She eased onto his lap for a snuggle. "Now, why don't you go blow off some steam with your morning jog." She paused in fear. "You haven't done that yet, have you?"

He set his mouth in a grumpy line. "No, I haven't."

"Good," she said in relief. "There's still hope of bringing that pulsing vein in your throat under control, then."

"What about Bob Williams?"

"Even a routine character check will no doubt take some time. Bob hates computers, so he'll have to find a clerk to help him. And the clerk will have to be free." She shrugged beneath her terry robe. "The system moves slowly."

Matt took her word for it and set out on his morning jog. Jill judged wrong, however. She had just stepped out of the shower twenty minutes later when Wilma called her to the telephone.

"It's your partner," she reported, her narrow, lined face set in curious confusion. "Surely you can't be that indispensable."

"Thank you very much," Jill intoned, taking the receiver in hand. "Hello, Bob."

"Hello there, operator."

"Cut it out," she scoffed, turning away from Wilma's interrogative look. "So, what have you got?"

"The news is simple and sorry. There is no Lieutenant Bruce Kildare stationed at Point Loma."

Jill clutched her robe to her throat as her damp body dropped a few degrees more. "Is that as far as you took it?"

"No. There is no Bruce Kildare on a naval base in the state of California. That's why I'm able to get back to you so fast. I hit a dead end right away. I did check on the rental car Kildare's driving. It was charged to Penny's corporation. She is one, you know, a corporation. It would probably be easy enough for Kildare to pull that off with a company credit card without too much trouble—if he's clever."

"Apparently he is," Jill conceded furiously.

"Another twist is that the car isn't on long-term lease. It's just rented for a couple of weeks, due back on Tuesday, after the holiday."

"Oh, no."

"I wish I could forge on. No place to go, though, without prints, or a photo, or something more."

Jill stared out the window over the sink into Wilma's small sunny backyard. She just couldn't help but hope for a happier report. But Matt was right. Penny needed more than a faithful friend right now. She needed a practical, collected cop on the beat.

"Jill?" Bob prompted. "Can you me feed more details?"

"You've been a big help already. It's up to me to act on this end."

"It's a tough deal. Travis told me he's the groom."

"Yes, that's right." She bit her lip, annoyed at Wilma's bold proximity. "So naturally time is a huge factor."

"That old auntie of yours still is butting into everything, isn't she?"

"Some things never change," she replied.

"Some things do," he noted with a chuckle. "You and Travis, I mean. Things must be pretty rosy."

"Yeah," she professed warmly, a smile curving her lips. "Who'd have ever guessed?"

"No need to always guess ahead, though, is there," he pointed out.

"Somebody else said the same thing last night," she admitted.

"And I know who. Give me a call back if anything else turns up."

"Thanks, Bob."

"Thank you," he returned with relish. "Now I can go into Chet's Green Door with the guys without an aura of anger hovering overhead."

Jill hung up the phone to find Wilma fussing with her flowers. She'd obviously already read the card. It was now propped against the Tupperware sugar bowl rather than the creamer.

"Lovely, aren't they, Aunt Wilma?" she said, swinging closer on her bare feet.

"Indeed. But that Roger has always been so thoughtful."

Jill gritted her teeth. When? Even in their most intimate days as teens, Roger had been nothing but a selfish show-off, incapable of a deep thought. But it was reasonable that Wilma would delight in him, being the epitome of surface herself!

"That call important?" Wilma asked, straining to keep real interest out of her voice.

"Nothing to fret about." Jill busily moved a couple of the daisies around.

"You sound upset, even now," Wilma pressed, her pale eyes keen.

If Wilma really cared for her, Jill would have been happy to share her business with her. As it was, she had no problem meeting Wilma's inquisitive stare without guile. "It's official business, nothing more. I have to go out for awhile. When Matt returns, tell him I went over to the Seacrest Motel."

"That's where we dropped Roger off yesterday after the luncheon," she observed knowingly.

"He's not the only one staying there," Jill retorted. "Even the groom has a room."

And it was only the groom's room that interested her. One way or the other, Jill was going to have it out with Bruce rat-fink Kildare.

It was a scant thirty minutes later that Jill was pounding on his second-floor door. The motel faced the sea with an open air balcony. The waves were kicking up quite a roar today, tugging at her apricot-colored jumpsuit and her knot of pale hair. She pounded all the harder to be heard.

It seemed he wasn't in. All the better for her purposes, really. Getting at the truth indirectly was probably her best shot. If she could just home in on a big lead. Bruce Kildare might be an alias, for instance. A real piece of ID would be useful, a license or passport. A piece of mail with the address of a business or a residence. Fingerprints would be best, but there wasn't time to see that kind of check through the channels.

For the first time in her career, Jill was cutting through bureaucratic red tape. She shook her head in an unconscious gesture of disbelief. It had to be Matt's influence on her.

Of course this move was more than a snip of tape. She was currently committing a crime to help a dear old friend in need. Breaking and entering was against the law, after all. But if she couldn't bend the rules for the sake of her old vulnerable, pregnant pal, she was no kind of friend at all. A jiggle of wire and the door popped open. Jill shook her head over the lax security and cautiously eased inside.

The shades were drawn tight against the windows, making the room quite dim. But Jill could see enough to make her way to a pole lamp near the writing desk. A click of the button brought a wan glow to the small mustard-toned room. Jill stealthily checked the closet and bathroom for Kildare, dourly noting that the place certainly didn't have a military order to it. The double bed was tossed. There were damp towels on the floor near the bathtub. Clothing was slung over every stick of furniture, even the television set.

Jill set her hands on her hips, inspecting the scene with a disparaging cluck. Some dream husband. Poor Penny. Jill sprang into action then, rummaging through the dresser, desk drawer, the two open suitcases, on the lookout for anything that would shed light on Bruce Kildare. There appeared to be nothing out of the ordinary. But the absence of anything bearing the man's name seemed odd. It was a trait of a con man.

The idea to toss the mattress was a halfhearted one. It was clumsy and a poor hiding place, considering maid service. But she had little to lose, considering the awful condition of the bed. It was this effort that inadvertently lead to her discovery. As Jill crouched at the foot of the bed for leverage, she spied something wedged beneath the large red vinyl writing chair across the room at the desk.

Jill abandoned the mattress and quickly tipped the chair on its back legs to find a large brown envelope secured to the burlap underside with masking tape. It would've gone unnoticed if the flap hadn't fallen open and into her line of vision, she realized.

This discovery was meant to be.

Jill quickly scanned the contents of the envelope. There were some handwritten notes, a soft-covered journal divided into days, broken down by the hour in places, and some packs of developed pictures bearing the logo of a local drugstore—all concerning Penny! This was exactly the kind of proof she needed to nail Bruce Kildare to the wall, force him out into the open as no good. She hastily returned everything to the envelope, shut off the lamp and headed to the door. He was concocting a blockbuster inside story for somebody. And there was only one man in town that she knew of who would be chomping for just such a scoop. And it just so happened he was handy.

"Good morning, Roger," she greeted briskly a few minutes later, three doors down the same windswept balcony. It had taken a good sixty seconds of rapid knocking to summon him, and her thinning patience was evident in her voice.

"What time is it?" Roger yawned hugely, regarding her with a glazed expression. Jill took a long, hard look at her old love in the stark daylight, unkempt and off guard. This was reality, the man Roger really was beneath his well-cut clothing! She'd obviously roused him and he apparently slept in his underwear.

Any illusions she'd been harboring for him died right then and there as she inspected baggy light blue boxers ballooning with sea air around his spindly legs and a white T-shirt pulled snug around his chunky middle. His tousled blond hair was showing signs of thinning to a widow's peak and his brows appeared uneven, as though they were routinely plucked. It occurred to her that he went to an awful lot of trouble to spruce up for public appearances. To his good fortune, his large frame held tailored clothes well, draped over his imperfections. At thirty, however, she felt he was far too young to have let himself go to this degree. It had to be due to his jet-set life-style, the lavish parties brimming with liquor and rich foods, the late night camping on doorsteps and peeking through windows.

"When I gave you my room number, I didn't expect a morning visit," he protested, injecting a note of suaveness into his tone and expression. She fought the urge to laugh at his unintentional stab at humor.

"We have to talk." She plowed past him, one arm curled around the brown envelope, the other barred against his belly should he protest.

But he didn't protest. He egotistically mistook her investigative motives for amorous ones. Jill came to realize that as she whirled to find his eyes roving the length of her jumpsuit. "Come to daddy after all, eh?"

Her blue eyes blazed with indignation. "Oh, shut up, you idiot!"

Roger froze in his tracks on the mustard carpeting. "What gives here, Jill? You've come to me. My room."

"I really came here to face Bruce Kildare," she railed.

Roger's jaw sagged in confusion. A yawn escaped his mouth. "Isn't he home, then?"

"No, he isn't! But look what I found under his chair."

"Under his . . ." Roger balked as Jill spilled the contents of the envelope on his open bed.

"Take a look at this stuff and tell me what's going on," she directed, thrusting a finger at the pile of papers.

Roger shrugged, dropping to the mattress. He sifted through the pictures, flipped through the journal. "This looks like an undercover investigation to me."

"Is he doing it for you?" she demanded.

"Huh?" Roger rubbed his bristled cheeks. "I don't know this character."

"This is the kind of snooping you do for a living, Rog."

"I know it. But why would I spy on Penny? She's a friend. And as far as I know, she has no juicy secrets."

"Do you understand how delicate her image is on public television?" she grilled, putting his shoulder in a death grip.

"Of course I do," he shot back, starting to get angry. "I really resent the fact that you think I could hurt her."

"I happen to be one person who's been betrayed by you, remember?"

He winced. "Yeah, I know. But I wouldn't dream of harming Penny with some kind of smear. We're like an old family, for cripe's sake." He raised a finger at her. "You had the right to take this one shot at me, and now I'm going to set you straight. I'm not in on this. Also, for the record," he added with a sigh, "I've never felt good about betraying you, believe me."

Jill bit her lip, lifting her eyes to the cracked ceiling. He was telling her the truth on both counts, she was sure of it. "I know I pressed too hard back then." With a resigned huff, she pushed the papers aside and sank down on the mattress. "You got scared and bolted. I was too clingy, looking for the warmth that Wilma refused to give. My bad luck it was at prom time."

"I wasn't ready for commitment yet," he admitted. "But I didn't want to take you to the prom, Jill." He slowly met her stricken look. "I deliberately picked that fight with you so I could take Gloria Simms."

Jill's eyes grew to surprised saucers. "Why?" was all she could manage to croak out.

"Because you were always the plain duckling, that's why. I knew your dress wouldn't be the best and Wilma didn't have the money to rent a limo or sponsor a fancy dinner in town. I couldn't come up with that kind of cash, either. But Gloria's folks could. She asked me to go before our argument, laid out the whole snazzy deal." He raked through his thinning hairline. "I'm sorry, Jilly. I just wanted to have the best of times. Something grand to remember."

"And you sacrificed my good time to do it."

"Yes."

"I guess it's just the kind of man you are." Jill averted her gaze, forcing airiness into her tone. "You've gone on to one lavish party after another, cashed in as a glorified tattletale."

"You're right."

Jill's eyes snapped to his.

He raised a halting hand. "I'm not saying I've taken the wrong course. I've had some pretty—no, some very good times. But the thrills have worn thin. The invitation from Penny to come back here, reconnect with you, it seemed so right, perfect timing."

"But I'm not available," Jill snapped, her expression more triumphant than apologetic.

Roger groaned in protest, reaching across the pile of papers to grasp her knee. "Now, about that, Jilly—"

A noise at the door cut him short. Roger and Jill reeled in surprise as Matt barged inside without knocking.

"Jill!" Her name tore out his mouth with galvanic force. "What the hell are you doing here?"

Chapter Thirteen

Matt's thunderous presence ejected her from the bed. But not before he'd seen Roger's hand on her knee. She knew it looked bad. Roger in his underwear. Her eyes misty. But Matt was her future. She was merely tying up some loose ends of the past. And helping Penny. Who desperately needed her for the first time ever.

"I've never been so glad to see anybody, Travis," she ventured. And she meant it. Surely he could see that.

"Tell me what's going on," he invited with false pleasantness. Roger flinched as Matt's hand flew up, but he was only shoving the door shut. Roger had a right to wonder. Matt did look lean and incredibly mean, dressed only in his ragged gray sweats, cut high on his sinewy limbs. He was a masculine power to reckon with.

"I will tell you everything in a sec," she promised, moving for the phone. "But I think it's best I call Penny first."

"I hope you're not going to invite her over, too," Roger complained, tugging at his T-shirt.

"The more the merrier!" Matt proclaimed snidely, balling his fists.

Jill sensed that Matt had overstayed his welcome. His hot temper was already getting the best of him. She bent over the nightstand, careful not sit down on the bed, and quickly punched in Penny's home number. "No answer." She hung up, then swiftly gathered Bruce's papers, shoving them into their original envelope. "Matt, we have to track her down fast."

"I don't know what that stuff is, Bannon," Matt growled, gesturing to the envelope in her hands. "But it saved your worthless life, lying between you and my woman."

"Matt!" Jill cried, aghast.

"This isn't over yet, Travis," Roger said with a faintly condescending smile. "I'm not through with Jill. And using your fists won't solve a thing."

"Penny's well-being is most important right now," she sternly reprimanded the pair. "She's about to marry a fraud!"

"It isn't my fault!" Roger said, automatically covering himself.

Matt's temper bubbled as his eyes snapped from one to the other in confusion. "Will somebody tell me what's going on?"

"I will," she assured. "On the way."

"I better come along, too," Roger decided, making a move to rise off the bed.

"No, Roger." Jill joined Matt at the door. "Give me—and Penny—some space to work this out."

"Oh, sure," he chortled. "Between the two of you, I'll end up swinging from a sturdy branch!"

"Well, we all can dream." Matt hustled out the doorway with Jill in tow.

Jill paused, turning back to snag the doorknob. "You should know better than to ever answer the door without your pants on," she scolded Roger in parting. "If those boxers had been briefs, Matt would've knocked your block off long before he spotted the envelope." With a mean squint, she closed him inside.

With a hand on her loosening knot of hair, Jill scurried along the narrow, windswept iron balcony after Matt's stalking figure, clattering down the stairs in her heels, then out into the motel's lot. She blocked his path, encircling him in her arms.

"Nothing happened up there, Travis. Believe me."

"Why were you in his room at all?" he demanded in a strangled voice. "The last time we spoke you were waiting for a call from Bob Williams. You insisted I jog!"

"Not to get rid of you!" she assured him. "Bob called back unexpectedly soon after you left. I felt I couldn't wait for you. Time is so precious. Didn't Wilma give you my message?"

"She told me you were over here at the Seacrest Motel, all right. Then she curled her mouth like this." He imitated the old lady's prune-lipped leer. "After dumping Roger Bannon here yesterday after the luncheon, she assumed I'd put two and two together and believe the worst."

"Oh, Matt." She pressed her head against his chest for a brief moment. "I'm sorry."

He cupped her face in his hands, raising it to his. "So what's going on?"

"Bob says there's no Bruce Kildare in the Navy," she hastened to explain. "That the car has no extended lease, as Kildare claimed, but a short-term rental charged to Penny's company. Do you know what this means? Kildare has no real roots here at all." Her explanation didn't loosen his granite expression. "Look, Travis, I swear that Bob's quick call back was a surprise. Unfortunately it was because he'd hit a dead end."

"So you came over here to get some new leads," he deduced grimly.

"Yes, exactly right!"

"That still doesn't explain what you were doing with Bannon, Jill," he said tersely.

"Bruce Kildare is compiling all kinds of information on Penny and this wedding, logging things that happen, snapping pictures of everyone."

"You think he's accumulating info for a story?"

"It rings like a tabloid exposé to me. You know, revealing Penny's pregnancy, wedding details. I'm assuming that he plans to marry her, then promptly betray her. Naturally, I thought of Roger's position on *Celebrity Circuit*, suspected he was in on it."

He absorbed the idea with grim relish. "Slick guys like Roger Bannon rarely get caught this way. How satisfying."

"Don't get your hopes up," she retorted. "He appears to be innocent. Once I calmed down—"

"On his bed," he clarified angrily.

"You should be glad his bed has that kind of tranquilizing effect on me," she hastened to say. "Anyway, Roger was of little help, though he could confirm that these notes and photos do make the beginnings of a story. For now, we're not sure who Bruce Kildare really is, or what he's up to."

Matt stalled for time to steady his emotions, reaching for the sunglasses hooked to the ribbed neck of his sweatshirt. "Your eyes were misty up there," he finally challenged.

Jill's stomach knotted in anxiety under his coplike interrogation. He was missing nothing in his efforts to monopolize and understand her. "Roger admitted to picking a fight with me back at prom time so he could take a flashy rich girl. Okay?"

Matt rolled his eyes, setting his glasses on the bridge of his nose. "And I thought I was a jerky kid."

"I'm sure neither one of you is in danger of receiving any retroactive teen spirit awards," she answered impatiently.

"He said he wasn't through with you yet," Matt quietly reminded her.

Jill stomped her foot on the blacktop in fury. "Well, he's wrong, okay? You're my man now, and nothing's going to change that!"

"Yes, ma'am." He offered her a snappy salute, unable to disguise his relief.

"Let's get going!"

"Lead the way," he invited. "I'll follow in Wilma's car."

Jill noticed her aunt's maroon Buick for the first time. "Wow, she never lets anybody drive that thing."

"Well, I don't think the motives were especially charitable, her hoping that I was racing to the scene of your infidelity. But it did save me cab fare."

Jill shook her key ring at him. "Ah, if you're going to start understanding my aunt that thoroughly, you're indispensable beyond my dreams."

Matt formed a cocky grin as she slipped behind the wheel of her Lumina, but it was a struggle. His heart soared at her declaration of ownership. But he forced himself to be realistic. Roger was still in there swinging, and she still had those old memories. He wouldn't totally count on anything until they were safely back in San Francisco. As much as he cared, he wouldn't let her break his heart during the sorting process. He just couldn't.

The first order of business was to go to Wilma's and regroup. Matt promptly popped into the shower and Jill moved around the kitchen ferreting out Wilma's address book, looking up some personal telephone numbers. She began to make calls in an effort to track down the bride. She eventually succeeded. Penny was at her mother's, taking a final fitting on her dress. Jill told Gwen Richman to keep her daughter put. She would be coming right over to have a candid talk about Bruce Kildare.

Jill was accustomed to flying off on her own when investigating something urgent—or with Bob Williams, who was always on alert—so it was tough to pause and wait for Matt.

She marched down the hallway to the bathroom and boldly rapped on the door. She paused in indecision when

Matt didn't respond. He probably couldn't hear her above the sound of the jet spray.

After a moment of deliberation, Jill decided she was confident enough in their new relationship to barge in on Matt's shower to prod him along. If he was surprised to see her when she rapped on the frosted doors enclosing the tub, he concealed it behind a leer of delight.

"You heard me out there," she scolded with a wizened look.

"Prove it, flatfoot," he growled playfully.

"How dare you test me, see if I would come in?"

"Gee, I'm glad you passed," he crooned, leaning out the glass door. "Join me," he suggested with a lazy look. "Auntie's away."

Her mouth quirked and her pulse accelerated. This was the purest form of sexual temptation that she'd ever been faced with. Matt, standing by so close. His soaked, soap-slicked body so touchable. She shifted on her feet, trying to get a closer look at his nude pantherlike form.

"Uh, uh, uh," he chastised, edging back behind the frosted barrier. "You gotta come inside for a peck."

"I tracked down Penny," she reported breathlessly. "She's with her mother. She's waiting—"

"We won't be long," he enticed, reaching out to stroke her throat.

"No, Travis, no!" She wheeled out of his drippy, groping reach.

"Okay!" His complaining grumble echoed out of the top of the enclosure. Moments later the water shut off.

"You know how important this is to me," she reiterated nervously.

"I know," he rumbled, grabbing for the striped bath towel she tossed over the door, hurriedly rubbing the terry over his short matted hair, down his beefy shoulders. It was probably unfair of him to make a try at seduction, but it really wouldn't have taken long, and he would've been far more assured of her commitment. Women often used words to make their points. Sometimes that wasn't enough. Sometimes a man needed to make his mark in a more basic way.

When he emerged from the bathroom five minutes later, dressed in blue jeans and a royal blue knit shirt, Jill was waiting for him in the kitchen with the bulky brown envelope tucked under her arm. The only thing she'd done to herself was unknot her hair, brush it loose and free to her shoulders. Just the way he liked it.

"You're ready?" she queried.

He hooked his fingers in his belt loops, scanning her length. "Yeah, but you sure aren't."

She squinted in confusion. "What do you mean?"

He grinned sheepishly, gesturing to her bottom. "I sort of left a damp handprint on your rear—"

"You what!" she screeched, doing some stretching and tugging at her apricot jumpsuit for a look.

"Sorry. I'm sure a moment in the sun will dry it all up."

"I hope so! It's too late to change. We'll just have to walk over there. It's only three blocks."

"Folks will understand," he said placatingly. "Look on the bright side, it gives credence to our cover."

"Things like this don't happen to me, that's all!" With a flounce she was out the door.

"Yeah, well," he called after her. "That's why you need me. To make them happen!"

WITHIN MINUTES they were moving up the front walk of the Richmans' family home. The white stucco ranch was twice the size of Wilma's, Matt noted, and the yard was regularly serviced by professionals. The trees were numerous and healthy, and the grass was putting-green perfect in texture and color. Matt had met Penny's parents, Gwen and Burt, yesterday at lunch. A nice savvy couple in the real estate game, geared for success. They wore it, lived it, preached it.

And Jill had been nurtured in oppression. So many subtle things around here had to rattle Jill's self-image. And who had been the one to bolster her ego, lift her out of her low times? None other than Roger Bannon. Bigmouthed Bannon, full of sweet talk and bull.

Jill skipped up the flagstone steps and rang the bell.

Matt sidled up beside her, having a cursory look around. "All clear."

"Huh?" She stared at him.

"Ten-four."

"Travis..."

He rocked on his heels with a roguish look. "I mean the handprint on your butt. It's evaporated into the atmosphere."

She was tempted to imprint his cheek, but Penny herself appeared beyond the screen, dressed in her bridal gown. "Come in, won't you?" Penny led them through the cool tiled entry hall to a screened-in porch out back with yellow cushioned patio furniture arranged around a large glass table.

Jill inhaled sharply at the sight of Wayne Smeed, seated on twin seats with Gwen Richman. The slick-haired manager was dressed formally in a gray suit and crisp white shirt. Gwen was dressed for business, as well, in a cream bow blouse and dark A-line skirt. By their set expressions, they appeared primed for action. How could they know it was necessary?

"Hello, Jill," Gwen greeted warmly with a trace of briskness. "Please, sit down."

Jill and Matt sank together on the larger sofa.

"I really didn't expect this kind of alert." Jill faltered, adjusting the envelope in her lap. She had hoped to tell Penny everything in private first, let her absorb the shock, then discuss options together.

Taking care with her flowing white dress, Penny settled in the only vacant chair. "Jill, if you want to talk about Bruce, I think it's best Wayne and my mother are here."

"Yes," Gwen agreed, turning her thin wrist to study the diamond-studded watch strapped there. "I have a house to show today—"

"On the day before Penny's wedding?" Jill gasped in surprise.

Gwen's laughter tinkled. "Yes, dear, it's an inescapable commitment."

"Yes. All right." Jill inhaled shakily.

"Jilly," Penny prodded with earnest green eyes. "You told Mom that you wanted to discuss Bruce candidly."

"That's right," Matt intervened with the sort of silky tone he used with distraught students. "Jill's uncovered some unpleasant truths—"

"Okay!" Penny flared, her veneer crumbling. "So you know Bruce Kildare doesn't exist! That's it, isn't it, Jill? You went digging around like a detective and uncovered my secret."

Jill and Matt looked at each other in shock, then focused on the bride. "Your secret?"

"Yes! There is no devoted fiancé, no lieutenant named Kildare. I made the whole thing up—with the help of Wayne."

"But why?" Jill asked, her thin brows arched in perplexity.

"Because my pregnancy is more than real," Penny blurted out in lament.

"Oh." Jill's eyes widened and her mouth fell shut.

"You can understand what such a scandal would do to her television image," Wayne explained with defensive vigor. "She would be through with children's television if she had a child out of wedlock."

Gwen flashed her daughter a fond look, then settled on Jill. "Even if she could weather the storm, people would speculate to no end on the identity of the father."

"As it happens, I love the father of my unborn child very much," Penny admitted with a sniff. "But he isn't free to come forward right now. He's trapped in a loveless marriage with a woman who's recently taken ill. It's put his divorce on hold. But I can't put the baby on hold, don't you see?" she whispered hoarsely. "I need a shill of a husband. A man to divert suspicion for the time being. Oh, Jilly," she intimated in a frantic rush, "I want this baby so badly. This is my chance to be a parent, and my lover's chance, too."

"Bruce is my nephew, an actor out of New York City," Wayne explained. "His surname is Smeed. We hired him to come in, play the groom, then supposedly ship off for the benefit of the press. In reality, he'll just go home to Manhattan, fall back into his own identity. He tinted his hair and shaved his beard for this role, so he looks remarkably different."

"She plans to eventually obtain a fake divorce," Gwen added. "After a discreet period of time."

Penny regarded Jill with a measure of embarrassment. "Sorry if you've been upset over Bruce. If only I could be more like you, mature, levelheaded, collected. I certainly don't expect you to understand how I could pull such a stunt. It must seem so darn silly."

Matt watched Jill expectantly, slipping a hand behind her back to give her an encouraging nudge. This seemed the ideal time to confess her charade, too.

"You're doing what you have to do, Pen," she murmured sympathetically, her spine stiffening under his rotating thumb. Matt had to be crazy, she inwardly fumed. She wasn't going to 'fess up to her pretension now. She didn't have a sensible reason for hiring Matt. She wasn't pregnant, her career wasn't on the line. Talk about silly....

Her motive couldn't be flimsier. She was too proud to be the last bridesmaid!

"Leave it to you to be so good at your job," Penny said in a halfhearted tease. "I almost hated to have you back, for fear that this would happen."

Jill completely dismissed her own circumstances with a light shrug. "Matt and I noticed things about Bruce together. His tinted hair, the rental car, tying his shoe with a granny knot. And the general feeling that he wasn't your type."

"I'm sure my conversation with Bruce on the way to the bachelor party didn't give you any comfort either, Matt," Wayne added with a sigh, looking more like a crestfallen uncle than a sharpy manager. "Bruce has become a bit petulant over the depth of his duties, grown dissatisfied with the agreed flat fee. And I've come to suspect he hoped that Penny might really fall for him."

"Naturally that wasn't about to happen," Penny put in, rolling her eyes.

Jill reached over to squeeze her friend's shaky hand. Her movement made the envelope in her lap crunch in re-minder—there was more to this story.

"So Bruce has gone along with everything," Jill probed. "All in all, you still think he deserves your faith?"

"He's my brother's only son," Wayne declared proudly, running his thumbs beneath his suspenders. "Family loy-alty means a lot. It's why I chose him."

Jill fingered the flap of the envelope. "I suppose he's one of these starving-artist types."

"He's sort of middle-class hungry," Penny responded with a shrug. "He's had some work on stage, in commer-cials. But he's still what you'd call undiscovered talent."

"But that's the way of show biz," Wayne philoso-phized. "It's his chosen path, so he has to take the knocks."

"I hate to report that he might be hoping to take a shortcut on the road to fame." With a contrite look laced with steel, Jill dumped the contents of Bruce's envelope on the table.

Angry energy enveloped the cheery screened-in porch as they all shifted through the photos and notes.

"It appears that he hopes to be seek fame and fortune from this situation," Gwen sputtered, tossing aside his journal. "He's written down things we've all said, described the clothes we've worn, who drank what. Personal private things! Sort of a kiss-and-tell deal."

"The scoop is so much bigger than I figured," Jill realized. "Not only could he give away your state of pregnancy, but he could unmask your marriage to him as a fake."

"And these pictures are mainly from my camera," Penny muttered in disgust as she rifled through them. "He took the rolls to be developed this morning. Said the shop was backlogged with the Memorial Day weekend rush and wouldn't have them ready until after the wedding. How clever of him to encourage me to take pictures for the sake of show. I'd know just what poignant moments to snap. Hell, I was his personal photographer, betraying myself!"

Wayne made an enraged noise, his large face reddening. "I'll kill that slimy little twerp with my bare hands!" The jewelry on his fingers glinted as he formed his hands into a viselike band. "My brother will be furious!"

"Roger wants you to know that he wasn't the contact planning to publish this exposé," Jill said, much to Matt's displeasure. Matt would have to try to understand. It was only fair to deliver the message.

Penny's perky face actually shined for a millisecond. "He's worried that I'd suspect him?"

"He does work for a tabloid," Gwen pointed out. "And knowing that cad, I'm certain he's been accused of plenty over the years."

"I wonder if Bruce has tried to market the story yet." Penny fretted with wringing hands.

"Probably not," Matt interposed, lifting his eyes from the hands clasped between his knees, gauging them to see if his opinion was welcome.

"How do you figure?" Gwen asked with real interest.

"Because if even a whiff of this situation leaked out before the ceremony, his scoop would be worthless. The story would become fair game, reporters would be camped out everywhere." Matt turned to Penny with a gentle smile. "My guess is that your original news, your simple wedding to a sailor, would only cause a mild ripple. But throw some spice into it with the pregnancy and fake groom, and the press would be hanging from your mother's rain gutters. No, I figure that Bruce wants to sell it after the fact, make it a complete package from start to finish."

"Then there just can't be a wedding," Penny announced, popping up out of her chair.

"Thankfully, I haven't alerted the legitimate press yet," Wayne said, tugging his handkerchief out of his jacket pocket to dab his perspiring upper lip. "We've been holding back until the final hour so we wouldn't have too many witnesses. Guess we'll just pull the plug on everything, including Bruce."

Penny bit back a sob as she stared at Bruce's notes. "Well, at least he doesn't have this groundwork anymore, thanks to you, Jilly."

Jill leaped up to hug her. "Just don't ask me how I got it, okay?"

"Where is Bruce now?" Matt asked.

"Getting the works for tomorrow," Wayne said with venom. "Wants to do Penny proud for the press coverage, he said. And it's all my treat. Haircut, sauna, massage, manicure."

"He'll bolt like a frightened deer if he discovers that envelope missing," Jill surmised.

"We can't let him get away without some sort of confrontation," Gwen remarked grimly. "Somehow, Wayne, you will have to shut him up."

Wayne nodded, pausing in thought. "I'll call him at that style emporium, tell him to go buy a new suit, on me. As much as I hate to spend another nickel on him," he griped with a wince. "I'll say that he should come straight to Rebecca's barbecue without returning to the Seacrest, that we're planning an extra photo shoot with friends and family."

Jill nodded in approval, giving Penny an extra pat. "He'll fall for it. The more pictures he can produce of this deal, the more money he'll figure to make." The proclamation brought a fresh round of tears from the bride, who clung to Jill like a drowning woman. Despite the circumstances, she couldn't help but turn a wistful smile to Matt. He was looking on in understanding approval. For the first time ever, Jill was really needed by one of her own.

Chapter Fourteen

Because of Penny's situation with Bruce and her pregnancy, the mood of the groom's dinner barbecue at Rebecca Lambert's that evening took on a wild-card atmosphere, in Jill's mind. She and Matt arrived at six, half an hour early. With Penny's final approval, it had been decided that all the wedding party would make an effort to beat Bruce's scheduled arrival, to discuss what had happened.

As it turned out, they appeared to be the first couple on the scene. They stepped inside the airy open-ceilinged foyer to be confronted by Rebecca and her husband, Charles. They were dressed for the evening in cotton shorts and pastel shirts of similar design, dashing around their tall Spanish-style home, picking up radios, magazines and plastic action figures.

"Come in and make yourself comfortable!" Charles invited with a good-humored bellow. Matt shook hands with their physician host. Matt already had a good feeling about him last night at the bachelor party. His grip was firm, his gray eyes clear. He looked to be about a decade older than his wife, with gray threaded through his dark hair. And he had the beginnings of a tummy, most likely from good home cooking. Oh, how Matt loved good home cooking.

He inhaled appreciatively. He could smell potatoes and pie, for certain.

"There's a man who wants to know what's for supper," Rebecca teased, moving across the marble-floored entryway to give each of them a hug.

"You have a lovely place, Rebecca," Matt intoned, noting that she was completely poised in her own element. And what a place to shine. This house was a mansion on the beach, a three-story vanilla-colored stucco. The abstract paintings on the walls were genuine. He'd just taken some of his students to an art fair on Fisherman's Wharf, and recognized the San Francisco area talent. And the furniture was antique, much like the stuff Rachel Harrington had crammed in her museum of an office back home. Somehow, Rebecca managed to give the sumptuous place a homey feel. He doubted there was much domestic help, judging by her remarks at the Cozy Kitchen reception.

"We like it here," Rebecca lilted, her dimples deepening. "But sometimes I wonder what it would look like immaculate." She took a couple of steps to the steep carpeted staircase, placing a hand on the black iron rail. "Josh, Emma! Come down for a junk pickup!"

A boy and girl, around the age of ten, appeared on the landing above. "Better come up here," an indignant Emma hollered, poking her face between the wrought-iron rails. "Josh knocked over my bookcase—"

"No, Ma, I fell 'cause she pushed me."

"He punched me."

"Anything we can do in the kitchen while you're away?" Jill asked hopefully.

Rebecca took a look at Jill's red silk pleated dress and shook her dark permed head. "I don't think so, Jilly. Why don't you just go out back to the deck. Take in the ocean view."

Matt was primed to protest, but Rebecca pressed her palms into their backs, giving them a shove. "Hurry on then, I have to scoot upstairs and referee."

Jill paused in the hallway, offering him a small smile of apology. "Sorry I suggested we dress up," she whispered.

Matt slid his finger under the knot of his tie with a grimace. It was a little more involved than that. She'd coaxed him into buying brand-new clothes! A gray oxford shirt with thin white striping and charcoal slacks. Useless threads he'd wear once or twice a year.

She compressed her scarlet lips under his glower. "Are you going to let it spoil your evening?"

"No, no." He heaved a sigh, loosening a little as he carefully folded the tie. "I can use the clothes, for chaperoning the prom, for instance. Guess the kids are tired of my brown slacks and tan shirt, anyway."

She took the tie and stowed it in her purse. "C'mon, let's go outside."

Both of them froze as they entered the family room and heard laughter drifting in through the windows. Jill picked up her step toward the sliding patio door. They weren't the first to arrive, but almost the last. A cursory look around told her the only ones missing were Penny and her people.

"Oh, man," Matt whispered in her ear as they stepped out on the redwood planking. "You and your insecurities."

Jill knew what he meant. Virtually everyone was dressed in casual clothing. Nothing inexpensive, but comfortable just the same. She'd been so determined to be recognized as a success, she'd gone overboard. This wasn't a silk and gabardine evening, it was a plain old cotton one.

Everyone chorused hello. Matt reviewed the players as he always did on these occasions as the hired husband. Alison and Tom Sherwood were the airline couple. They were looking at the Lamberts' double burner gas grill. Gayle and Tom Fairchild, owners of the restaurant that held their luncheon yesterday, were seated on redwood chairs with floral cushions with their baby between them, exchanging words with Roger Bannon, a few feet away at a portable bar, set up close to the safety rail.

"Don't you look fetching tonight, Jilly!" Roger openly ogled her body in the clingy red silk.

"Thank you very much," she replied with pleasure. She still couldn't help wanting Roger to feel a loss. It was childish and purposeless, considering that she could never fall for him again. But she was finally facing her feelings, and she liked the rush it brought her. Dabbling in a little sweet revenge was exciting.

Matt gritted his teeth over the flirty exchange, realizing he needed space to breath. He broke away to the rail at the opposite side of deck to admire the view on his own for a minute.

Jill fussed over the Fairchilds' baby, watching Matt out of the corner of her eye. He looked drop-dead handsome, poised at the rail with his shirt sleeves rolled up to his elbows, the sea breeze rippling through his short brown hair, the sun tingeing it a golden color. He turned ever so slightly to watch a gull swoop down, giving her a better view of his profile. He struck a rough-edged silhouette against the sky, reflecting his personality with clarity.

The more bonded she felt to him, the more questions she had about what made him tick. What was it like to be a reformed rebel? Despite his successes at school and with the Harrington Agency, he didn't like to be hemmed in too tightly, and he didn't like to dress up much. She liked to dress up. Not in a flashy way, but in a subtle, elegant fashion. It added to her ice-princess image at work, but she couldn't bear for anyone to think—as Roger had—that she couldn't make an upscale showing. Matt was smoldering over their overdone image. But she couldn't help it. She didn't like that old gray duckling perception they had of her. She'd much rather be overdressed than underdressed.

Matt balled his fists as he gazed down the steep sloping beach below. So she'd actually dressed up for Bannon. The pieces fit. The jerk hadn't considered her flashy enough back in high school and she was out to show him she could dazzle anybody anywhere. Why couldn't she simply dismiss him for the surface bounder he was?

Rebecca's voice drew him around. She and Charles were circling with glass trays of appetizers. Matt forced himself to saunter closer to the crowd, a smile frozen on his face. Penny and her parents were crossing the threshold of the sliding door single file. Obviously it was time to face the issues. Like Jill, Penny was dressed to the limit in a soft gold dress that played well with her short cap of red hair. Like Jill, she was here to make a statement, make a proud showing. The women were so different, yet so alike—each finding reason to scam the crowd with fake husbands!

Jill moved up to Penny, giving her hands a squeeze. Matt shook his head, trying to rein in his simmering temper. These people meant so much to her. More than anything, he wanted her to feel the same way for him! He just had to get her out of here, home to San Francisco. Her life was pretty bland back there. She'd have all sorts of time for him. Time to learn to be crazy and mussed up.

Jill searched her friend's disquieted green eyes with her concerned blue ones. "Would you like me to explain?"

Penny shook her head. "Thanks, but this is my problem."

Rebecca used her organizational skills to quickly direct everyone to chairs and the picnic table benches. No one dreamed of protesting under her snappy direction. Jill chose to stand by near the door between Matt and Penny.

Penny stood before all of them with her hands clasped under her chin. "Where to begin," she started with a false laugh. "Some of you know what's going on, some of you don't."

"We aren't a jury around here," Rebecca said, giving her a one-armed hug as she passed by with a tray of shrimp puffs. She set them on the table and slid onto the end of the bench beside Charles.

"No, you're my dear friends." Penny blinked, nibbling at her lip. "You see, I've tried to pull a fast one on everybody—the whole nation, really—and I've gotten caught."

The deck fell silent as Penny outlined her pregnancy, her search for a stand-in husband. Wayne's efforts to produce his nephew for the job. She slanted Jill a grateful look as she explained how Jill became suspicious, couldn't resist digging into Bruce's background.

Murmurs of disapproval made Jill bristle. But Penny quickly set the record straight. "It's a good thing she did what she did," she proclaimed. "It turned out that Bruce was going to play the role, then sell the truth to the highest bidder!"

The rumble shifted to an upbeat note, and a short round of applause followed.

"Guess I just can't turn off the cop in me," Jill told them, flushing with pleasure.

"Which makes you a turn-on," Roger raved, tipping his glass of beer to his mouth.

Jill could sense Matt stiffen even from a few feet away. She strolled over to set her hand on his arm with a comforting pat.

"So there you have it." Penny lifted her hands in a helpless gesture. "I haven't heard from Wayne or Bruce."

"You don't think they've taken off to hawk the story, do you?" Alison asked with her characteristic bluntness.

"No, I don't," Penny promptly denied. "Wayne's my right hand."

"Thank you for those kind words, sweetie." Wayne Smeed emerged from the kitchen in a sport shirt and slacks.

"I haven't heard a word from Bruce," Penny reported nervously.

"And you won't." Wayne kissed her lightly on the cheek. "The louse appeared at my door about an hour ago for a little extra cash, and I let him have it. Put the fear of Uncle Wayne into him." The gleam in his dark eyes matched the polish on his shoes. "He was like a whipped pup when I told him you had all the evidence he'd collected. I threatened him with the things he fears most, his autocratical father and being cut out of my will." He aimed a thumb at his puffing chest.

"Thanks, Wayne." Penny turned to the guests, seated in their places with uncertain expressions. "Enough trouble," she announced with effort. "We don't get together much anymore, so let's just enjoy this reunion."

A ripple of relief rose in the air and people began to mix and mingle.

Jill moved a little closer to the agent, still struggling with lingering questions. "Wayne, when did Bruce decide to fink on Penny? He was willing enough at first, wasn't he?"

Wayne exhaled in resignation, accepting a whiskey and soda from Roger, who'd appeared at his side full of curiosity, too. "We guessed right on a lot of counts this afternoon. Bruce did become frustrated when he set his romantic sights on Penny and she didn't tumble for him. And then he did get a brainstorm concerning Roger Bannon here."

Roger raised his hands in self-defense. "I swear I didn't have dealings with him. I wouldn't hurt a friend like Penny."

A sour grunt rose from Matt's belly, but he forced it down. He had to make it through this ordeal.

"That's right," Wayne confirmed. "He just assumed by your profession, your dandy manner, that you'd be thrilled to push his story to your tabloid. Jill was right when she suggested that he wanted to have the whole story wrapped up before he shopped it around."

"Oh, Matt said that," Jill corrected, casting him a proud look.

"And I'm not a dandy," Roger complained, causing everyone to roar with knowing laughter.

Matt started when he felt a hand on his shoulder. He turned to find Charles Lambert smiling at him. "Rebecca believes you're more than qualified to brush sauce on her chicken. Are you willing?"

Jill nudged Matt playfully with her elbow. "Matt's more of a defrost man."

"So am I," the doctor confided. "My wife runs this house single-handedly."

"I'd be glad to help out," Matt replied, leveling a look at Roger as he stood by indecisively. The reporter started to drift toward the drink trolley, squaring his shoulders and sucking in his stomach as he moved.

Rebecca appeared with a platter full of boneless chicken breasts. "So have you nailed my helper?" she asked her husband.

"Yes, dear," Charles reported with a mocking huff. "Matt can't wait to brush on your special secret sauce. The job you don't ever trust me to do."

"You just refuse to put a thick enough layer on the meat, Charles," Rebecca complained, setting the tray on the barbecue's side shelf. "And you refuse to wear the right equipment." Before Matt knew what was happening, Rebecca had removed the terry apron from her waist and was looping it around his neck.

He blanched as he look down at the rooster figure draping his chest. "What's this?"

"Protection, silly," Rebecca replied matter-of-factly.

"Should work," Roger gibed from behind the drink trolley, missing nothing of their exchange. "Nobody's going to crowd cockadoodledo!"

Merry laughter filled the twilight. Matt grimaced, turning away to apply sauce to the strips of meat with a resounding slap.

Jill hovered nervously at his side. "Ignore him," she whispered.

"We could all ignore him if I hurled him over the deck," he muttered.

Jill gasped as he slowly turned to reveal his dark brooding look. She couldn't believe the depth of fury sheened in his coffee-colored eyes. "Surely you can control yourself," she asked. "This party means so little in the broader landscape of our future."

"If you meant that, you'd have told them the truth about us, Jill." He leaned closer, his breath a harsh burn on the curve of her ear. "Are you playing this out only to bait Roger, see if you can win him back?"

"No." She swallowed, discovering that her throat was almost swollen shut. "I'm just trying to live down my wallflower youth. As you're trying to live down your rebellious past."

"I'm making the effort to let go of my lingering anger," he pointed out. "Called Bob Williams to show my good faith. You've done nothing to right your position, haven't shut down Bannon for good, haven't confessed our real status to your friends. I think you better reexamine your values. Decide where you stand and take a stand!" With that he turned to his task, shutting her out.

Jill closed her eyes, summoning the fortitude to go on. He was wrong, wrong, wrong! Wasn't he?

Dinner was served buffet style soon after. Food was set up on an island in Rebecca's huge stainless steel kitchen. It gave the guests the freedom to move around, eat inside or out. When Jill wandered into the foyer with her plate and glass of wine, she didn't expect company.

"Hey, there, Jilly."

Jill flinched as Roger's hand rested on her hip. "You smell like a distillery."

"Maybe because I'm drinking my dinner," he slurred, lifting his glass in a solo toast.

"Seems like a dumb idea."

His pale blue eyes glistened with mischief. "I'm in the dumps and it's all your fault."

She sighed hard, looking down the hallway for a sign of Matt. He had been right. She was playing a foolish game, baiting Roger just to watch him squirm. "I sincerely doubt it," she denied, making an effort to edge by him with her plate and glass.

"Give me a kiss. C'mon." Roger pressed her back into the plaster wall, puckering up in her face.

Jill couldn't contain her emotions. The sight was too much. She burst into giggles. "Oh, Roger, you used to do the same thing back in high school—when you pushed up against the lockers between classes."

"And you liked it," he reminded her. He drew his hand up to her breast and was just closing his palm over it when he felt two huge hands clamped to his shoulders. It was Matt, prying him loose, tossing him into a stumble. "Hey," he blubbered, sloshing his drink down the front of his linen shirt. "I didn't mean anything."

Rebecca marched up the hallway from the kitchen in her Reeboks, taking Roger's glass away from him. "You've had enough. You're acting like a fool!"

Roger stumbled, then sagged against the wall, his thinning pale hair tumbling across his forehead. He frowned as he noticed his friends forming a cluster around him spouting chuckling remarks. "You think I'm a sore loser, don't you?" he asked thickly. He glared at all of them, eventually focusing on Matt alone. "Thanks for not belting me one, Travis. That's what you do best, isn't it?"

Matt's strong features grew incredibly fierce. This clod had an angle. Bannon's pale eyes were amazingly clear, suggesting that he had an incredible tolerance for alcohol. Bannon obviously welcomed this moment. He wanted Matt to lose it.

The truth hit him like lightning. Roger Bannon knew. About him. Probably about everything. "I'd close my big mouth if I were you," Matt suggested coldly. It was an empty threat, one Matt knew wouldn't stick. Bannon had been working up to this climax all along. Did Jill understand? He doubted it. She didn't look worried enough. "Maybe we better go now, Jill," he suggested tersely.

"Can't go now," Roger griped, grinning at Jill. "You haven't made your announcement yet."

The realization finally struck home on her delicate features. Matt watched her brow lift a fraction, like it did when she was on the scent of something. She was mentally piecing it together. Tabloid journalists had lots of sources. Roger had done some advance digging on her, probably to see what his chances were to score. He'd come up with some juicy information.

"You know what I mean," Roger purred patronizingly. "Matt Travis has a little juvenile record, for starters."

"Those records are sealed," Jill cried out angrily, aware of all the sagging jaws in the background.

"Sure they are," Roger crowed. "But gossipy neighbors, people on the street, have long memories. And greedy needs. A little cash gets 'em talking."

"Maybe you'd like to lie down for awhile," Rebecca suggested brightly.

Roger patted her curly head as one would a friendly puppy's. "I'm just getting warmed up. Seemed so strange to me, Jilly, that you'd fall for a guy who slugged a cop."

"What!" Jill hadn't meant to reveal surprise, but that's what Matt had done? If only he'd told her first!

"Bob Williams," Matt told her flatly, shoving his hands in the pockets of his new slacks. "At the grill."

"Yeah, he's a robber. Travis was accused of driving a getaway car from a grocery store robbery."

Jill's eyes widened to blue saucers. "That can't be!"

"Oh, it can be," Roger assured with a bobbing head. "Tell her, Travis."

Matt's gaze was steady, his tone modulated. "You just did."

Roger's head lolled. "Well, we'd all be frantic if Jill had married some kind of con, now wouldn't we, gang?"

Charles pushed his way through the group jammed into the hallway. "Roger, I'm calling you a cab."

"But she didn't marry some con," Roger continued on. "She isn't married at all! Are you, Jilly?"

"No," she answered quietly, studying the toes of her suede heels.

"What's going on, Jill?" Penny questioned, openly aghast.

"It's like Roger said. I hired Matt to come home with me to play my husband." She forced a smile. "So you see, Penny, you and I are back to square one. Still the last bridesmaids."

"That wouldn't bother you, Jill," Gayle protested, tossing her curtain of caramel colored hair. "Being the only single of the bunch. Would it?"

Jill shrugged.

"Well, I guess this job is a crash and burn," Matt muttered in defeat. "Thanks for dinner, Rebecca." With that he spun on his heel and charged out the front door.

Jill stared blankly at her dumbfounded friends for a brief moment, then raced after him.

"Travis! Wait! Please!"

She breathed a sigh of relief when his shadowy form halted in the middle of the long, winding driveway. She darted between the parked cars, plowing right into him on the incline.

"Oh, Matt, if only you'd given me some advance warning."

"Is that what you chased me out here to say?" he roared in amazement.

"I just mean that it's a pretty big secret, you can't blame me for being stunned."

He lifted a hand in a frustrated gesture. "I didn't know it would come out. Never has."

"Does Rachel Harrington know?"

"No, Rachel doesn't know," he mimicked. "It would take a real creep to dredge it up, too."

She couldn't argue that Roger was exactly what he seemed. "Didn't you think I could handle it?"

"I would've told any woman I really loved all about it. In time." He seized her shoulders for an electric moment. She hoped he was going to kiss the hurt away with the kind of physical gesture he was so comfortable with. But he didn't. He used her tactic, the verbal exchange. "I wasn't ready to tell you yet. You weren't ready for all-out trust."

"Yes, I was!"

"I advised you not to bait Roger Bannon. Not to pay him back for past slights. But, oh, no, you just had to take a shot at him. Spur him into action."

She squealed indignantly, wrenched out of his hands. "You're blaming me for what he just did?"

His mouth thinned as he stared into the starry sky. "Partly. He kept it bottled up for quite awhile. I don't think he would've taken it further than you or me in his efforts to test our bond. He didn't want you angry, Jill. He just wanted you." As Matt had himself.

They paused in the stillness, stewing in their own juices.

"You know what you need most, Jill?"

The husky question floored her. She knew. She needed him. But her old defenses were higher than ever. Now she didn't even have the minimal respect of her friends to fall back on. They had to view her as downright pathetic, just the image she was trying to avoid. But an encouraging word from him right now would mean the world. Give her a foundation to build on again. She inhaled a shaky breath, summoning the nerve to put herself out there on the line. "What do I need most, Travis?"

"Time. Time to sort out your feelings. Plot new direction."

"Huh?"

He grasped her chin, massaging the tender skin of her lower lip. It trembled under the pad of his thumb, causing him to swallow hard. How could he still be affected when she'd made him feel like a felon? Without verifying one single fact? Without bothering to take him on an ounce of faith? Maybe his body was quaking because the last of his compassion was draining out of him.

Her voice was hushed and dismayed when she spoke. "You're dumping me? Here and now?"

"Some space is necessary," he stated with level firmness. "You don't know what you want."

"My whole life is space," she cried in a panic. "I'm on my own, dammit, always have been! You don't understand."

"I do understand," he argued flatly. "We're alike in a lot of ways, you and me. We brood, we make mistakes with people. Hell, I even underestimated Bob Williams for far too long."

"You slugged him!"

"Thanks for the reminder."

She gave him a melting look. "Oh, Travis!"

Matt stepped back a little. "I'll make sure Rachel doesn't bill you," he said in parting.

"I already paid in full!"

His mouth curled in a wry smile. "You're just too efficient."

"How will you get back to Wilma's?"

"I'll walk," he called over his shoulder. "Please stay here, Jill. I've had my fill. And I'm sure Wilma will be more than happy to take me to the train station tonight."

Jill watched him disappear down the curving boulevard, a shadow in the glow of the streetlights. And to think she'd thought life had dealt her her most embarrassing night way back in 1983. Who'd have ever guessed she could top it, drag her first love and her last love together for one big circus of humiliation. But she'd had some help, hadn't she? Roger had a hell of a lot of explaining to do. And she had all night to listen!

Chapter Fifteen

Many of the party guests soon drifted down to the beach below the house. Nobody was comfortable anymore, faced with the shock over the two phony marriages. Charles begged off to put his children to bed and Tom Sherwood and Ray Fairchild wandered into the family room for a look at the Lamberts' wide screen television. Wayne and the elder Richmans left altogether.

It was the original old crowd that gathered on the sand for a heart-to-heart talk.

A chill raced up Jill's spine as she stood on the shore, letting the cool breeze whip her fair hair and red dress like silken banners. Roger loped up beside her, wise enough not to touch her.

"Guess you hate me, Jilly."

She flicked him a lethal look. "Guess you're just the same old Roger. Looking out for number one, stirring up controversy just for entertainment."

"Why did you pretend with him?" he beseeched in confusion. "Did you want to hurt me that badly?"

"No." She stared out into the dark tossing sea. The wash of the water was the only sound for a spell. She realized that they were all waiting for her answer. Penny, Rebecca, Gayle and Alison. They were all closing in on her from behind. "Not that it hasn't been fun watching you squirm, Roger."

"Why did you do it?" Penny seconded, linking her arm in Jill's. She stared out to sea with her, patiently waiting for a response.

"Because I've always been last, that's why," she confided, her voice steeped in emotion. "My whole life, always last. Never felt good enough, had less of everything."

"Couldn't you leave all that behind you?" Alison queried in bemusement. "You're a respected police detective now."

"I still find coming home difficult," she choked out. "A reaffirmation of all my disappointments." She turned to face the semicircle they'd formed around her. "To me, being the last bridesmaid was rock bottom. The closure on our youth, the final division between us." She threw her hands in the air in frustration. "I could see the nightmare in vivid color, all of you with your families, inviting me to holidays. Chin up, kiddies, it's our turn to have Auntie Jill. Must have pity, she has nobody. It's the pity I can't stand. It's always been veiling our friendship."

To her chagrin, Penny erupted in laughter. "Oh, Jill, sweetie. We've always looked up to you. You got the best grades—"

"Because I spent twice as much time studying," she dryly rejoined.

"It paid off," Gayle said. "You made it. That's the important thing. The bottom line."

"We could never pity you," Alison scoffed, pushing her long, caramel-colored hair from her face. "Sure, we hated the way Wilma was, but that kind of sympathy is a good and positive thing."

"My kids think you're a hero, being a cop," Rebecca chimed in. "If I hadn't laid down the law, they'd have been all over you tonight."

Jill's teary eyes glimmered with pleasure. "I didn't know any of this."

"So where did you get Matt?" Gayle asked, rubbing her hands together with glee. "He's really a doll."

"I called 1-800-HUSBAND," Jill confessed uncomfortably, digging her toe into the sand. "It's a service geared to professional women who need a partner for a special occasion."

"Hey, I've heard of that outfit," Roger put in, not wanting to be forgotten.

"Well, Matt's affection for you sure wasn't an act," Penny exclaimed.

"Neither was his irritation," Jill added with a wince. "Oh, I've wrecked the best thing that's ever happened to me!"

"I'm your consolation prize," Roger purred, edging closer.

"Oh, shut up!" she cried, pounding on his chest. "You gobble up girls like a glutton at a smorgasbord. Matt really cared about me, and together you and I flubbed it up— teamed up for one last fiasco!"

"Lots of girls like me," he retorted with a hurt expression. "I thought you still did, too."

"I'm ultimately to blame for what's happened to me," Jill was quick to point out. "But you helped! The only good man I've ever stumbled across and he's gone."

"You girls are impossible!" he blustered in denial.

"Jill deserves your hide, Roger," Rebecca scolded. "The least you can do is listen."

"No, Bec, I'm finished," Jill declared with a sniff, wiping her cheeks with the back of her hand. "Penny's in the biggest jam, with her pregnancy, her on-screen reputation at stake."

The petite redhead shrugged, her hand stealing to her tummy. "I guess I'll just have to come clean, risk losing my job. Though I really feel it's unfair that I need to produce a husband right now," she vented angrily, "pretend to play house for the right-wing conservatives."

"Maybe you should dial 1-800-HUSBAND, Pen," Rebecca suggested. "The wedding arrangements are all made, all we need is the groom."

"Hey, yeah!" Jill snapped her fingers as inspiration struck her. "Bec's right. All you need is a man. A shill. Even an empty pompous shell will do...."

If Roger didn't recognize the description, he couldn't miss the human circle closing in on him. "Oh, no, girls..." He reared back in terror. "I like my single existence."

"It'll just be pretend," Penny cooed, drawing a fingernail across his cheek. "I won't touch you or anything."

"But I can't go hide out after the ceremony like that actor could." He balked. "My name will be in the paper with yours—and it will be a lie!"

"Wonder how it will feel to be on the other side of the dubious story," Jill cracked with glee. "Cheesy journalist trapped in marital snare with television star!"

"You're pretty good with headlines, Jilly," Gayle praised. "We'll draw up our own press releases."

"But ladies will consider me out of circulation," Roger spat out in horror.

"It'll only be about a year," Penny said soothingly. "Celibacy can be a snap. Just read all about it in that paper you work for. It was on page one last week, right below the Elvis-cloning story."

He inhaled sharply. "What if I refuse?"

Jill twisted his collar in her fingers, drawing him close. "You've always gotten your own way with all of us, Roger. You're a classic moocher tag along who never pays his dues. Just think back on all the times we helped you with homework, lied for you to your folks, lent you money for your car—"

"Let you copy biology tests!" Rebecca blurted in confession.

Time froze as everyone turned to Rebecca in shock.

"Hey, I wasn't born head of the PTA, you know!" she declared saucily with a hand on her rounded hip.

Jill turned to Roger as he tried to edge away. "In a way, you're marrying all of us, returning our favors with one simple act of kindness."

"Five ladies and no sex!" he squawked. "Even a eunuch would be ticked."

"All I'd ask is that you live at my place for the time. Be discreet with your trysts," Penny explained seriously.

"Oh, man, oh, man," he fretted, rubbing his forehead.

"As if you've got anything to lose." Gayle huffed. "You have no ties to anyone."

"And you know Penny has a beautiful mansion up the coast," Rebecca wheedled. "A swimming pool and everything!"

"Well . . ." he mumbled.

Jill smoothed his collar and presented him to the group. "Guess who's getting married in the mornin'!"

They all cheered, making an attempt to haul Roger into the ocean. He dug his feet into the sand in protest, allowing his heavy body to go limp in their grip. "Don't even think about it, girls. This ship is drydocked."

"Oh, c'mon," Alison taunted. "Might be just the born-again christening you need! All the trouble you've caused this trip."

"I want to stay dry," he insisted, sounding far more sober than he had thirty minutes ago up at the house. "I—I want to go after Travis to apologize."

Jill regarded him with wonder. "You do?"

"Yeah, it's been eating at me since he left. I did toy with you unfairly, Jilly," he admitted with reluctance, his eyes dropping to the sandy beach. "I didn't know just how much you and Travis meant to each other until I watched you part ways out in the driveway. I'd come to town to claim you, and he was standing in the way. I did some checking with the help of a coworker, and found out he was a hired hand, a stand-in husband. I guess I went a little nuts. It was wrong of me to wreck things for you. Maybe, given the chance, we can fix them.''

"It's a real nice idea," Jill relented, folding her arms across her chest to fend off a chill. "But he said he wanted to be alone, and he meant it!"

"Ah, hell," Roger objected with a wave, "men don't always mean what they say. They just say it louder than you girls do."

"No, I just can't see it," she muttered. "He meant it."

"Jill, now you're being stubborn again," Penny said in warning.

"Lacking faith in yourself again," Rebecca added. "Whatever happens, you're still the special person you've always been."

"Maybe there still is hope tonight." Jill reconsidered under their expectant gazes. "Guess it can't hurt anymore than it does right now."

"Yeah!" the girls chorused. "Let's go cut him off at the pass!"

The lot of them piled into Jill's Lumina and Rebecca's van, peeling over to Wilma's more modest street.

Jill's heart pounded hard with fresh hope at the sight of Wilma's car parked in the carport. The six of them charged the small house like bandits. Jill burst inside first, halting in the living room where Wilma was settled before the television watching a hospital drama. "Aunt Wilma!"

"Come back with your tail—" Wilma cut herself off guardedly as she craned her neck to find that Jill had backup. She slowly rose from her chair. "So what's going on?" she asked evenly.

"Where is Matt?" Jill asked, simply, impatiently.

"Took off in a taxi ten minutes ago," she replied jovially. "He was storming around in your room for awhile, so I just went in there and had a chat with him."

"What did you say, Wilma?" Penny demanded anxiously.

Wilma threw up her thin arms helplessly. "He was blazing around like a bull, confused, angry, didn't know what to do with himself."

"And?" Jill prodded, her fists clenched at her sides.

"Said you had a fight." Her curlered head bobbed in self-congratulation. "Of course I figured that out for myself!"

"Wilma, could you give us a bit more to go on?" Roger requested with one of his most dazzling smiles.

She preened at him. "Why, certainly, dear. I pointed out that perhaps the fight evolved because he was no match for you, Roger. He didn't like that at all, and sputtered that he wasn't even really married to Jill, that I was bound to find out all about it anyway. I let him spill the whole story, despite his rude manner."

"Then what happened?" Jill demanded staunchly.

Wilma smiled primly. "I told him to go, of course. Called him a cab myself, sent him out to the curb to wait. Imagine, the nerve, accepting my hospitality under false pretenses."

"You had no right to interfere!" Jill raved brokenly. "He was stalling to see if I'd come after him, I know it!" A round of groans filled the room. They were just a little too late.

"You've behaved disgracefully, Jill," Wilma scolded, shaking a bony finger. "If you have a brain in your head, you'll drop to your knees and beg Roger to take you back."

Jill's mouth dropped open in shock, and a foreign squeak popped out. She turned to Roger, to find that even he could not believe it.

"I'm so sorry, Wilma," he intoned in convincing sincerity. "But I cannot accept any such offer from your niece."

Wilma's face crumpled. "Oh, darling boy, don't be so hasty. Please. The tongue-wagging this town will give her this time will sink the Ames name for certain."

"That's not true!" Alison protested with vigor. "Jill is respected by all of us. We love her!"

Wilma pulled a thin smile as she shook her gray head. "It is only Roger who can bring her up to your standard of living. Only Roger who can give her a place with your kind."

"Aunt Wilma!" Jill cried in a strangled voice. "You've done impossible damage here, driving Matt away. You had no right to do that!"

"I am only trying to right things for you," she assured crisply, her body ramrod straight. "All these years, you've never understood, never appreciated my efforts to steer you to your betters."

"You misunderstand, Wilma," Roger intervened in a liquid baritone. "It's you I cannot stand."

"What!" she bellowed, her hollow chest quaking.

He nodded, his full face crumpling with regret. "I would propose to the captivating Jill in a flash, if it weren't for you, skulking around in the background, pretending to be some sort of society icon."

Wilma's complexion went white, her glare reflecting pure venom. "How dare you?" she seethed. "I've always treated all of you wonderfully."

"Everyone but me, Wilma," Jill accused in a small voice. "What good could your social angling do me, if you withheld your approval?"

The woman's wrinkled face was sheeted in fury. "You got what you deserved. Always. This stance you children have taken against me here is intolerable."

"We aren't against you," Penny explained. "We're just pro Jill. And tonight we're trying to make up for all the times when maybe we didn't make that clear enough."

"Roger and I aren't even considering marriage," Jill felt compelled to admit with a crooked, sad smile. "He just said those things to make you think a little bit. Now, if you'll excuse me, I plan to pack my things. Penny most likely needs me tonight and I plan to be there for her.''

"So you're off again, without a man," Wilma crowed in parting.

Jill felt a painful lurch in her heart. Matt was gone for now. Maybe forever. But one way or the other, that would have to be settled on her return to San Francisco.

"Yes, Aunt Wilma," she eventually conceded. "I am still unattached. But I guarantee you," she said, turning to beam at her friends, "I'm going to be just fine."

Chapter Sixteen

"You don't want me to make another pot of coffee, do you, Matt?"

Matt's reply to his father amounted to a distracted grunt. He had way too much on his mind to pay attention to every word Chet uttered.

It was ten the following Wednesday morning, an hour before the Green Door opened for the lunch crowd. Chet was puttering around behind the bar, checking his soda tanks, washing glasses in the portable washer. Matt was seated on a center bar stool with the early edition of the San Francisco *Monitor* spread out in front of him. He'd been so dumbfounded by the wedding picture he'd found in the entertainment section, so flabbergasted, that he'd cut out of school for awhile, homing back to the nest to brood.

Matt heaved a rueful breath. Naturally, Penny Richman's official wedding portrait was bound to sting some, with all those familiar faces staring at him. Especially Jill's lovely face. The grainy picture didn't reveal anything with clarity. How was she? Did she miss him?

Apparently the ceremony had gone on without Bruce Kildare, with a clever shift of players. Roger Bannon was dressed in the jazzy tuxedo, standing beside the bride. Unbelievable casting! But he was named in the caption as the groom. The attendants flanked the couple, females fronting the bride, males fronting the groom, forming a pyramid on a hillside. For the umpteenth time his fingers counted down the women, then the men. As arranged, members of the old clique were partnered with their husbands. Wayne Smeed had been added to the lineup, taking Roger Bannon's place with Jill, so Roger could take Bruce Kildare's place beside Penny. He paused with a pensive expression, trying hard to imagine, not for the first time, the commotion, the camaraderie, ultimately wishing he'd been able to see things through. Dammit, he'd liked most of those people.

But he'd left of his own free will. No, she made him leave! he thought, pounding the bar. What was a man to do? The charade was a shambles by then. Roger was all over her like a soggy blanket. He stared at his reflection in the rectangular mirror spanning the wall behind his father. Lord, he looked bad. Clean-shaven and all, but his skin was pale and his eyes were vacant. His mouth formed a grim line under his mustache.

"I mean, it seems like you're glued to that stool and it's a school day," Chet chided loudly. "Ten o'clock in the morning. All the kids are sittin' at their desks and their teacher is moping over some wedding picture in the paper."

"It's my free hour and it's the last day of class," Matt grumbled. He slurped the last dribble of coffee from his mug, then set it down with a thud. "Hey, can't a man get any refills around here?"

Chet's gaze narrowed as he leaned across the bar. "Go back to school, you lazy slug!" He straightened up, whisking the mug away. "Just like when you were a kid, Matt. I have to tell you to go to school. Order you to do it!"

Matt dismissed him, running his fingers over the dog-eared edges of the section. "How did Penny end up with Roger Bannon?"

Chet froze with a frown. "I thought you said Jill wanted that guy."

"I don't think Jill could grope her way out of a revolving door right now," he snapped angrily, "much less choose a man!"

"He's attractive, like the bride," Chet observed, studying the picture upside down. "Girls like that kind."

"Well, that tuxedo he's wearing is covering a lot of loose flesh," Matt muttered, his face darkening in contempt.

"Well, at least Jill is still free," Chet remarked, turning to the stainless steel coffee maker behind him to start a fresh pot.

"So? You think that matters to me?"

"Hell, no," Chet said, pursing his aged lips. "You always skip class to mope around here."

"Some guys need more than a second chance, it seems," a third masculine voice bellowed. The Travis men turned to find Detective Bob Williams filling the doorway, dressed in one of his old shiny suits. "Playing hooky, Travis?"

"If you're tracking down doughnuts, we're fresh out," Matt gibed, his eyes dropping to his paper.

"I thought we'd declared a truce," Bob challenged, easing onto a stool near Matt. "Cup of coffee, Chet?"

Chet set a fresh steaming cup in front of him.

"He gets coffee?" Matt complained.

Chet leaned across the bar on his forearms as if to share a confidence. "It's the Green Door's policy to give surly customers the bum's rush. Nixing their refills usually works."

"Okay!" Matt slapped his newspaper into a messy bundle.

Bob put a detaining hand on his arm. "I was sorry that you and Jill didn't make a go of it. And it's like I told her from the start, your record was nothing."

"She sure thought it was a big something!"

"No," Bob objected, "she was just reeling from having her cover blown."

Matt's dark head bobbed. "So she told you what happened, then."

"She had to tell somebody!" Bob shot back defensively under Matt's accusatory look. "Didn't sound like anything that can't be patched up."

"She thought I was an armed robber! Just because that toad Bannon told her so!"

"I explained that you drove a getaway car away from a grocery store robbery under the influence of bonehead ignorance at the ripe old age of fifteen," he hastily assured him. "That you didn't know anything about the holdup and that you slugged me here in the grill out of panic, because you thought I was trying to corner you for driving without a license."

"She buy it?"

Bob's large featured faces brightened. "With your temper? Of course she did!"

"Just for the record," Matt said with effort, "I don't blame you for my time in the juvy. Guess you've just been a symbol of the worst time of my life. It was wrong to take it out on you."

Bob's bald head gleamed under the amber lighting as he nodded in understanding. "Yeah, well, Jill's story is much the same. The trips back home to those weddings, the collection of dresses in her closet, it all symbolizes failure to her." He lifted his beefy shoulders. "More than anything she wanted to shine back home, and the works sort of crumbled around her at that barbecue. Would've been tough to say all the right things to all the right people in the heat of the controversy."

But she hadn't even come close to handling it right, Matt thought with stinging recollection. They'd been making so much headway, drawing closer, acting as a team. Then wham, it was gone! She flushed under Bannon's flirty remarks. He charged up, made one last-ditch move for her. And to top it off, she foundered over his teenage mistake! The fact that she managed to reach him so quick, hurt him so deep where few people could reach him, certainly hadn't given him any comfort. How dare she do all that?

Matt fought to keep his expression benign as he slipped off the stool, digging in his brown twill jeans for his key ring. "Gotta get back to Hill."

Chet raised his hands at him in a helpless gesture. "Glad you finally know it!"

Matt swatted the air with his newspaper and began to weave through the tangle of tables full of tipped-over chairs. Bob called his name as he neared the back exit. His shoulders stiffened under his tan knit shirt and made a reluctant half-turn.

"Any message for Jill? I'm catching up with her at the station this afternoon."

He paused, blowing air between his teeth. "I'll be seeing her sometime."

"That's all?"

"Yeah. It's as accurate as I can get. And you know how she thrives on accuracy."

The older pair hooted in reprimand, but he kept on walking, right out the door. They just didn't understand how it was. Jill had left him feeling vulnerable, like an abandoned baby in a stroller. In the center of a mall. At the height of Christmas shopping. Dressed in only a diaper. Lost in a sea of legs.

He shook the image away as he climbed into his Jeep. He revved the engine hard as his vision changed shape. The teeming of shoppers' legs transformed into Jill's legs, long, lean and luscious. And he was all grown up. In bed. And those legs were wrapping around his body like silken bonds. He took a hard turn out of the grill's lot, nearly tipping over. He righted the vehicle to the blast of car horns from both directions. Somehow, some way, he'd have to find a way to reconnect with her. Or he'd have to drive her from his heart forever. Unfortunately, neither option seemed possible.

A WEEK HAD PASSED since they'd made love in her old bed.

Jill tossed a half-eaten frozen turkey dinner in the trash Saturday night, then flopped back on her white sofa in front of the television. She picked up the remote control and began to channel surf, sailing through cartoons, news and a football game. She finally settled on a station showing an old black and white movie. She sank deeper in the cushions as Bette Davis chewed the life out of some guy.

"Go, Bets, go," she mumbled, sipping from a can of cola on the end table. "Sock 'em and rock 'em for all of us!"

Their one-week anniversary... Jill tipped her head back on the cushion. She could see Matt if she closed her eyes. Clock his descent as he ever so slowly lowered his body over hers, with that crooked little smile of his. She tingled all over as she remembered the roughness of his hair-dusted body, grazing over hers with a tantalizing burn.

It was no ordinary Saturday. It was prom night for many of the local schools. Jill's favorite night of the year! She rolled her head toward her large closet where she'd hung her old blue dress over the open door. She didn't know why she'd displayed it. Just to wallow in her mistakes, perhaps. Showing up Roger had been a hollow victory. Though it had been a howl to shove him into the groom slot. His good deed of a lifetime!

The dress still looked pretty damn good to her, price tag and all, she decided, studying it with interest. How ironic that her young neighbor Krista now found it to be totally stylin', absolutely cool. The news that Roger had deliberately dumped her before the prom because she wouldn't have dressed ritzy enough was agonizingly interesting—and ironic. His glory days were probably over, and a member of the new generation thought this dress was the greatest.

The man was a fool. Even a bigger fool than she was—if possible.

She would get through this night with flying colors, she assured herself. Krista and Mandy were coming by to primp up for prom, use her makeup and hot rollers, rummage through her accessories for matches to the formals they were borrowing. Every dress had its own shoes and handbag, she'd assured them. Some even had jewelry.

The chime of the doorbell startled her. It was barely five-thirty. Seemed too early for the girls. Jill leaped to her feet and remembered she looked a sight in pink sweats, with her hair piled atop her head in a mop. It was funny. After Matt had messed her up a little, she found she liked it. But not for company. The bell rang again in summons. Well, somebody was in for a treat. There was nothing she could do but answer. She checked the peephole, then swiftly swung open the door.

"I wasn't expecting to ever see you again!" she said in hushed surprise.

"I know it. May I come in?"

Jill stepped aside, giving Rachel Harrington entrée. The agency owner was dressed in sharp counterpoint to Jill's sloppiness in an eggshell sweater dress with a leather belt and shoes, her brown hair woven in a flawless French braid.

Rachel inspected Jill's disheveled appearance, not quite concealing her surprise. "I hope I'm not interrupting."

"No," Jill assured her with forced brightness, sinking back on the sofa. "Sit down, please."

Rachel glided to one of the immaculate chairs in the small living room, crossing her legs with a rustle of nylon. She spoke as she rummaged through her small clutch purse. "You'll be pleased to know that I've brought you a full refund, including your deposit."

Jill's mouth sagged open as Rachel leaned over to hand her a check. "I can't accept it, really," she protested, holding up her hands. "I got my money's worth. Actually straightened out of lot of old misunderstandings, with my friends and my aunt.''

''For the better, I hope,'' Rachel said with warm surprise.

Jill studied her hands for a moment. ''Let's just say that the truth brought a measure of closure to a lot of things. My friends have convinced me that I am wonderfully single and my aunt believes I am hopelessly so.'' She smiled wryly.

''I think I understand,'' Rachel said after a pensive pause. ''But I must insist that you take this money—''

''Why, because it's really Matt's money?'' Jill demanded on a shriller note.

''I never said that. This check is cut from the agency book.'' Despite the denial, Rachel's sheepish expression confirmed Jill's suspicion.

''Well, you'll just have to reimburse him. He can't afford to start paying off the jobs-gone-wrong.''

''That won't be a problem anymore,'' Rachel intimated, tucking the check in her purse. ''He's quit the agency entirely.''

Jill's delicate face creased with worry. ''Can he afford to do that?''

''He'll get by,'' Rachel predicted on a cheery note. ''He had no choice but to bail out, really. After your encounter, he's convinced himself that he can't play the fill-in husband anymore with the necessary objectivity.''

Jill leaned forward on the sofa. ''This is my fault, Rachel. I spoiled the agency job for him.''

''No, you didn't,'' Rachel scoffed, golden flecks twinkling in her eyes. ''But it is your fault.''

''How?''

''You spoiled him for all other women, that's how!'' Rachel lamented with equal measures of frustration and joy. ''The motherly instincts in me are happy that he's finally been smitten, but the businesswoman in me is crestfallen. He's one of the best husbands I've ever had. Could put anyone at ease. Always came through—'' She broke off, remembering that he'd stalked off the job with Jill. "Let's just say he was very good at what he did and will be sorely missed."

"Maybe given a little time he'll be back," Jill forecasted. "Odds are you'll see him long before I will."

"Odds are neither one of us will be seeing him," Rachel said with candor, focusing directly on Jill. "Do you love him?"

"He might just be too impossible to love," Jill said, pouting.

"Oh, you two! A couple of hardheads!"

"Why did you really come here tonight?" Jill demanded, her patience all but evaporated.

"To repay you and to perhaps advise you," Rachel admitted, clicking her purse shut. "I've known Matt for quite awhile, and he's hardest on the people who get close. The thing is, his lion's act is nothing more than a smokescreen, a way to conceal his fragile heart. This whole thing in Santa Barbara really hurt him."

"It hurt me, too!" Jill quickly retorted.

"No question," Rachel softly sympathized. "I don't know exactly what went on, but it's somehow left Matt believing that you could never want him enough. As I say, I'm not judging or advising. I've been absolutely forbidden to discuss this with you at all."

Jill managed a small smile. "I know, you're just delivering the check."

"Right!" Rachel rose to her feet. "I just wanted you to know how things stand. If you feel like making a move, I'm certain you won't be turned away."

"Strong women don't crawl."

"Of course not," Rachel intoned, clasping her hand for a farewell shake. "But even a strong woman wants a warm bed. And if it's as easy as tossing extra tinder on dying flames, why not take the chance? If the fire doesn't flare, you've only lost a little of your tim—ah, timber."

"I'll think about it," Jill promised, seeing her out. But she already knew that Matt was justified in expecting her to make the first move. She had acted like a flighty teenager with Roger. Intent on making a certain impression on everyone, she'd turned a deaf ear to Matt's discomfort, glossed over his attempts at courting.

But how to send him a message without taking too huge a chance? Watching him walk off down Rebecca's driveway had been an agonizing ordeal she could not repeat.

Jill paced around the room, suddenly catching sight of her old prom dress still hanging on the edge of the closet door. A slow smile spread across her face. There was a way after all. And Krista could help her. Without even understanding the hows and whys.

MATT WAS STANDING sentry later on that evening in the gymnasium of Hill High, the senior class prom in full motion around him. The four-piece combo parked on stage were playing a soulful Whitney Houston song. The young female singer didn't have much strength in her voice, but the kids didn't seem to mind. They were contentedly swaying around the floor under the soft blue lighting and glittery cardboard stars, dressed in formalwear that aged them a good five years in appearance. It also gave them adult ideas. Matt was fresh from pulling apart a frisky couple behind the bleachers. His mouth formed a smug line as he rocked on his heels. The kids couldn't believe he'd found them. But nobody knew the tricks better than a reformed rebel!

He was strolling down a side aisle with his hands in the pockets of his charcoal dress slacks when he saw her hovering near the entrance. The beautiful blond in that distinctive sapphire dress. He froze in his tracks and stared. The glittery stars hanging from the ceiling suddenly seemed real, the music pure sweet Whitney herself. Jill had come to him. Broken down, given in. But what a risk! In that crazy old dress full of memories!

His legs were like lead under him. But he was cutting across the dance floor at a brisk pace anyway, his pulse pounding in his ears. He'd come to know that blasted dress as Roger's folly, a symbol of his stupidity. With a closet full of choices, why select that dress?

The important thing was that she was here, he schooled himself on a steadying breath. The room was dimmed for romance, and she still had her back to him. He realized that she must've come with Krista and Amanda. Amanda was at her side, speaking to her in lively animation. He couldn't wait to see her eyes, twinkling with sensuality and affection. She had to feel those things, to come this far.

Finally, he was close enough to reach through the crowd and place his hand on her shoulder. "Hey," he crooned.

She spun around. "Hey!"

Matt blinked. He was staring into sparkling eyes, but they belonged to young Krista Sundin. She was wearing Jill's dress.

"Hey, Coach, you okay?" Krista and Amanda flanked him with concern.

He forced a chuckle. "Yeah, guess the noise is getting to me."

"So, how do you like my dress?" Krista asked, stepping away to twirl around, make the flared hem ripple.

"Charming." He was filled with relief and disappointment. Jill had known better than to wear the recycled dress for him. But she hadn't summoned the guts to come. He clenched his fists at his sides. Didn't she understand that he couldn't risk her rejection all over again?

"Jill said to be sure to say hello to you right away," Krista announced perkily, stopping on a dime.

"What!"

Krista laughed as his features lit up. "Crazy, huh? I promised I would, though, because it was part of the deal. I actually get to keep this dress!"

"Oh, I am so glad to hear it," Matt erupted in relief. It was a sign, after all. Jill was ready to try again. Rachel had certainly pegged them right earlier in the week. They were a couple of hardheads for sure. This was obviously the best Jill could do. Like him, she was reluctant to make a grandstand play. But it was her turn. And this was right. Exactly perfect. When Matt jolted out of his reverie, the girls' dates were on the scene, spiriting them away. "So, Krista," he began haltingly. "Jill say...anything else? Like is she at home tonight?"

"Oh, no, she's not at home," Krista chastised saucily.

"No?" he repeated bleakly.

"She's out in the parking lot, by your Jeep—" Krista caught her breath as Matt sprinted past her and out the double steel doors.

Jill hailed Matt from a distance of several yards. He wasn't surprised. A security guard hired for the dance had her pinned against the Jeep and appeared to be questioning her.

"Hurry up!" she called out on a desperate note. "Please tell this man who I am!"

Matt sauntered up with his hands clasped behind his back. Jill's heart skipped a little. He was wearing the clothes he bought in Santa Barbara, the black slacks and gray oxford shirt.

"What seems to be the trouble?" he asked in a deep, playful timbre.

"Oh, Mr. Travis," the guard greeted him, pushing up the brim of his uniform hat with a sigh. He looked a little frazzled, but Matt would've expected nothing less. "This lady is trespassing. Claims to know you."

"Really?" Matt's brows jumped. "She have any ID?"

"In this outfit?" Jill screeched. "C'mon!"

Matt rubbed his mustache to conceal his smirk, lazily inspecting her pink sweats, her tousled knot of blond silken hair. "I thought I knew her, Ed. But the lady I know never has a hair out of place."

"How would you like your nose out of place, Travis?" Jill curled a fist and tried to snake it around the guard. Ed took hold of her wrist, causing her to squeal in outrage. "I'm damn sick and tired of tangling with you, Ed!"

"You frisk her yet, Ed?"

Jill's expression sheeted in horror. "Travis!"

The guard's face clouded. "How does she know your name, Coach?"

Jill's blue eyes glittered with scorn. "Tell him or I'll kill you."

"She belongs to me, Ed," Matt confessed with a chuckle. "Isn't that right, honey?"

"I'm not so sure anymore, you beast!" Ed loosened his grip and she promptly wrenched free.

"Thanks, Ed," Matt murmured, capturing Jill in his arms before she could stray. "Thanks for looking out for my girl."

"Why didn't you tell me who you are?" Ed wondered in bewilderment. "That you're the coach's girl?"

"I wasn't sure I was!" she exploded. "It seemed simpler to tell you that I'm a detective."

"Against the law to impersonate police personnel," the guard scolded, his heels clicking across the parking lot.

"But people always believe I'm a cop," she said, staring after the guard, waving his flashlight between rows of cars. "The one time I dash off without my purse."

"You're just too pretty in pink to pass yourself off as a tough detective," he purred. Matt leaned back against the Jeep, pulling Jill against him. "Too soft and cuddly and disheveled." He gave her hair a ruffle. "A man doesn't anticipate that kind of trouble from this kind of kitten."

Jill sighed, losing steam. "Oh, Matt..."

"I love this impetuous side of you," he rasped against her ear.

"I don't think I have the stamina to behave this crazy very often," she fretted apologetically. "You ridden in a teenager's car lately? Krista's boyfriend offered me a ride, and in the name of convenience I agreed! He's missing part of his taillight, he didn't make more than a rolling stop right out on the boulevard—"

"Jill, honey," Matt said, pressing his fingers to her lips. "He's a good boy. I'll speak to him. Tomorrow."

"Okay," she relented, with a sweet smile. Cupping his clean-shaven cheeks in her hands, she dropped her mouth to his.

"Mmm." He drew his hands along her back, indenting her softness into his length.

Her lips broke from his, planting kisses all over his face. "I'm so glad you want to try again, Travis."

"Thank you for coming, honey. All I needed was a little sign that you were willing. This was such a nice surprise, the answer to my dreams."

"I didn't know how long it would take you to spot the dress on Krista," she intimated sheepishly.

"Try thirty seconds."

"It seemed like years in the hands of security man Ed," she grumbled.

Matt tweaked her nose. "Everything went perfectly. The moment I realized it was Krista in the dress and not you, I knew we were home free."

"Not..." To his surprise she broke into laughter. "Oh, Travis, I knew better than to flaunt that dress in your face. Giving it to Krista is my way of telling you that I'm all done with past regrets."

"I figured that out," he assured her.

"Of course, but doesn't it feel good to hear me say it?"

"Know what would really feel good?" he asked with roguish look.

"What?" she wondered warily.

"Having a date for the prom."

Jill gasped. "But I'm not dressed for it!"

"Oh, c'mon," he urged, straightening up, tugging at her shirt. "I wanna dance with my girl."

Jill smiled, tracing a finger along his cheek. "Okay. Guess I'm finally going to make it to the prom."

Matt linked his arm in hers, and they strolled up the lot toward the gym. "The mood is just right. The ceiling is like the heavens, and the music... You'll swear to God it's Whitney Huston up there on stage."

Jill's doubtful laughter rang through the night. "Oh, Travis, you must have been an impossible romantic back in school."

"Just impossible," he confided. "I'm at my best right here and now. I've got a brand-new girl, and shaken loose my anger over the bad old days."

"Hmm, you're still trouble, though," she fretted, slowing her pace.

"What!" he bellowed.

"You took my sweater and never gave it back."

"Well, you come home with me tonight, and we'll search my place top to bottom till we find it."

"Starting with the bedroom?" she asked, clinging to his arm.

He nodded, with twinkling eyes. "Starting with the bed."

And there are more husbands!
Turn the page for a bonus look at what's in store
for you in the next 1-800-HUSBAND book.
It's a sneak preview of

THE COWBOY HIRES A WIFE
by Jenna McKnight
November 1995

*"Whether you want him for business... or
pleasure, for one month or one night, we have
the husband you've been looking for. When
circumstances dictate the appearance of a man in
your life, call 1-800-HUSBAND for an
uncomplicated, uncompromising solution.
Call now. Operators standing by...."*

Don't miss
#605 THE COWBOY HIRES A WIFE
by Jenna McKnight!

Chapter One

Wade had sought advice from every woman he knew on the rodeo circuit. He'd even called his mother. They all said the same thing. "Ignore Missy's tantrums."

He kept his eyes glued to the road, whistling along with a Clint Black tune. He prayed for Jen to return soon and hoped she wouldn't take a bullwhip to him for turning her normally sweet-natured daughter into a little foot-stomping terror.

Missy started with a sniffle, then escalated into full-scale, tears-streaming-down-her-cheeks, sobbing.

He pulled into Howard Johnson's and parked in the shade of a billboard. "Here we are. Hojo's, just like you wanted. Put on your dress, Sprite."

"It's wrinkled!" Her face was blotchy and screwed up with all the anger only a naive six-year-old would dare turn on him.

Wade knew better than to laugh, but it was *soooo* tempting. He covered his mouth with his hand, under the guise of checking to see if he needed a shave, which he did.

"There's nothing I can do about it now. Put on some jeans."

"No! I like dresses!"

"Well, I'm going to eat. You can stay here if you want."

Wade was as good as his word. His mom had told him that was the number one rule with children. He stepped out of the RV, closed the door behind him, and stretched the kinks out of his back. He got more knots from dealing with one little girl than riding the rankest bull.

He needed help.

He found it as he slid into a booth where he could keep an eye on the door of the RV. That's when he got a good look at the billboard he'd parked under.

"Coffee?"

He favored the aging, apron-draped redhead with his best smile. "What do you know about that ad on the bill-board?"

She squinted out the window. "1-800-HUSBAND? Wouldn't know. I'm on my third one, and I didn't need help gettin' any of 'em." She raised a carafe in each hand. "Reg'lar or decaf?"

He pushed his cup toward her. "Sweetheart, I need all the caffeine I can get right now."

His attention wandered back to the billboard. It would make a helluva lot more sense if somebody advertised wives. Lots of men needed them. There was always laundry to be done. And shopping. And cooking.

The more personal aspects he could handle himself, but Missy added a ton of work to his life. One little spot on a dress. Or one little wrinkle...

If someone hired out husbands, surely wives were available, too. This was supposed to be the land of equal opportunity and no sex discrimination, after all. "You got a pay phone?"

The waitress looked at him, the billboard he was still staring at, and then back at him. "*You're* gonna call?"

Deep in thought, he rubbed one hand over his rough whiskers. "Yeah, I think I might."

"Well, sugar, they'd be crazy not to hire you."